TRULY,
MADLY,
DEEPLY

Other Life-Changing Fiction™
by Karen Kingsbury

Lost Love Military Series
Even Now
Ever After

Forever Faithful Series
Waiting for Morning
A Moment of Weakness
Halfway to Forever

Women of Faith Fiction Series
A Time to Dance
A Time to Embrace

Cody Gunner Series
A Thousand Tomorrows
Just Beyond the Clouds
This Side of Heaven

Red Glove Series
Gideon's Gift
Maggie's Miracle
Sarah's Song
Hannah's Hope

Life-Changing Bible Story Collections
The Family of Jesus
The Friends of Jesus

Children's Chapter Books Ages 8–12
Best Family Ever—Baxter Family Children (Book 1)
Finding Home—Baxter Family Children (Book 2)
Never Grow Up —Baxter Family Children (Book 3—2021)

Children's Picture Books
Let Me Hold You Longer
Let's Go on a Mommy Date
We Believe in Christmas
Let's Have a Daddy Day
The Princess and the Three Knights
The Brave Young Knight
Far Flutterby
Go Ahead and Dream with Quarterback Alex Smith
Whatever You Grow Up to Be
Always Daddy's Princess

Miracle Story Collections
A Treasury of Christmas Miracles
A Treasury of Miracles for Women
A Treasury of Miracles for Teens
A Treasury of Miracles for Friends
A Treasury of Adoption Miracles
Miracles—A Devotional

Gift Books
Forever Young: Ten Gifts of Faith for the Graduate
Forever My Little Boy
Forever My Little Girl

e-Short Stories
The Beginning
I Can Only Imagine
Elizabeth Baxter's 10 Secrets to a Happy Marriage
Once Upon a Campus

www.KarenKingsbury.com

KAREN KINGSBURY

TRULY, MADLY, DEEPLY

A Novel

ATRIA BOOKS
New York London Toronto Sydney New Delhi

ATRIA
BOOKS

An Imprint of Simon & Schuster, Inc.
1230 Avenue of the Americas
New York, NY 10020

First Atria Books hardcover edition October 2020

ATRIA BOOKS and colophon are trademarks of Simon & Schuster, Inc.

For information about special discounts for bulk purchases, please contact Simon & Schuster Special Sales at 1-866-506-1949 or business@simonandschuster.com.

The Simon & Schuster Speakers Bureau can bring authors to your live event. For more information or to book an event, contact the Simon & Schuster Speakers Bureau at 1-866-248-3049 or visit our website at www.simonspeakers.com.

Interior design by Lana J. Roff

Manufactured in the United States of America

1 3 5 7 9 10 8 6 4 2

Library of Congress Cataloging-in-Publication Data
Names: Kingsbury, Karen, author.
Title: Truly, madly, deeply : a novel / Karen Kingsbury.
Description: First Atria Books hardcover edition. | New York : Atria Books, 2020.
Identifiers: LCCN 2020021145 (print) | LCCN 2020021146 (ebook) |
ISBN 9781982104382 (hardcover) | ISBN 9781982104405 (ebook)
Classification: LCC PS3561.I4873 T78 2020 (print) |
LCC PS3561.I4873 (ebook) | DDC 813/.54--dc23
LC record available at https://lccn.loc.gov/2020021145
LC ebook record available at https://lccn.loc.gov/2020021146

ISBN 978-1-9821-0438-2
ISBN 978-1-9821-0440-5 (ebook)

Dedicated to Donald, my husband of thirty-two years and the love of my life. And to our beautiful children and grandchildren. The journey of life is breathtaking surrounded by each of you, and every minute together is time borrowed from eternity. I love you with every breath, every heartbeat. And to God, Almighty, who has—for now—blessed me with these.

1

Walking barefoot in the silky white sand of Karon Beach on the island of Phuket in the Andaman Sea, Tommy Baxter felt a million miles away from reality. Beside him was the only girl he had ever loved, a girl he had met his freshman year at Northside High School. The one who had his whole heart.

Annalee Miller.

"I'll remember this as long as I live." Tommy slid his fingers between hers, their pace slow and easy. "Every detail."

Her pale blond hair danced over her bare shoulders in the Indian Ocean breeze. "When I write the story of my life"—she smiled up at him—"this page—being half a world away from home with you—will always be my favorite."

And Tommy could barely breathe. Those green eyes had captured him the first time he saw her and they held his heart still. They always would.

The start of their senior year at Northside High was weeks away, but they still had a few days left on Phuket. Visiting the western beaches of Thailand with Annalee's family was something they had looked forward to since May.

"The fishing boat leaves in two hours." Annalee looked out at the water. "God gave us the perfect day." She slowed a bit. "Let's go back. I'm a little tired."

Concern washed over Tommy the way it had yesterday when she mentioned needing more rest. "How did you sleep?"

"Good." Annalee looked at him. "Don't worry, Tommy. It's the time change. That's all."

Yes, that made sense. After all they were eleven hours ahead of Indiana. But hadn't they been here long enough to be used to the change? Everyone else in the group was rested by now.

Tommy held her hand a little tighter. "Maybe you should get to sleep earlier tonight."

"Okay." She didn't look troubled. "Good idea."

They took their time on the way back. Tommy surveyed the string of five-star hotels that marked the beach, the same beautiful stretch of shoreline that had been devastated by the tsunami of 2004. But there was no sign of that now. The beaches of Phuket had made a resounding comeback. Tourism was at an all-time high.

Vacation wasn't the reason Annalee's family was here this week, though. The Millers had come to the mountainous rain-forest island for work. Annalee's parents ran Each One International, a ministry with offices across the world. The goal of Each One was to reach the least and lost in various cities, care for their physical needs and provide safety, and to tell them about the love of God.

Here at Karon Beach, Annalee's parents had been

taking meetings with local Each One leaders. Tommy was bunking with her younger brother, Austin, and Annalee shared a room with her parents. The rooms had been comped by the hotel manager, who was familiar with the work Annalee's parents were doing. The stay wasn't just a vacation. Annalee's parents were being briefed on the work ahead.

According to Annalee, so far they had received very valuable information.

Tommy filled his lungs with the sweet salty air. The days here on the shore had seemed like they'd last forever. But the hard part of the visit would happen tomorrow. That's when the group would head to Phuket City and Patong's seedy Bangla Road. Annalee's parents had warned them that the day would likely involve rescue work.

"Let's sit for a while." Tommy searched her face. Annalee's freckled cheeks were tan from the days on the beach. But her beautiful eyes didn't look right. "Or maybe you should take a nap. Before the fishing trip."

Annalee shook her head. "I'm okay." She nodded up the beach to their chairs. "This is good."

They sat and stretched their legs. Annalee took a deep breath. "Senior year. How can it be?"

"The days flew." The sun cast a thousand diamonds across the water. Tommy turned to her. "You're sure about Indiana?"

"I think so." She linked her pinkie finger with his. "I like NYU. But I'd rather be close to family."

They had both applied early to Indiana University in

Bloomington, an hour from home. All Tommy's aunts and uncles lived there, along with his papa John Baxter. Tommy was deciding between Indiana, Harvard, Duke and North Carolina.

But there were days Tommy wasn't sure about any of them. "I still think about the military. I could graduate in May and head to the recruiters' office." He raked his hand through his short blond hair. "Someone has to do it."

"True." They'd had this conversation before. Annalee wanted him to go wherever God was calling him. She understood the military would mean they'd be apart. Maybe for years. "If you become a soldier, you'll be the best they ever had."

Tommy ran his thumb over her fingers. This was one more reason why he loved her. She had no designs on his life, no ulterior motives. Not like his parents did. He glanced at her. "Of course, I could still be a doctor." He winked at Annalee. "Which would make my mother happy."

"We don't have to have all the answers." She leaned her head back and closed her eyes. "I feel God's Spirit here. In the touch of the wind and the soft of the sand."

"Mmm." He couldn't look away, couldn't take his eyes off her. "I feel Him here, too."

RAIN FELL EVERY other day in July in this part of Asia, but not that afternoon. Sunshine drenched the beach as Tommy helped Annalee onto the fishing boat. Her parents and brother and two fishing guides were already on board.

Tommy slipped as he stepped inside, and Annalee caught him. "Whoa!" He found his balance.

"Good thing I feel better." She laughed. "You're not easy to catch."

"True." At six-foot-three, Tommy was easily nine inches taller than Annalee. People often mistook him for a college athlete. He gave Annalee a side hug. "Just testing you."

Dan and Donna Miller sat at the front of the boat with the guides. The goal was to catch a marlin for dinner. Austin stayed at the back with Tommy and Annalee.

They were a few hundred yards offshore when they spotted the first dolphin. Five more surfaced nearby. About the same time their captain and guide, Hans, cut the engines. "Dolphins know what's about to happen." Hans was a veteran fisherman. Backward baseball cap, soggy unlit cigar between his sun-scarred lips. He pointed to the choppy water near the boat. "Lots going on here."

"Can I jump in?" Austin ripped off his shirt and jumped onto one of the bench seats. "I've always wanted to swim with dolphins."

"Not on my watch!" Hans motioned to Austin. "We're chumming the water, boy. Dolphins aren't the only animals we'll attract."

Austin looked over the edge of the boat. "I hadn't thought about that." He took a step back. "Reef sharks, right? But I read that they don't bite."

"A man lost a foot to one a few years ago." Hans raised his weathered brow. "Stay in the boat."

The guide outfitted everyone with a rod and reel. Even Annalee. Which was a good sign. She had said she wouldn't fish if she wasn't feeling strong. *Finally*, Tommy thought to himself. *She's past the jet lag.*

An hour later, Austin caught a yellowfin but it broke free from his line. Then minutes before they returned to shore, Tommy felt a sudden strong tug on his reel. "Hey! I got one!" The fish doubled his fight, and Tommy dug his heels against the inside of the boat and bent his knees. "Someone help!"

Mr. Miller rushed over. He grabbed Tommy by the waist and the two of them fought the fish with all their strength.

"It's a marlin!" Annalee's father was first to see the spikes along the upper part of the fish. "This is the one!"

"Reel it in slowly, gentlemen." Hans was at their side. "There you go . . . that's it!"

Ocean spray whipped their faces, but Tommy and Annalee's father held on until the monster fish was up and over the boat railing. The two high-fived, both of them out of breath.

"I can't believe it!" Annalee put her hand on Tommy's shoulder. "It's the size of a shark!"

She wasn't far off. Tommy had seen pictures of marlin, but nothing had prepared him for the behemoth catch. Hans helped Tommy and Mr. Miller hoist the fish up for a picture. Then they dropped it into an oversized tub of ice.

Tommy was still breathing hard as he turned to Mr. Miller. "Thanks for the help!" Tommy wiped the seawater from his face. "That was crazy!"

"Teamwork." Mr. Miller put his arms around his wife and Austin. "That is one massive catch."

"Congratulations!" Hans measured the fish and faced them. "Biggest marlin of the year!" He grinned. "Most tourists come back with nothing. You're a sporty group!"

Back on the beach Hans prepared the fish and cooked it over an open flame. What they didn't eat, he would take to a nearby restaurant, where people from the village would line up for free fish.

When Hans was gone, Tommy sat with Annalee and her family at a table near the water and Mr. Miller prayed over the meal. "This day in the sun was a dividing line, Lord. I can feel it. Today we see what life is like with Your grace and goodness." He paused. "Tomorrow we will see what it is like for the lost children of Phuket."

The man's words were sobering. Tommy was aware they would be working tomorrow, but until now he hadn't thought of exactly what that meant. He looked at Annalee's father. "You remember last summer my family and I took that trip to Africa. We painted orphanages and made bracelets with the kids." He hesitated. "Will it be like that?"

Mr. Miller shook his head. "We do oversee an orphanage in Phuket." His tone grew heavier. "I'm afraid another issue has taken precedence for this trip."

"The rise in tourism has brought an increase in sex trafficking." Mrs. Miller took her husband's hand. "Twenty minutes from here, there's an open-air beach market where children are sold." She explained how Each One was working with local law enforcement officials to close down trafficking rings. "In the meantime kids from all over Asia are still brought here as slaves. We rescue them, but sometimes the young ones don't even know where they're from."

Tommy thought about his younger sister. Malin was twelve now. If someone kidnapped her and forced her into . . . He couldn't finish the thought. He'd do anything to protect her. "So . . . you rescue these kids, and then . . . where do they go?"

Annalee's dad explained that Each One had recently opened a safe house. It had forty rooms and as many trained volunteers. The goal was to get the victimized children safe and fed and then to reunite them with their families. If their families could be found.

"What if the kids don't have anyone?" Annalee's shoulder brushed against Tommy's. "I guess . . . I didn't know how bad things had gotten here."

Austin anchored his elbows on the wooden table. "I talked to Dad about this before we left. I asked the same thing." He looked at his father. "What if the kids don't have anyone?"

"That happens sometimes." Mr. Miller was quiet for a moment. "An orphaned child is most vulnerable for this wicked business."

"So sad." Tommy couldn't get his mind around it. "What happens next? At the safe house?"

Mr. Miller crossed his arms. "Some kids stay until we can find them a home. A safe place where they can have something they are desperate for." He hesitated. "A family."

When dinner was over, Annalee and Tommy moved to the same pair of chairs they'd sat in earlier. The sun was setting, casting streaks of pink and yellow across the vast blue sky.

For a while they didn't talk. The sounds of the gentle waves on the beach and the wind in the palm trees nearby was enough. In the distance, the cry of a macaw echoed through the hills.

Tommy took Annalee's fingers and brought them to his lips. The two of them had made a deal when they started dating. They could hold hands and hug, they could kiss. But nothing more. Not till they were older. Not till the time was right.

But there were times when keeping their promise was all but impossible. Last year at prom when Tommy took Annalee home, and her parents had been gone. They had stood on her front porch and he had taken her face in his hands. Their kiss had stirred feelings in him that stayed with him still. God alone had kept him from crossing lines with her that night.

Here on this beach, Tommy felt the same familiar draw.

She turned to him. "You're going to be mad."

"At what?" He slid his chair a little closer, so his bare knee was touching hers. "Never at you, Annalee."

"Not me." She stared out at the ocean. "Tomorrow. The monsters trafficking children." Concern tinged her voice. "You can't fight them, Tommy. They'll arrest you."

His heart warmed as he studied her. "You know me."

"Yes." She looked at him again. "Promise me."

Now it was his turn to look at the water. If he had his way they would round up every trafficker in Phuket, put them on a boat and set them adrift in the Indian Ocean. But God's ways were higher. He wouldn't do any good by taking the law into his own hands. Especially here in Thailand. "I'll follow your dad's lead." He kissed her hand again. "I have this strange sense I'll know about my future after tomorrow. . . . You ever feel that way?"

"At times." She stood and stretched. "Maybe we'll both live here and work for Each One someday." A smile lifted her pretty lips. "Then I could walk this beach with you whenever I wanted."

The sunset was hitting its peak, the sky a canvas of colors that took Tommy's breath. He stood and put his arm around her shoulders. "How do you feel?"

"Perfect." She faced him, careful to keep a few inches between them. Thailand didn't approve of public displays of affection. Tourists weren't held to the same standard, but even hugging could be considered rude. She touched his cheek and the sensation lingered. She smiled. "Walk with me?"

"Yes." He clenched the muscles in his jaw and hesitated. "I don't want the sun to set."

She smiled. "Me, either."

They walked at the water's edge, slower than before. "I wish we were older." Tommy kept his gaze straight ahead. "Finished with college and sure of what we want to do." They were out of view of the public now, alone on the most secluded stretch of sand. There wasn't another person in sight.

"Mmm." She waited. "Sounds wonderful."

"And I wish this wasn't a mission trip." Tommy slowed to a stop and faced her. "But our honeymoon."

Annalee looked at him, straight through him. "I wish that, too."

They had talked of growing up and getting married before. Just not on an empty stretch of sand half a world away from home. Tommy moved closer. One inch at a time. The electricity between them was so strong, he couldn't stop himself. Even when he knew he shouldn't kiss her here.

"This day, being with you here . . . it was perfect." His words were a desperate whisper against the sound of the surf. "You're the most beautiful girl I've ever seen, Annalee." He took hold of her other hand and his body moved closer still. "Your eyes . . . your heart."

"Hold me?" Annalee looked over her shoulder. "No one can see us."

She didn't have to ask twice. He eased her into his arms. *This is heaven*, he thought. And he could only imagine what it would be like . . . if this were their honeymoon. His cheek brushed against hers, his lips a breath away from hers. "Annalee . . . I want you."

"I wanna kiss you." She searched his eyes. "We're alone out here."

Tommy ran his fingers through her hair and framed her face with his hands. "Me, too . . . I want that more than my next breath." His lips were so close to hers he could smell her sweet breath.

Son . . . be careful.

The words blew across Tommy's soul and made him catch his breath. He took a half step back and exhaled hard. He didn't have to ask if the voice was God's. The Lord spoke to Tommy often. He was familiar with His tone and timing. *Yes, Lord . . . I hear You. I will obey.*

Tommy put his hands on Annalee's shoulders. "Can you imagine? Getting picked up by the police for kissing in public." He laughed, trying to keep the moment light. "I don't think your parents would like that." He ached for a way around the local rule, but there was none.

She took a step closer and rested her head on his chest. The warmth of her through his thin white T-shirt almost made him kiss her anyway. Her arms came around his waist. "You're right." She breathed deep in his arms, and the sensation was more than Tommy could take. She lifted her face to his. "Maybe tonight. When it's dark."

With a strength not his own, Tommy separated himself from her. "Really?"

"Yes." Annalee's eyes sparkled. "When everyone's asleep."

Tommy wanted nothing more. But no matter how

great the idea seemed, he wouldn't allow it to happen. He couldn't disrespect her parents like that.

They turned around and walked back toward the hotel, slower than before. Soon enough the sun would slip below the water and darkness would cover Phuket. Tommy would meet up with Austin in their room and they would talk pro basketball and players the Pacers were looking to trade or the starting lineup in the coming season.

But for now there remained the warm feel of sand on their toes and the touch of salty beach air on their faces. And Annalee Miller's hand in his.

That most of all.

2

Annalee felt sick even before she stepped out of bed. But it wasn't jet lag. This time the work ahead of them weighed on her. Not until yesterday did she fully grasp what they'd be dealing with on the streets of Phuket today.

Once she and Tommy parted ways for the evening, the reality of what was happening on this island hit her hard. She had barely been able to sleep. Girls and boys in their early teens and younger being sold in the open marketplace. Twenty minutes from here.

It'll be okay, she told herself. *God will lead us where we need to go.* She stood and looked around the room until she found what she wanted. Three vitamin B capsules and two bottles of water. A few minutes later Annalee felt stronger. She grabbed her Bible and stepped outside onto the balcony. Her parents were already in the lobby, meeting with the local Each One coordinator about the work ahead. Annalee still had thirty minutes before the group was set to meet for breakfast.

The air smelled of fresh jasmine. Annalee stretched her legs on the chaise lounge and opened her Bible to

Philippians, chapter four. God's Word was her companion and best friend. The voice of the Father spoke to her from the pages of a book that transcended time.

But of all the verses in all the chapters in all the books of the Bible, this part in Philippians was her favorite. She had the fourth chapter nearly memorized, but today more than ever she needed to see the words. Soak them into the depth of her soul.

Rejoice in the Lord always. I will say it again: Rejoice! Let your gentleness be evident to all. The Lord is near. Do not be anxious about anything, but in everything, by prayer and petition, with thanksgiving, present your requests to God. And the peace of God, which transcends all understanding, will guard your hearts and your minds in Christ Jesus.

With every word, Annalee felt peace come over her. The passage filled the cracks in her heart and convinced her she would survive this day. Whatever terrible realities they saw.

Annalee knew a little about sex trafficking. They had talked about it at school. How to avoid being trafficked. Don't talk to strangers. Don't chat with unknown people online. Don't hang out at the mall alone. That sort of thing. But today she would see helpless kids being sold and abused for the sake of someone else's greed. Bought for a sickening selfishness.

Her eyes found the words again. *Do not be anxious about anything, but in everything . . .*

She closed her Bible and set it on the nearby table,

but even still the Scripture stayed with her. . . . *And the peace of God, which transcends all understanding, will guard your hearts and your minds . . .*

A gentle breeze blew off Andaman Bay this morning. Annalee stood and breathed deep. She stretched her arms over her head and for the next ten minutes she ran through a series of stretches. As she did, she remembered last night and the boy who lived permanently in her heart.

Tommy Baxter.

Nothing about Tommy was ordinary. He'd been the star basketball player on the Northside varsity team since their freshman year. Apparently, Tommy played the game just like his father had once played it. Mr. Baxter was a lawyer now, but back in his high school days, Luke Baxter had been first-team all-state.

No surprise that Tommy played like his dad. He looked like him, too. One of Annalee's greatest joys was watching Tommy run up and down the court, driving to the hoop. Northside fans had come to expect twenty points a game from Tommy Baxter. But they didn't expect the way he lived his life off the court. If Tommy had been like every other popular jock at school, he wouldn't be with her family here in Thailand.

In fact, they wouldn't have dated at all.

ANNALEE'S DAD WAITED till after they were done eating before turning the breakfast conversation over to Niran, their guide for the day. Niran and his wife ran the newly opened safe house near Phuket City and today he would take them to Bangla Road near Patong—the beach not far from where they were staying.

"You will see things today that will stay." Niran tapped his temple. "Here. In your mind and soul." Niran was maybe in his sixties. He told them how when his children had grown and gone, he and his wife felt a driving desire to help.

"So many children." Niran's eyes narrowed. "Those lost little ones, they are our family now."

Tommy stayed by Austin as they walked to Niran's van. Annalee walked with her parents. There would be no hand-holding for them today. As they set out, Annalee studied the architecture. This was her first time to Thailand, and the pastel buildings and Chinese accents surprised her. This developed city wasn't the sleepy place she had expected.

Niran pointed out highlights as they made their way to Patong. "Everyone lost someone in the tsunami. It doesn't matter how many years go by, we remember." He slowed the van and pointed to a park just ahead. A battered boat sat on a cement platform. "That police vessel saved eighteen adults from the waters that day." He nodded. "There are many tributes."

As they drove into Patong, the building fronts changed. The signs and displays looked seedier. Cheaper. Same with the hotels. Niran pointed again. "Hotel rooms here are a mere fraction of what they cost at the beaches of Karon and Kata." He set his jaw. "Many rent by the hour."

They parked in a big lot at the beginning of a long stretch of road where outdoor market vendors lined the sidewalks. They stepped out of the vehicle. Niran gathered them close, as if the passersby might hear them. "This is Bangla Road." He stared down the road-way. "Here we rescue children every week."

A bad chill ran down Annalee's arms.

"What are we going to do?" Austin was only sixteen, but he had a heart for their parents' ministry. He al-ways had.

"We will walk." Niran pointed toward the busier parts of the street. "Make eye contact with the children and you will see. They know who I am. If they are afraid, they will look away."

"These children are property," Annalee's father added. "They are owned by dangerous people, men in most cases."

Niran nodded. "You will take my lead."

Annalee looked at Tommy and for a few seconds their eyes held. The reality of this was clearly more than either of them could believe. She walked between her parents and Tommy stayed by Austin.

Their pace was slower than Annalee expected.

Not four buildings down Bangla Road, she spotted a pair of young teens walking toward them. The girls wore skimpy short skirts, bikini tops and high heels. Nothing like the typical beach attire worn by most women on the street.

Annalee felt her heart skip a beat . . . something was

wrong with these girls. The situation was obvious, like Niran had told them. Annalee's dad stopped and she and her mother did the same thing. But Niran hurried on. That's when Annalee saw the men.

One trailed the girls. The other leaned on a nearby tree with a cell phone. Before Niran could say something, two white men in bold Hawaiian print shirts walked up to the girls. The guys looked like tourists.

The distance between them was too great for Annalee and her family to hear what was being said. But in seconds the man with the cell phone was at the girls' sides. The two white tourists passed what looked like a handful of cash to the man with the phone.

And just like that, the girls took a hard turn toward a hotel, the tourists close beside them. A few doors down they disappeared through the doorway of a building. In English, the sign read, MASSAGE PARLOR.

Annalee felt sick to her stomach. *Did that really just happen?* The man with the cell phone met up with the guy who had been trailing the girls, and again money seemed to be exchanged.

Niran looked heartsick, but he kept walking. The others caught up to him. They had missed the chance to help the two girls. Annalee had a feeling there would be more.

Bangla Road bustled with an ethnically diverse mass of tourists. Most of them seemed to be looking for a kind of fun that was illegal in other countries. Niran had told them the nights were worse. The things that could be bought and sold would hurt their hearts. He kept the details to himself. He didn't have to say anything. Here in the Phuket sunshine, the sex slave industry was in plain sight.

Five more buildings and Annalee spotted a thin girl in the crowd ahead. She was walking toward them, and like the two others, this one wore high heels and heavy makeup. But as they got closer, Annalee gasped and covered her mouth. The child couldn't have been more than ten years old. Dirt streaked her see-through shorts and top, and her hair was teased to twice its normal size.

Suddenly a Thai man, maybe fifty years old, came alongside her and shoved her. Hard.

The girl fell to the ground and scrambled to her feet. Blood trickled from one knee and terror screamed from her eyes, but she didn't cry out. The man grabbed her little chin and forced her to look into his face. He barked something at her, then he dropped back into the crowd behind her.

"They are beaten if they don't make eye contact with potential clients." Niran spoke softly as they walked.

They were close enough now to see the girl was crying. She seemed desperate to avoid the eyes of passersby. Too terrified, too hurting to look up. Even if it meant a beating, apparently.

Annalee caught a determination in Niran's eyes. He took a few running steps through the crowd and put his hand on the girl's shoulder. Annalee and her family were just a couple feet behind, but they stopped. This was Niran's territory.

Whatever Niran said, the child nodded. Tears trickled down her cheeks. And like that the angry Thai man was there at the girl's side. He shouted something at Niran and then Niran whipped out his wallet. The police had given him a badge, a way of identifying himself as an informant.

Anything could happen at this point, Niran had told them. But a trafficker would rather lose a child slave than lose his freedom. And Thailand's government was very hard on convicted sex traffickers.

It only took a few seconds for the Thai man to understand what was about to happen. Niran already had his cell phone out. Like a seasoned athlete, the perpetrator turned and ran for his life. He was halfway down the block when Niran stooped and talked again to the little girl.

She was still crying, her black eyeliner running down her face. Niran turned to Annalee's parents. "We need to get her to safety. The child told me she's been that man's slave for three weeks. He said he'd kill her if she got away."

Before they took the girl back to the van, Niran directed her to the nearest bench. When she was seated, the child's feet didn't even reach the ground. Annalee looked around. No one seemed to notice the scene playing out here. Tourists, too busy bartering for a better priced T-shirt to see a child sex slave being rescued. Too busy to notice other trafficked children mixed in with the summer crowd.

Annalee and the group formed a shelter around Niran as he worked. He said something to the girl and she ran her hands over her cheeks and nodded. Niran removed the heels from her young feet and slipped them into his backpack. From inside one of the pockets he pulled out a pair of sandals and gave them to her.

Her hands shook as she slid them on.

And in that single act, the child no longer looked like a sex slave. She was a girl in need of safety and shelter and family. With the change of shoes, the child looked like she might be Niran's daughter. Niran motioned to Annalee. "Hold her hand, please."

Annalee took the child's hand and at the same time, the girl looked up. Her eyes welled with fresh tears and then she did something Annalee hadn't expected.

The girl smiled.

"It's okay." Annalee figured the child didn't speak English. But she had to try. The girl clung to Annalee's hand. As if her life depended on it.

The group hurried down the street with Niran in the lead. Even still Annalee wasn't sure what would happen once they reached Niran's van. Would the child really go with them? She was young and thin and scared, but she didn't know them. Annalee and her family were clearly not from Thailand, and Niran was a complete stranger.

Still, the child didn't hesitate.

Niran helped her into the van and forty minutes later they drove through a set of double gates to a sprawling compound. Part of that time, Niran talked on the phone, no doubt preparing his team for the arrival of the girl. Behind the chain link and razor wire was a large white brick building. The place wasn't glamorous but clearly this was the safe house. More like a safe hotel. They parked and a woman met them as they got out of the van.

"That's Som, his wife," Annalee's father explained to the others.

The woman took the girl and gave Annalee's group a traditional greeting. Hands together and a slight bow. As she left with the child, Niran turned to them. "She looks forward to meeting you later."

They walked toward the front door. Annalee still couldn't believe it. "How . . . old is she?"

Niran gritted his teeth. "Eight years."

Like someone had kicked her in the gut, Annalee reeled toward her mother. The child was barely more than a baby. How could this happen? She stole a look at Tommy.

His eyes flashed with rage. "Mr. Niran . . . can I ask you a question?"

"Of course." Niran's eyes were teary.

"Where were the police?" Tommy clenched his jaw. "If we could see those girls so easily, why couldn't they? Someone in authority should be rescuing these kids."

Annalee agreed, of course. They all did. Ending the problem of sex trafficking in Phuket seemed simple enough. Arrest the guys with the children, lock them up and throw away the key. That would stop traffickers from thinking they could steal boys and girls and sell them on Bangla Road.

Niran shook his head. "They are smart, these men."

He looked disgusted. "They say they are Grandpa or Uncle. The kids usually agree."

"Why?" The question was out before Annalee could stop herself. "Don't they want to be rescued?"

"It's complicated." Niran crossed his arms. "Traffickers confuse the brains of these children. They threaten to kill their parents or families. It's very precise how they treat their victims, like a science. Captors know how to keep their slaves."

"Of course, it's not just here." Annalee's father looked at each of them. "The United States has the same thing. Even Indianapolis. It's just harder to see."

Niran nodded. "I'm afraid so." He looked toward the front door of the safe house. "We cannot help every child. But today, we thank God for saving that little one."

Yes, Annalee thought. She closed her eyes for a few seconds. *Lord, restore this child of Yours. Give her new life here. And help Niran and his wife save more boys and girls.*

And suddenly she had a glimpse of the future. She could see herself working with rescued girls, giving them a safe place to live and heal, saving them from their wretched existence. Right in her own city.

In the vision she didn't see only herself working with broken children. She saw someone else. But his face wasn't that of a stranger. It was the face of the only boy she had ever loved.

Tommy Baxter.

3

Basketball practice let out early that September afternoon, and Tommy was thankful. He had agreed to take Annalee to a doctor's appointment, a checkup. Just to see why she was still tired. Everyone figured she had mononucleosis. Something she might have gotten when they were traveling, and the virus was still lingering.

Her parents were out of town so today it would be just the two of them.

Routine, he told himself. *No big deal.*

They were a month into their senior year at Northside and all of life lay stretched ahead of them. Today wasn't going to change that. She'd get the official diagnosis for mono, follow the doctor's orders and get better. After talking to God about Annalee, Tommy had a sense everything would be okay. Annalee wasn't dealing with anything serious.

She couldn't be.

He took another five three-point shots and swished them all. His routine to end every practice.

Across the court Coach Anders entered the gym

from the locker room and walked toward him. "Got another call from a scout. University of Michigan." Coach was a veteran. He'd worked at Northside for nearly two decades. "You telling your parents about these offers?"

Tommy smiled. "They know." Not for a minute did he want to play college basketball. He'd made that decision a year ago. He wasn't tall enough for the NBA and college hoops would take too much time. He didn't need the scholarship. His grades would take care of that.

Coach had a basketball under his arm. "We're talking full ride. Division I programs."

"No thanks." Tommy led the way to the locker room. "Someone else out there wants it more than me. You know that."

"True." Coach Anders shook his head. "I'll never understand you, Baxter."

That was okay. Lately, even Tommy's parents struggled to understand him. "You could at least try a season of college ball," his dad had said to him a few days ago. Tommy listened, patient. But his decision never wavered.

He bid goodbye to his coach. Then he showered, grabbed his backpack and walked across campus toward the library. Annalee would be waiting for him there.

He saw her before she saw him. Did she look thinner? More frail? She wore a white button-up sweater and her shoulders looked practically bony. Weight loss was a symptom of mono. She should've gone to the doctor before this. But what if . . .

No. Annalee was fine. Her weight loss was just a part

of the virus. Or maybe she hadn't lost weight. Maybe it was just the way she wore the sweater. Yes, that was it.

They walked to the parking lot and he helped her into his black Jeep. Before they reached the road, she turned to him. "Tommy . . . you aren't afraid, right?"

"Me?" A strange panic welled up inside him, but he hid it. *Don't be worried*, he told himself. He forced a laugh. "Of course not. This is just a checkup." He reached for her hand. It felt colder than usual.

She nodded and settled into her seat. After a minute she checked the time on her phone. "We're early. My appointment got moved back an hour."

"Well then . . . I have an idea." He turned at the next light and headed to Benson's Bakery on Main Street. Oldest Indianapolis creamery around, and Annalee's favorite.

A smile lifted her lips. "You're not taking me for—"

"An iced vanilla latte?" He kept one hand on the wheel, his eyes on the road. "Yes, Annalee, I am. After what happened last time . . . I think it's only right."

She laughed and the sound was music in the air. That, combined with the wind in the trees and the bright blue sky, made Tommy relax. Everything was going to be fine. Annalee would receive her mono diagnosis, get better and move on with life.

"By the way." Annalee shifted in her seat and stared at him. "I forgive you for last time."

"Good." He grinned at her. "I told you I'd make it up to you." The store was just ahead. *This was good. Her favorite coffee and funny stories.* Everything was going to be fine.

Annalee's eyes danced. "I mean . . . what was your excuse again? Lack of balance?"

"Like I said . . . I was reaching for your door." He raised his brow. "Trying to be a gentleman."

"I'm just teasing." Her laughter remained. "It was an accident."

"But who does that?" Tommy parked in the lot adjacent to Benson's. "I reach for your door and hit your iced latte. Straight into your face."

"It was fun explaining it to my parents." She took a deep breath. "I laugh every time I think about it."

As he stepped out of the Jeep, Tommy did an exaggerated bow. He eased her into his arms and his eyes held hers for a long beat. "Happy to keep you entertained."

For a moment, all he wanted was to kiss her. But if she had mono, he'd better not. They'd been refraining just in case. He worked his hand through her silky hair, his voice a whisper. "Just don't replace me, okay."

Annalee stifled a laugh. She looked like she wanted to kiss him, as badly as he wanted to kiss her. But it couldn't happen now. Not until her diagnosis.

Finally he stepped back and she took his hand. "Don't worry, Tommy Baxter." She smiled at him. *Those green eyes.* "I won't replace you."

"Same." He didn't look away. "Not now or ever."

It's just a checkup. Mononucleosis. Nothing more.

He bought a large drink for her and a small iced tea for himself.. They were almost back to the Jeep, talking about his basketball team and her chemistry class, when it happened.

A deafening screech came from the nearest intersection. Tommy turned and saw a gray sedan jolt to a halt, but the driver didn't stand a chance. A new model pickup blazed through the red light without braking. The truck barreled into the side of the sedan and somehow kept going.

"Tommy!" Annalee dropped her coffee and took a few steps toward the intersection. "The driver!"

Already smoke poured from the sedan's engine and the hint of a flame curled up from under the hood. Several cars stopped, but no one got out. Tommy threw his drink and took off. He looked over his shoulder at Annalee. "Call 9-1-1!"

He rushed toward the car even as the fire grew. Other cars pulled up to the intersection and skidded to a stop. One guy opened his car door and stood, but he didn't move, didn't run toward the flaming sedan.

Only Tommy did that.

Everything shifted into slow motion. He couldn't see anything but the car and now something else. A woman frantically struggling inside the twisted wreckage. She looked like she was trying to free herself.

Tommy reached the sedan and grabbed the driver's door handle. It wouldn't budge. The heat was intense and getting hotter. Flames moved over the front of the car toward the windshield. *It's going to blow*, Tommy thought to himself. *God, help me, please. It's going to blow!*

With a strength greater than his own, Tommy finally jerked the door open. "Come on!" He took hold of the woman's arm. She was older, maybe in her late seventies. "You have to get out!"

Sirens sounded in the distance, but it didn't matter. Tommy didn't have time for fire trucks or ambulances. A half a minute or so was all he had to get the lady out. Seconds, even.

"Help me!" the woman screamed. "I . . . I can't get my seatbelt off!"

Smoke was filling the car, the heat suffocating both of them. Tommy held his breath and reached over the woman. *God, please* . . . Tommy pushed the seatbelt button again and again. "Come on . . . please." And suddenly . . . it released.

The smoke and heat were definitely getting to the woman. She choked and gasped, struggling to breathe. There was just one way Tommy was going to get her out of the car alive. He hooked his arms beneath hers and pulled with everything he had.

With a supernatural speed and strength, Tommy dragged the woman across the intersection to the nearest curb. At the same time an explosion ripped through the vehicle and shot it ten feet off the ground.

Hovering over the woman, Tommy watched, horrified. *God, you saved us. Thank You.* He had no words, just gratitude. A fire truck pulled up and an ambulance behind it. The scene unfolded in a rush of motion. People running about, passersby and drivers crowding to the intersection. Paramedics hurried up to the woman and took over. One man asked Tommy to step back.

Which he did.

All the way back to the spot near Benson's where Annalee stood pinned to a brick wall. Her face pale, her whole body trembling. "Tommy."

He took her in his arms and held on. No one seemed to notice them. The flaming car had everyone's attention now—not the guy who had pulled the woman from danger. Tommy didn't care. The driver was safe now, that was all that mattered.

The woman was safe.

"You . . . you could've been killed." Annalee pressed her forehead to his chest. "You're crazy."

"Someone had to help her." Tommy was shaking now, too. The adrenaline catching up to him. "She . . . she wouldn't have made it."

Annalee looked up at him. "You had seconds. That's all."

Everyone should've run to her, Tommy wanted to say. "She needed help." He cradled her head in his hands. "It's okay." He breathed the words into her beautiful blond hair. "God was with me."

A police officer walked up and took a report. What happened and who hit who. "You dragged her from the car? Before the explosion?"

"Yes, sir." Tommy slid his hands into his jeans pockets. "I did."

The officer studied him. "You're a rare breed, son." He

patted Tommy's shoulder. "Kind, compassionate. Selfless."
His eyes softened. "We could use a few more like you."

"Thanks." Tommy wanted to say it was no big deal.
Running toward the burning car wasn't something he
took time to consider. "Anyone would've helped her."

But he was the only one who did.

The police officer finished taking notes, while across
the street the ambulance pulled off with the woman inside. A tow truck moved what was left of the sedan. The
cop looked up from his notepad. "She's breathing well."
He narrowed his eyes. "She'll be okay . . . because of you."

When the officer was gone, Annalee took Tommy's
hand and stared at him. "Anyone would *not* have helped."
She looked over her shoulder at the intersection, and
turned to Tommy again. "Only you."

"Anyway . . ." He'd had enough of the conversation.
He forced a smile. "You lost your coffee again."

"Seems to be a theme." She linked arms with him
and pointed at the gutter. Their empty plastic cups still
lay there. She picked them up and tossed them into a
nearby trashcan. "Looks like we need to come back.
Maybe after the doctor."

He laughed and held the door as she climbed into his
Jeep. That's what they would do. After the doctor figured
out her mono and sent them on their way, they could
come back here and pretend like he hadn't rescued a
woman from a burning car and she hadn't had to go get
her fatigue checked out.

Because by then everything would be fine.

• • •

THE DOCTOR WAS an internist. A specialist in internal medicine. Tommy read that on the man's door as they entered his office. Annalee checked in and sat beside him in the waiting area. Tommy took her hand. "You worried?"

"Not at all." A few swipes and she opened her texts. "Look." She smiled and held the phone up so he could see it. "My mom asked the same thing."

Tommy studied her. She didn't look as tired today. Her cheeks were pink, her green eyes bright with life. He watched her texting her mom back. "What're you telling her?"

"Same thing." She slipped her phone in her purse and leaned back. "I'm sure it's mono, Tommy. Plus, doctors like to rule out things. That's all."

That sounded right. Of course her primary doctor had suggested this specialist. Annalee had been tired since the trip to Thailand two months ago. And she had a cough she couldn't shake. Sometimes—if Tommy was honest—Annalee seemed out of breath from nothing more than crossing the street. He tapped his foot and looked around the office.

Framed beach art hung on every wall. One painting looked like Phuket. He gave her hand a soft squeeze. "Seems like yesterday, walking Karon Beach."

"Mmm. Yes." She breathed deep. "I feel better today. So, that's good."

"It is." Tommy gripped the arms of his chair. Why was he so anxious? "Open gym went well."

"I can't believe it's your last season." She didn't look away, didn't blink. "I'm glad I get to watch you play. One more year."

Something inside him relaxed. They had so much ahead. The rest of the fall semester and then Christmas break and the games would start. Tommy loved having Annalee in the stands. She and her parents sitting next to his family.

"Annalee Miller?" A heavyset nurse stood at the doorway. She had kind eyes.

Annalee stood and gave him one last glance. "I'll be right back."

This is routine, he told himself. His eyes landed on the beach painting again. Otherwise her parents would be here. His phone buzzed and he checked it. His cousin Cole Baxter Blake texted him a few times a week. This time about a girl he was seeing at school. The conversation helped Tommy pass the time.

Seven minutes later, Annalee walked through the door holding a piece of paper. Tommy stood to meet her and immediately two things troubled him. First, the appointment hadn't taken nearly long enough. Even the most basic exam should at least take twenty minutes. The other thing was more obvious.

Annalee looked scared to death.

When they were out in the hall, she stopped and faced him. "I need a scan. It's two floors down in the hospital wing." She held up the piece of paper. "They want me to do it now."

Tommy's mind began to spin. "A . . . a scan?" He shook his head. "For what?"

"My lungs and chest." Annalee looked up. "The doctor drew blood to check for mono. But he heard something, when he listened to me breathe." Her smile didn't reach her eyes. "It's probably all part of the virus."

The floor didn't feel solid anymore, and Tommy couldn't find his voice. As they entered the elevator, he focused on the place where Annalee held tight to his elbow. Standing next to him. Where she'd been as far back as freshman year.

At the imaging department, he held the door for her. They were barely inside when a tech stepped into the waiting area. "Annalee? We're ready for you."

She turned a weak smile toward Tommy and waved.

"It could take an hour," the woman told him. "If you'd like to have a seat."

Annalee moved through the door with the tech and Tommy was alone in the room. This one had nothing on the walls.

He sat down and clasped his hands. Why was it going to take an hour? He squeezed his eyes shut and tried not to think about it. But the questions came anyway. How far away had they taken her? And what about her parents? Should he call them and tell them or had the doctor done that already?

It's just routine, he told himself. *She's probably had*

mono for months. Which can't be good. But her grades were still amazing and she still laughed at his jokes. So she wasn't that tired. Not too sick, like something more serious.

But what if . . . ?

No way he could finish the question, so he let it dangle against the backdrop of his pounding heart. And in the sterile cold of the waiting area, Tommy Baxter did the only thing he could think to do.

He dropped to his knees.

4

The trip to New York City was in twenty-four hours and Reagan Baxter could think of little else. She parked her Acura at the lot near Indianapolis's Downtown Canal Walk and looked up. The leaves were starting to turn. Weather reports said it was going to be a beautiful autumn.

But first they would take their New York trip.

She spotted her sister-in-law's SUV. They had arranged this walk a week ago, a chance to talk about the visit to Ground Zero. For the first time, both families would return to Lower Manhattan for the anniversary of 9/11.

The lives they'd lived back then, the losses they'd faced were topics Reagan and Ashley Baxter Blake rarely talked about. All of them had lived in Bloomington, Indiana, when the terrorist attacks happened. But at the time, Reagan's parents lived in Manhattan. Her dad had worked in the North Tower, on one of the top floors.

He had died there.

Eventually, Reagan had married Ashley's brother,

Luke, and the two of them had moved to Indianapolis and raised a family. Tommy, Malin, and Johnny, who was a second grader. Their story was heartbreaking and hope-filled, a marriage that had survived great losses. But it stood as a beacon for all their family.

Beauty from ashes.

For Ashley, it was her husband, Landon, who had painful memories from his time in lower Manhattan. In 2001, he had been hired by the Fire Department of New York and would have been there that September 11, but a work injury in Bloomington had set him months be-hind. He was well enough when the attacks happened that he dropped everything and took a bus to New York that terrible day to look for one particular missing fire-fighter.

His best friend, Jalen.

Landon had worked at Ground Zero until he and a team of firefighters found Jalen's body in the mountains of debris. Landon returned home and in time he and Ashley married and had a family. Ashley's life had been equally full. She and Landon had Cole, nineteen; Amy, fourteen; Devin, twelve; and Janessa, eight. They had lost one baby just after birth. But what they had was rich and true and beautiful.

And all of it born from the ruins of 9/11.

Now this year they had finally all gotten vacation days around September 11. Nineteen years had come and gone since their lives were changed that Tuesday morning, and now the trip was tomorrow.

Reagan had looked forward to this walk with Ashley so they could talk about the past before flying to La-Guardia. Reagan met up with her sister-in-law in the parking lot and the two hugged. Ashley blew at a wisp of her hair. "You packed?"

"Hardly." Reagan laughed. "You know me. Last minute."

"Me, too. Landon keeps me in line." Ashley unzipped her windbreaker.

"How were things at the gallery?" They made their way to the path.

"Amazing." Ashley's pace was slow and easy. "I sold three paintings this week."

For years Ashley had displayed her artwork at a gallery an hour south in downtown Bloomington, where she and her family lived. But her reach had expanded. Now she was selling paintings at a gallery in Indianapolis, too. "Congratulations." Reagan smiled. "I'm not surprised. You're so talented, Ash."

"Thanks." Ashley stared at the river. Not many people were out on the three-mile canal loop this afternoon. "So . . . tomorrow."

"I know." Reagan lifted her eyes. The sky was crystal blue, the faintest breeze stirring the trees that lined the walk. "I haven't been back since my mother moved."

"When did she leave New York? Not long after 9/11, right?"

"A few years." Reagan nodded to a bench up ahead. "Want to sit? The sun feels good."

"Sure." Ashley took the spot beside her and they

looked at the water. "Such a pretty area . . . here in the middle of the city."

"I love it." Reagan came here often. She would bring lunch to Luke at his nearby law office and then walk for an hour. "My mother moved to Florida the year after Luke and I married. So, yeah. It's been a long time since I've been back."

"Me, too." Ashley crossed her arms. "Every time we think about taking the trip, something else comes up. Or we make other plans."

Reagan understood. "I can't believe I'll be standing at Ground Zero tomorrow."

"Your mom never remarried?" Ashley faced Reagan. "Is she . . . lonely?"

"She's not." Reagan pictured her mother's sweet face, and she felt the corners of her lips lift. "She helps out at a local children's home. And Tuesdays she attends a singles Bible study. Fifteen people her age without spouses. That keeps her busy."

"I can't imagine . . . what she went through that day." Ashley narrowed her eyes and looked off. "Your dad goes to work, ordinary day, and without warning he's trapped in the worst terrorist attack to hit the United States."

"His view from the eighty-ninth floor of the World Trade Center was breathtaking." Reagan could still remember the time she and Luke visited him there, mere months before 9/11. "Life felt untouchable up there. He had no idea what was coming."

Ashley sighed. "Landon talked to Jalen's parents.

Sometimes they visit Manhattan on the anniversary." She sat a little straighter. "Not this year."

Reagan remembered the sadness of Jalen's death, too. Landon and Jalen were both firefighters, best friends from college. "How many days was Landon at Ground Zero looking for him?"

"Too long." Clouds had covered the sun. Ashley stood. "I hate thinking about it. Let's walk again."

For a few minutes they moved along the path without saying anything, lost in the memories of that long-ago time. "Tommy's definitely joining us. Not sure if I told you."

"You did." Ashley smiled. "I wish Cole could come. He has eighteen credits this semester. Too busy to get away." They enjoyed this, talking about their kids.

"Tommy's asking about his grandfather." Reagan stared straight ahead. "They're a lot alike. I see that the older Tommy gets."

Ashley nodded. "The trip will be good for him. Good for us all." She took a deep breath. "Even if it's draining."

They kept on and at the end of the walkway they stopped at Quills for coffee. The air was cooler, ushering in the thunderstorms forecast for that night. "The weather . . ." Ashley sipped her latte. "It's like life. You never know when the blue skies are going to disappear."

"True." Reagan had once heard a speaker refer to the journey of life, and how only God could get them through the lightning and wind. *Let the Lord drive*, the man had said. *He knows how to get His people safely home.*

Ashley pointed to a family of ducks. "Aww." She walked to the water's edge and Reagan followed her. "Look at them. Not a care in the world."

Reagan watched the ducks swim off. "How's Amy?"

A smile started in Ashley's eyes. "Every day is a miracle." She breathed deep. "When I think how things could be. I'm just . . . thankful. No other words."

Several years ago Amy had come to live with Ashley after a terrible car accident took the lives of Ashley's sister Erin, her husband and their other children. Only young Amy had survived the crash, and since then she had lived with Ashley and Landon and their family. Amy was fourteen now. Reagan sighed. "Her mannerisms, the things she says remind me so much of Erin."

"Me, too. Like Erin left fingerprints on her little girl's heart." Ashley's eyes welled up. "Amy misses her mother every day. But she's doing so well. She really is."

They walked back to the path and when they reached the parking lot, Reagan turned to Ashley. "I'm so glad you and Landon are going with us. No one else . . . no one gets what we all went through."

Ashley hugged her. "You and Luke . . . the two of you were apart for an entire year after 9/11."

"We'd be apart still if it wasn't for you." Reagan hadn't talked about this since she and Luke married. But the truth remained. "You chased him down . . . and brought the two of us back together."

They talked a few more minutes about their families. How Ashley's dad—John Baxter—was doing well and how each of their kids was faring in school this year. "I'm glad they're staying home." Ashley looked at Reagan. "Remembering 9/11 won't be easy."

"But it's part of our journey." Reagan took hold of Ashley's hands and gave them a slight squeeze. "A part where God was definitely driving."

"Yes." Ashley stepped back and checked the time on her phone. "I better go. See you tomorrow!"

Reagan climbed into her car and thought about all she still had to do, all that the next few days would bring. Tommy was taking his girlfriend to the doctor this afternoon, so he'd been distracted. Not focused on the trip to New York. At least he was no longer talking about joining the military instead of attending college. There would be time for that after getting his degree, if Tommy thought it best.

For now, Tommy had the grades to do anything with his life. He could be a doctor or a lawyer. Anything he wanted, really.

Before she started the car, Reagan stared at the tallest buildings in Indianapolis. The ones right across the canal. Her eyes found the offices on the top floors. Lights shone from the windows and Reagan could picture life on the other side of them.

People in their offices, talking and working on computers, making a dent in the day's workload and planning ways to hit the goals and demands of their jobs. All with the prettiest views of the city. Just like life had been that Tuesday in New York City. Not for a minute did anyone up there that morning think they had so little time to live.

Her father wouldn't have thought that, either.

She headed to the interstate. Malin and Johnny would be back from school by now, doing their homework. Reagan's mother would arrive later that night from Florida to stay with them. And Luke's father, John Baxter, was going to spend the weekend with Ashley's kids.

All so that for just a few days they could go back again, back to the events of a time the nation would remember forever. For everyone else it was history. But for Reagan and Luke, Ashley and Landon it was something more.

It was personal.

ASHLEY TOOK HER time on the hour-long drive back to Bloomington. Her dad and stepmom were already at the house, getting Devin and Amy and Janessa ready for a four-day weekend together. Tonight, dinner was pizza— so Ashley and Landon could focus on packing.

Like she had told Reagan, her time at the art gallery had gone exceedingly well. God continued to give her inspiration for her paintings and people kept buying them. But there was something she hadn't told Reagan.

Landon's cough was worse.

He wasn't fighting a cold and he didn't have bronchitis. No fever or chills or congestion. Just a cough. Worse

than last year at this time. Maybe—if she was honest—
Landon was a little short of breath. And possibly more
tired than he should be.

So last night after Landon and the kids were asleep,
Ashley had moved into the art space next to their bedroom, opened her laptop and started searching. It wasn't
the first time she'd been concerned about Landon's
health and certainly it wasn't the only situation where
she'd turned to the Internet for answers. Years ago
Landon had struggled with lung issues, but then, miraculously, he had gotten better.

Maybe this was only a low-lying virus. Possibly he
was struggling with seasonal allergies. Either way, last
night Ashley suddenly had to know more about the current risks for people who had spent months sorting
through the pile at Ground Zero.

She had long known there was a causal relationship
between the toxins at Ground Zero and the undeniable
spike in premature deaths among those exposed to
them. But she hadn't googled the situation in a while.

From the room down the hall, Landon's cough had
broken the silence.

And before it stopped, Ashley began the search.

Ground Zero and cancer
Ground Zero and lung disease
Deaths associated with Ground Zero

She found a police memorial site where a number of
fallen officers from New York City looked to be in their
forties and fifties. *Strange,* she thought. She hadn't been

looking for a police memorial. So Ashley began to click on the names of the deceased and her blood ran cold. Almost all of them had died the same way.

9/11-related illness.

And so Ashley looked back through the years and what she found horrified her. Twenty-three New York police officers died on 9/11. But since then nearly 250 police officers had died of illnesses connected with 9/11.

Landon, of course, was a firefighter. So that led Ashley to her next search. What about firefighters who worked at Ground Zero? Again the numbers were staggering. Since 9/11, more than two hundred firefighters had died of cancer or other diseases connected to those events.

Then there was the big picture. Ashley had learned last night that more than ten thousand people exposed to toxins around Lower Manhattan after the terrorist attacks had now died of illnesses as a direct result. Recently, the city of New York had opened the Memorial Glade at Ground Zero. A new $5 million walkway to honor first responders who had died since the terrorist attack.

All of which meant one terrifying thing.

Landon's cough needed to be checked out.

Ashley had also researched specialists who handled cases related to 9/11 and she'd found a doctor in Lower Manhattan. Then before fear changed her mind, she booked a consultation for early afternoon tomorrow. As soon as they arrived in the city.

Convincing Landon hadn't been easy. "It's nothing," he had told her earlier this morning. "Allergies, my love. Every fall, remember?"

"Sneezing, sure. Itchy eyes." She had put her hands on his shoulders and looked straight at him. "Your cough is worse, Landon. You need to see someone. Just in case."

He had finally agreed and now Ashley was consumed with the sickening possibilities. *Lord, let it be nothing. Landon is everything to our family . . . to me.* She could see him as clearly as if he were standing in front of her.

Tall, still dark hair. As fit as he'd been in his firefighting days.

Landon was the Bloomington fire chief now. He spent his days at a desk—managing his department and being the liaison for community relations. But back in the day he had been involved in a number of deadly fires—one where he saved the life of a little boy and wound up in the hospital fighting for his own life.

But all that had been only kindling to the toxins he was exposed to at Ground Zero, working fourteen-hour days until he helped find the body of his best friend, Jalen. Ashley tightened her jaw. *Let it be a cold, Lord. Heal Landon, please.* All day she had silently talked to God, begging him for peace. Remembering words from the Bible to soothe her anxious soul.

Do not worry about tomorrow, for tomorrow will worry about itself.

Cast all your anxiety on Him, because He cares for you.

Whatever is true, whatever is noble, whatever is right,

whatever is pure, whatever is lovely, whatever is admirable—if anything is excellent or praiseworthy—think about such things. . . . And the God of peace will be with you.

Come to me, all you who are weary and burdened, and I will give you rest . . .

Over and over and over.

Traffic back to Bloomington was light so Ashley pulled into the Baxter house driveway sooner than she'd expected. Tomorrow at this time not only would they be in New York City, remembering the events of nearly two decades ago. They would have answers about Landon's health. And as much as Ashley wanted to know, she wasn't relieved at the thought.

She was scared to death.

5

Annalee sat on a cold metal chair a few feet from an enormous donut-shaped machine. The scan would take place in a few minutes. Until then, the tech had told her to wait. Already she'd been here longer than that. She looked at the flat surface extending into the donut and the panel of instruments beside it and she had just one thought.

She wished Tommy were with her.

Why did he have to wait in the other room? Didn't the medical people understand how nervous she was, how frightened she felt even doing this? A shiver ran down her arms. She pulled her phone from her purse and texted her mom.

The doctor ordered a scan for me. It was in the same building, so Tommy brought me here. I'm waiting now for the tech so we can get it over with. Do they use a scan to diagnose mono? Honestly, Mom, I'm afraid. Please pray.

Almost as soon as she sent the text, her phone rang. Annalee wasn't sure if she could be on the phone in this place, but she didn't care. "Hello?"

"Honey, why didn't you call me earlier?" Her mother sounded frantic. "I had no idea they'd order a test the same day."

Annalee closed her eyes. "Me, either." She sucked in a quick breath and blinked. *Don't panic,* she told herself. *Stay calm.* "The doctor said . . . it could be mono. He took blood."

"Okay. Yes . . ." Her mom released a long breath. "That's what we've been thinking. I had mono when I was in high school. It's terrible." She hesitated. "So that must be why they're doing the scan." She sounded relieved. "You just need more rest. Like we've been saying."

The doctor had agreed Annalee had all the symptoms of mono. An occasional fever, zero energy and most mornings she woke up with sheets wet from sweating. Night sweats, the doctor called it. Whatever she was dealing with, the tests today would tell the story, and then she could move on to getting better. She cleared her throat. "You've heard of that, right? Scans for mono?"

"Yes. I think so." Her mother's answer was a little too quick. "They're probably looking to see if your spleen is enlarged. That's something they would see on a scan."

A woman wearing a white coat walked into the room.

"I have to go." Annalee dropped her voice to a whisper. "I'll call you later."

"Okay, honey. Your dad and I . . . we're coming home tomorrow."

Annalee set the phone in her purse and lifted her eyes to the woman. "Is it time?"

"Yes. I need you to remove your clothing and jewelry." She handed Annalee a hospital gown. "And change into this." The woman smiled, but it didn't change her serious expression. "I'll give you a few minutes."

While Annalee did what the woman asked, nausea formed a pit in her stomach. *Why am I worried?* This couldn't be anything serious. Her mom's sister had died on the mission field in Kenya last year. A family could only take so much heartache.

It has to be mono.

The woman returned and helped Annalee onto the flat table. Then she handed her a pair of earplugs. "You'll want these. The test is loud . . . it can last as long as an hour depending on what we see."

She'd never worn earplugs. She took a minute to figure out how to make them work and then Annalee lay flat on her back. Her heart picked up speed and raced against the wall of her chest. The earplugs made the sound louder. *Peace,* she prayed. *Please give me peace, God. Calm me down.*

As the table slid into the tube and the test began, Annalee remembered something her father had told her. *If you're stuck in a difficult situation take yourself somewhere else. Remember a happy time or relive some meaningful moment.*

With her eyes squeezed shut, Annalee did just that. So she was no longer in a cold tube with loud scary sounds happening around her. She was on her parents' back porch a week ago telling them about a decision she'd made. A decision about her life.

Her parents had made hot cider. Austin was at football practice so it was just the three of them. Like it was happening again, Annalee could smell the cinnamon from her warm mug and see the looks of anticipation in the faces of her parents.

"God has spoken to you?" Her dad sat opposite her, all of them in rocking chairs.

"He has." Annalee had never been more sure about a career path. "I know what I want to do." And then she'd told them. "I want to help trafficked children here in Indianapolis." Annalee's heart soared at the possibility. "I'm thinking of developing an app."

The idea was straightforward. Hotel workers would download the app, which would connect with local law enforcement agencies. If a front desk employee suspected a trafficker was bringing a child into a hotel room, the worker could notify authorities anonymously through the app. If the tip turned into an arrest or a rescue, the hotel worker would receive a reward.

Her mom's eyes had lit up. "I like it." She looked at Annalee's father and then back at Annalee. "Who funds the reward?"

"It would be a charity." Annalee had tried to think of everything. "People would donate knowing that the reward money would only be given out if police were able to take action."

They had talked for another half hour about how an app like that could start in Indianapolis and spread to the entire nation or even the world. Her parents agreed that hotel workers were often the last line of defense for trafficked kids. In the United States and even in places like Thailand.

Annalee blinked and the memory disappeared. Shrill beeps and whirring sounds filled the tube—which was four inches from her face. Maybe closer. She tried to take a deep breath but her lungs wouldn't fill, wouldn't expand correctly. Were the walls of the cylinder closing in?

Another memory. That's what she needed. Again she squeezed her eyes shut and this time a different face filled her mind. The handsome face of Tommy Baxter. He had taken her on a date two weeks ago, before her mom had made today's doctor appointment. Back when her fatigue wasn't so draining and she was still sure her tiredness had something to do with the trip overseas. Not this dreaded mono.

She pressed her back against the hard platform. Once more, Annalee could hear Tommy's voice as they set off that day. He had looked at her from behind the wheel. "You ready for your Super Surprise Saturday?"

A smile had filled her heart. "Super Surprise Saturday?" She'd laughed. "What does that even mean?"

"It means you deserve the world. So this isn't our average movie night." Tommy had grinned at her. Then he'd handed her a pink envelope. She could still smell his cologne like he was here with her again. "Open it."

She had known immediately this was going to be a forever memory with Tommy. Inside the card was a poem.

School has started, senior year.
Summer's gone no beaches here.
Still I thought I'd take a chance
Take you out and find romance.
First stop on our night of fun
The chicken place, a 2.1.
I love you always, Annalee

   P.S.—We don't have to be in Phuket for you to take my breath away. That doesn't rhyme . . . but we do.

Love, Tommy

"Are you serious?" Annalee had closed the card and looked at him. "We're doing . . . what . . . a scavenger hunt?"

"We are." He had looked so handsome. Crewneck navy sweater and dark jeans. His hair still blond from the summer sun. "I'm at your beck and call, my fair princess. Think about the clues. Where to first?"

"Uhh." She looked at the card again. "Chick-fil-A?"

"Ding-ding-ding. You got it! *That chicken place.*" He grinned at her. "Let's go!"

She hadn't understood the 2.1 part until they got inside the fast-food restaurant. One of Tommy's friends from the basketball team was working behind the counter and Tommy steered them to his line. When it was their turn, Tommy gave her a soft nudge. "Go ahead . . . place your order."

A laugh caught her off guard. Whatever this was, Tommy's friend had clearly been expecting them. There was a line forming behind them. Annalee tried to compose herself. "I'll have a 2.1 . . . I think." She looked at Tommy. "Right?"

He shrugged at his friend. "The princess wants a 2.1. My treat, of course."

Tommy's friend had Annalee's meal ready. Grilled chicken and a side salad. Her favorite. He handed her the food. "There's the two." He chuckled and pulled another pink envelope from beneath the counter. Annalee's name was written across the front. "And here's the one."

When they were back in his Jeep, she opened the card and found another poem. The journey led them to a pottery craft store where they made matching mugs and then left them to be fired in the kiln. Next was a stop at her favorite coffee shop, where they shared a pair of pumpkin spice lattes.

"You don't even like pumpkin." She had given him a funny face as they got into the Jeep again. "What are you doing?"

"Seeing things from your side of the fence." He took a sip and shuddered. "Just this one time, anyway."

Here in the tube she relived each moment.

At each stop the cashier was ready with a pink card, and each card held another poem, another hint for the next stage of their adventure.

The next poem led them to a custom cookie store. Behind the counter an older woman seemed to recognize

Tommy as soon as they walked in. Tommy grinned at her. "My princess has an order, I believe."

Annalee was getting used to this. "Yes . . . I'd like a 2.1 please." She laughed. "Whatever that means."

"Well . . ." The woman giggled. She had to have been in her eighties. This must've been the highlight of her week. "Today only . . . a 2.1 is this." She lifted a small pizza-sized box from beneath the counter and opened the lid.

Pink writing on a pair of enormous chocolate chip cookies read:

Princess lovely
Girl so fair . . .
I think we make
A lasting pair!

Tommy winked at her. "Pair . . . get it? Two cookies. Because we're the perfect duo!"

Again Annalee laughed. The woman gave her yet another pink envelope, and this one directed the two of them to the Fishers Topgolf, twenty miles northeast of Indianapolis. On the ride there, Tommy played Broadway show tunes. Hits from *Hamilton* and *Dear Evan Hansen* and *The Lion King*.

They sang at the top of their lungs and laughed at how they had been in the school musical together fall of their freshman year. He had been Frank Butler in *Annie Get Your Gun* and she'd been Annie. That was how they met.

A "showmance," they had called it.

The noises in the tube were louder now. Annalee squeezed her eyes more tightly shut.

Don't think about it. You're at Topgolf now.

Topgolf turned out to be the last stop on their list of adventures that night. A few times a year, Tommy golfed with his dad and uncles. But Annalee had never done more than miniature golf. That night nearly every time she took the club and tried to hit the ball, she made some mistake.

First, she had accidentally tipped the ball, causing it to roll off the platform in slow motion and down into the scoring area below. As if the wind had blown it off the putting surface. For her next turn, she hit the ball straight at the course map directly in front of her. It had ricocheted off the hard surface and barely missed her face as it settled into the wasteland below.

Both of them had collapsed in a hug of giddy joy, holding each other up so they wouldn't fall to the ground laughing. When Tommy could finally breathe again, he had looked at her. "You're the only one who needs a helmet at Topgolf."

Noises from the scan grew louder again.

Focus, Annalee told herself. *Stay with the memory.*

On the drive home, she and Tommy sang again and talked about musical theater, their love for it and the reasons neither of them had stayed with it. Annalee had shifted her attention to choir. And Tommy played basketball. Which meant neither of them had time for school musicals.

Still, it was one of their dreams to spend a weekend in New York City. Walk the insanely busy streets and catch a few shows. Tommy was going with his family for the anniversary of 9/11, but that was a different sort of trip.

Annalee could still see Tommy's profile as he pulled his Jeep in front of her house late that night. He put the car in park, then turned to her. "And that, Annie, is how a princess should be treated."

Annie.

The noise around her faded, and her heart was filled again with the sound of Tommy's voice. Calling her Annie. For her, it was a silly nickname, the one Tommy used when he wanted to make her smile.

He was the only one who ever called her that.

Tommy had helped her carry the cookies and her handful of pink cards as he walked her up to the door. He faced her and took hold of her hands. The night air had been chilly, so he stood close. As if he might shelter her from more than the cool evening, but from anything that would ever dare come between them. Whatever might try to hurt her.

They set their things down on the nearest rocking chair and Tommy took her in his arms. "All night . . . I kept waiting for this. You and me, alone." He took her face in his hands and kissed her.

Just long enough to tell her what he wouldn't dare say with words.

Because they knew better than to let a moment like that linger. Instead she had watched the muscles in his jaw flex, something that happened when he was making a difficult shot on the basketball court. Whenever he had to work extra-hard.

Like he had to work to not keep kissing her. His breath had been warm on her face, and when he said goodbye he leaned close. Ever so slowly his lips touched hers once more. Only that.

"You deserve the world, Annalee." He handed her the cookie box and searched her eyes. "The least I could give you was a Super Surprise Saturday." He was a few steps down the walkway, then he looked back and grinned. "Oh . . . and next time we might skip Topgolf!"

The memory lifted. *There.* She had done it. The scan was nearly finished, and because of her father's advice Annalee had avoided thinking about it all this time. Thinking about the possible reasons the internist had ordered it. She blinked her eyes open and then closed them again.

This is nothing. It has to be nothing.

There was high school to finish and college to conquer and people to help. She had Tommy Baxter to spend her whole life loving. This health situation was just a reminder for her to take better care of herself. In a week or so she'd get the results. Mononucleosis. And she'd rest up—as long as she needed.

Then she would get on with her life.

The machine made a loud thumping, like someone was trying to jackhammer their way into the cylinder. She held her breath. How much longer did she have in here? And why was she having trouble breathing? When could she get back to Tommy in the waiting room?

She had no answers, no way of knowing how much longer she had to stay in the suffocating tube. But she knew what to do about it. And just like that she could feel herself climbing into Tommy's Jeep and he was sliding behind the wheel, smiling at her.

"You ready for your Super Surprise Saturday?"

6

Tommy's stomach hurt. He stood and walked up to the receptionist. "Annalee Miller?"

This time it was a guy behind the counter. He didn't look old enough to work at a hospital. "I'm sorry?"

"Annalee Miller." Tommy forced himself to stay calm. "She's been in there thirty minutes. Do you know how much longer?"

The guy checked something on his desk and then on the computer screen. "Uh . . . looks like she has another half hour or so." He hesitated. "There's a cafeteria and a coffee shop on the fourth floor."

Coffee. That would help. Tommy nodded. "Thanks." He had to get out of here before he shouted at someone. What possible reason could there be for a scan to take this long? He walked out the office door and headed down the hall.

Already he could breathe better.

A cup of black coffee and ten minutes later, Tommy was back in the waiting room. This time he wasn't alone. An older man sat on one side of the room, eyes downcast, wringing his hands. A carved wooden cane leaned on the chair beside him.

Tommy studied the guy. Was he here for himself or waiting for someone he loved?

The man glanced up and nodded as Tommy took a seat against the adjacent wall. The look in the man's eyes said this wasn't about his own health. He was waiting for someone. Maybe the future hinged on whatever news the man might hear today.

Same as Tommy.

From the floor beside him, the man lifted a thermos, unscrewed the lid and took a sip. "Still hot." He set it down again.

Tommy nodded. He didn't feel like talking. What was taking so long? *A magazine*, that's what he needed. He sorted through the ones spread out on a long coffee table separating the rows of chairs. The one on top said: CLIMATE CONFUSION? GLOBAL WARMING OR AN ICE AGE?

Tommy thumbed to the article. Something about a Greenland iceberg gaining size over the last few years, and temperature readings cooling in the depths of the ocean. He closed the cover. The last thing he wanted was to read about the climate while Annalee was a few doors away sliding in and out of some metal tube. *Poor girl.* She hated elevators. The scan must've made her feel terrible.

Scripture. That would help. He pulled his phone from his jeans pocket and opened his Bible Promises app. A quick scroll and he found what he wanted. Love. Bible verses on love.

I have loved you with an everlasting love . . .

For God so loved the world . . .

Dear friends, let us love one another, for love comes from God . . .

Every line, every word spoke to him. God loved him . . . and He loved Annalee. Tommy's breathing slowed and he settled into the cushioned seat. This was mono, nothing more. Everything was going to be fine. The doctor was just being thorough, making sure he didn't miss anything. God wasn't going to let anything happen to her.

She was too good. She had too much to do for Him.

Tommy stretched out his feet and laced his fingers behind his head. The man across from him looked up. "You waiting for someone?"

"I am." Tommy looked at the waiting room door and then at the man. "My girlfriend's getting a scan."

A crooked smile tugged at the man's lips. "Mine, too."

The old man had a girlfriend? Something about that put Tommy at ease. He leaned forward. "How long have you two been dating?"

"Oh . . . we're married." The man winked at Tommy. "Fifty years. She'll always be my girlfriend."

Tommy chuckled. "I like that."

The smile faded from the man's face. "Etta's fighting cancer." He clenched his fists and relaxed them again.

"This scan . . . it's her last chance. If the cancer is worse, then . . . there's nothing more they can do."

"Oh." Tommy had no idea what to say. "So it could be . . . good news today?"

"That's the hope." The man glanced at the waiting room door. "It'll take a miracle." He crossed his fingers and tapped both hands on the wooden arm rails of the chair. "Hoping the stars line up for her."

All his life growing up, his parents had taught Tommy and his siblings to pray for divine appointments. They didn't need to go to a foreign country to be smack in the middle of a moment only God could set up.

A moment like this one.

"I'm Tommy Baxter." He stood and shook the man's hand.

"Ernest Jones." The man gripped his knees. "You can call me Ernie."

"Okay." Tommy didn't have to ask God for the words. He knew from experience the Lord would give them. "Mister Ernie, you mentioned it'll take a miracle. Are you a praying man?"

The expression on Ernie's face changed. "There was a time. In my younger days."

"Oh." Tommy took his time. "What changed?"

"Life." The older man narrowed his eyes. "People get sick. They die. It makes me mad."

"Yes. . . . My grandma Elizabeth died way too young. Cancer."

The spark faded from Ernie's eyes. "See what I mean?"

"Right." Tommy nodded. "I remember something my aunt Ashley told me. She lost her third baby at birth. But the few minutes she lived, everyone in the family gathered around the hospital bed and prayed over that little girl. We sang and celebrated her."

Ernie's face softened. "That's sad."

"Before the birth, my aunt knew her baby was sick. She and my uncle were ready." Tommy kept his eyes on the man's. "My aunt had come to believe the miracle was even getting to hold her little girl at all."

"Yeah. That's what people tell themselves." Bitterness colored the man's tone. "I say the little girl should've lived. That is . . . if God was watching over her." He looked off. "If people were praying."

Tommy thought for a moment. "I guess it's all in the way you look at it. If God isn't real . . . then what?"

The door opened and a different tech wheeled an older woman into the waiting room. She had shoulder-length silver hair and her eyes immediately turned to Ernie. Tommy hurried to hold the door. At the same time Ernie was on his feet, moving to her wheelchair. "Was it better this time . . . less scary?"

Tommy wanted to watch the two of them, love personified. But he had an idea. He grabbed a piece of paper and pen from the receptionist and scribbled down his email address. Then he waited not far from where Ernie was still helping his love, Etta, get situated.

The man started to push her wheelchair toward the door when he seemed to remember Tommy. He turned to him. "I take it you *are* a praying man, then?"

"I am." Tommy handed the slip of paper to Ernie. "I promise to pray for your wife . . . if you'll let me know how the test comes out."

The man hesitated at first. But then he found that lopsided grin again. "I'll do it." He took the paper and patted his wife's shoulder. "Etta, this is Tommy. My new friend."

"Hello." She looked back and smiled. "You seem like a good one."

When they were gone, Tommy did what he'd told the man. He asked God to give Ernie and Etta a miracle. For two reasons. So Ernie would know that God was real and that He cared about every person, every prayer.

And so that the man might have a little more time with his girlfriend.

Tommy checked the time on his phone. Still another fifteen minutes before Annalee's test would be finished. If he married her the way he planned to, one day they might be back in an office like this and Tommy might be talking to some young gun about his girlfriend of fifty years.

His Annalee.

He had never planned to have a serious girlfriend through high school. Tommy had been too focused on sports, too busy with his peers and his family. Back in middle school, guys his age with girlfriends always seemed to be pretending. Acting older than they were.

Back then the girls towered over the boys and no one could drive.

Made more sense to spend his free time dribbling a basketball.

But all that changed his first day at Northside High.

Tommy leaned back in the waiting room chair. He had taken theater class because it counted as a music elective. That and two of his buddies from the team had also signed up. The rowdy social kids sat in the front that day. Ms. Elmer told them they were going to do a production of *Annie Get Your Gun,* and she expected everyone to participate.

Singing was something Tommy had gotten from his mother. They sang church songs and country favorites around the family piano. But that was it. Tommy was just okay—not the sort of gifted it would take to make a career. Which was why most of his friends didn't know he could sing at all.

Not until the first day in theater class.

That morning, his group flirted with a few girls, all of them joking about being the leads. Ms. Elmer taught them the first verse of one of the songs. Then she asked students interested in being a lead to sing the verse solo at the front of the room, one at a time.

Tommy had never been afraid of much, so he was the first to raise his hand. If he was going to be in musical theater, he might as well let the teacher know what he could do. He sang that day with the confidence of someone who had been performing all his life.

His buddies gave him a standing ovation, high-fiving him and hollering over the fact that Tommy could do more than shoot baskets. Ms. Elmer nodded her approval. "Very nice. We have some real talent this year."

The girls in their friend group took turns singing for Ms. Elmer and then his guy friends sang for her. Only a few could even remember the words.

That's when it happened.

Ms. Elmer called on a girl from the back of the room. When she came forward a sort of hush fell over the class. None of them had ever seen her before. Blond hair spilled over her shoulders and when she turned and faced the class, her green eyes took his breath.

Most beautiful girl Tommy had ever seen.

"Class, let's welcome Annalee Miller from Ohio. She and her family just moved to Indianapolis." Ms. Elmer's smile told everyone she knew more about what was coming than they did. "Annalee?"

What happened then was something Tommy would remember as long as he lived. Annalee began to sing and the sound filled the room. They might as well have sold tickets for the performance she gave that morning. Hers was the voice of an angel and when she finished, the other girls knew they were competing for second place.

Tommy's teammates hurried him along when class ended, but just once he looked back at Annalee. She was gathering her things from the last row of seats and for the slightest instant their eyes met.

From that moment on, Tommy had been in love with Annalee Miller.

It came as no surprise a week later when Annalee was cast as Annie Oakley and Tommy, as Frank Butler—less because he was so talented and more because no one else in the program could sing on pitch.

Week after week of rehearsals, Tommy and Annalee were in the same scenes, working together, blocking their movements, side by side, singing duets. And in all that time Tommy learned practically nothing about her. Only that her parents were missionaries who had relocated to Indiana, and that she had one younger brother named Austin.

Otherwise she was an enigma.

Annalee was friendly while they worked on the show, but after rehearsal she would hurry off. When Tommy saw her in the lunchroom each day, Annalee sat by herself, usually reading. And she looked quite content about the fact.

Like she quite enjoyed the alone time.

Finally the night of the show, Tommy took a chance. After the applause died down and the curtain fell, while he and Annalee were still in the dark of the stage, he took her hand. He would never know what had been more surprising about that moment. The fact that he'd been brave enough to make the move, or what happened next.

Annalee didn't pull away.

"I don't want the show to end," Tommy had whispered. "Could you still be my Annie?"

And she had done the exact thing Tommy had hoped she would do. Annalee Miller had laughed. "Why, yes, Frank Butler." She had kept her voice low. The rest of the class was a few feet away in the wings. "I'd love to be your Annie Oakley. And I'm still a better shooter."

They had laughed, their faces close to each other. And they'd been together ever since. Every now and then she was still his Annie and he was still her Frank. Back then his friends hadn't understood the attraction. "She's so quiet," they would tell him. "Sure she's pretty. But she's always reading a book."

Tommy would only smile and nod. No one else had to get it, but him. In the seasons since then, Annalee had sat near the top of the bleachers with her family for every one of his basketball games. And when he didn't have practice after school he sat in the choir room and listened to her sing.

He could pick her voice out of a hundred-person ensemble.

As the months and years went by Tommy never tired of Annalee. Hardly. Instead he found more things to love about her. The fact that she didn't care about the popular crowd like so many of his friends. And she was smart, too.

When she and Tommy would walk the canal path in downtown Indianapolis, Annalee would talk about her classes and what she was reading. Frank Peretti's *The Oath* and Randy Alcorn's *Deadline* and *Dominion*. Francine Rivers's *Redeeming Love*.

One of her favorites was C. S. Lewis's *Mere Christi-*

anity. They'd sit on the swings at White River Park and she'd talk for hours about a single facet of one chapter. "C. S. Lewis used to be an atheist. Did you know that?" She didn't wait for his answer. "If everyone read his book, the whole world would believe in God."

Other girls her age obsessed over makeup and Instagram and who was liking who. They were addicted to Snapchat and Twitter. Annalee didn't care about any of that. She wasn't on social media and the only time she used her phone was to make plans with Tommy or her family and choir friends.

"What could Instagram teach me, that I can't learn in a book?" she would say.

The fact that she wasn't like every other girl at school only made Tommy fall harder. At the end of their junior year, he started talking about forever. Especially one night when he had brought her home from a coffee date.

They had stood facing each other on her front porch, and Tommy had put his hand on her shoulder. "Annalee, I want to marry you one day," he'd said. He wasn't kidding.

She must've seen that in his face because she brought her fingers to his cheek. "Isn't that the way the story ends, Frank?"

"Yes, it is, Annie." And the two of them had moved closer, their hearts beating hard, until finally—for the first time—they kissed.

Tommy still wasn't sure how he pulled away from

Annalee that night when she had to go inside. He could remember smiling even after he got home.

And so life had gone with them. His parents loved Annalee and her parents loved him. One night a year or so ago, his dad said it best. "Some people just find the right thing early."

The fact that they were young didn't bother Tommy. He had no interest in dating other girls. There *were* no other girls, not ever. Only Annalee. His Annie.

As if on cue, the door opened and Annalee walked into the waiting room. She looked more tired than before. Weaker. She smiled, but it didn't reach her eyes. "Hi."

Like Ernie twenty minutes ago, Tommy was on his feet and at her side. He put his arm around her. "How was it?"

"Fine. I'll know next week." She leaned into him. "I want to go home, Tommy. Please."

They didn't talk on their way to his Jeep, didn't sing on the drive back to her house. Neither of them brought up the plan to get coffee. Instead, Tommy helped her inside and visited with her brother for a few minutes. Before he left, he pulled Annalee aside and stared straight into her eyes. "This is just a virus."

She nodded, but she looked away.

"Annalee . . . I mean it." She had to agree with him. If she didn't believe she was okay, then his certainty would crumble and everything would fall apart. He hugged her for a long while and when she was settled on the sofa, he headed home.

The whole drive he prayed and believed. The test was just a precaution. Tommy gripped the steering wheel and his eyes lifted to the blue sky. No clouds in sight. Not for Indianapolis. Not for days.

And definitely not for him and Annalee.

As the night played out, a single silent prayer stayed with Tommy. As he ate dinner with his family and played Scrabble with Malin, and as he did his homework and headed upstairs for bed. The words consumed him every few minutes.

Please, God, don't let her be sick.

God, please heal her.

Please, God.

Until finally he fell asleep.

7

No one else knew about Landon's doctor appointment.

So when the five of them arrived at LaGuardia Airport that Thursday, the day before the anniversary of 9/11, Ashley had to remind herself to act normal. Of course, the reason they were here was somber. Which meant no one asked questions when she wasn't her usual talkative self.

The group took an Uber to the Ritz-Carlton near Central Park. Luke's law firm had connections with the hotel management, so both rooms were comped. But it was just after eleven and the rooms weren't ready.

Ashley spoke up first. "Landon and I have a few spots we want to visit." She smiled at her brother and his family. "Let's meet up at the museum at two. Would that work?"

"Definitely." Reagan put her arm around Luke's waist. "I want to show Tommy where his grandpa worked."

They left their bags with the bellhop and Landon grabbed another Uber for the ride to the doctor's office, near New York University Medical Center, a few miles from Ground Zero. A decision had been made to continue federal assistance for people sick with 9/11 illnesses. So if Landon had something seriously wrong, he would be entitled to compensation. Of course, Ashley cared much more about getting Landon help than a settlement.

Dr. Michael Berg was one of the leading experts in the area.

Ashley held Landon's hand in the back of the SUV while their driver maneuvered through heavy traffic. "Big lunch crowd." Landon tried to make small talk with the man.

The driver shrugged. "It's always like this."

Ashley looked out the window as they traveled south along the Hudson River. Every block or two she could just barely make out the new World Trade Center. She looked over the water at the Statue of Liberty.

For the most part, New York looked like the city she remembered, the one it had been before 9/11. The one it was once again. As if the terrorist attacks never happened. Only Ground Zero would be totally different.

Landon coughed twice and then again. Ashley pulled a water bottle from her purse and handed it to him. Never mind what had been rebuilt. The terrorist attacks had happened. She lived with the proof every day. Especially lately.

Dr. Berg's office was on the forty-third floor in a towering medical building. They checked in and waited a few minutes before Landon's name was called. Up until now, Ashley had been stoic. But as they took their places in two chairs near an examination table she felt her heart skip a beat.

Don't panic, she told herself. Landon had struggled with lung issues before. He'd been short of breath and diagnosed with signs of early damage. But this time his cough seemed more pronounced. Ashley reached for his hand and felt tears spring to her eyes. *Not Landon, God. Please . . . not him.*

"Hey . . ." Landon put his hand on her knee. "Baby, what?"

"I . . . I can't." Ashley wiped the tears from her cheeks and stared at him. "I survived everything leading up to this. My own health scare and my mother's death. The loss of our little Sarah hours after she was born. Erin's family and the accident." Her throat felt tight, like she couldn't draw a full breath. "I survived because God gave me *you,* Landon. That's the only reason."

"Love, I'm here. I'm not going anywhere." He put his arm around her shoulders and eased her close. "Everything is still fine. I believe that."

Ashley nodded. *I can't live without him, God. . . . Don't take him from me. Please.*

"Say something." He put his finger beneath her chin and lifted her face to his. "Come on, baby."

"I love you." She blinked back another rush of tears. "That's all. I love you, Landon Blake."

Her head was still pressed to his shoulder when Dr. Berg joined them a few minutes later. The man was in his fifties, maybe. Pleasant and fit. He asked Landon to sit on the table. "This was supposed to be just a consultation. But I had a cancellation." He checked his folder. "If you have an hour, I'd like to go over a few things and do a few tests."

"Absolutely." Landon released his hold on Ashley. "We'd like answers."

"And yes"—the doctor glanced at Ashley—"illnesses related to 9/11 are very real and very dangerous." He sighed. "We know now that toxins filling the air around Ground Zero in the days and weeks after the attacks were deadly."

Ashley pressed her fists into her middle. She didn't want to hear this. She wanted to grab Landon's hand and run back to the airport. Board the first flight to Indianapolis and get home to Bloomington as fast as they could.

But Dr. Berg was still talking. He explained that he would draw blood and do an X-ray. Then he would do a PET scan.

"If you haven't eaten yet today." The doctor put his stethoscope to his ears.

"Actually, I haven't. Just in case." Landon smiled. "I'm ready for you."

He looked calm and relaxed and it hit Ashley. Landon had always been like this. Able to stare danger in the face. She and Landon had met in fifth grade, but long after that—when Ashley was in her early twenties, she had come back from a wild time in Paris, pregnant and alone. And when her longtime friend Landon Blake pursued her, she thought him too safe. Because he was a good man. Too good for her.

She smiled. How wrong she had been back then. No one took danger on more quickly than Landon Blake. Whether he was putting out a fire or marrying her.

Or here, facing tests that could define their future.

Dr. Berg listened to Landon's lungs for a long while. A few times Landon coughed and the doctor had to step back. Was that concern on his face? Again he listened and after a minute or so he smiled. "Your lungs, Mr. Blake, sound surprisingly healthy." He hesitated. "I'd still like to take a closer look."

Next he sprayed a numbing agent into Landon's mouth. "This might feel a little strange." The doctor checked his watch. "In a minute, I'll slide a camera into your mouth and down your throat. Lung damage often shows itself in the esophagus."

Ashley crossed her arms tight in front of her as she watched Dr. Berg thread the camera into Landon's mouth and down his throat. Landon didn't even flinch. Another ten minutes and Dr. Berg pulled the tube clear. "Beautiful! Your tissue looks pink and healthy." He shook his head. "You were at Ground Zero for quite some time, is that right?"

"Yes." Landon exchanged a glance with Ashley. "Until we found my buddy. He was FDNY."

Dr. Berg pursed his lips. "I'm sorry." He paused. "I hear that a lot."

Of course he did. Ashley stared at her hands for a

long moment. Hundreds of firefighters were caught in the collapse of the buildings that day. Their FDNY coworkers were naturally the ones searching through the pile of smoldering toxic debris. And most of them—like Landon—didn't leave till the last body was pulled out.

Dr. Berg took Landon for his scan, and Ashley waited in the exam room. She thought about the crazy timing of this test. Their nephew Tommy had just sat in a waiting room while his girlfriend, Annalee, underwent a similar exam.

The PET scan would check all of Landon's soft tissue, every organ and especially his lungs. If there was cancer growing anywhere, the test would show it. Ashley paced in the small room. Every tomorrow hung on what Dr. Berg found in the next hour.

Ashley pictured their older son, Cole, in his sophomore year at Liberty University. Cole, who Landon had adopted when he married Ashley. Back when Cole wasn't even in kindergarten yet. Now Cole and Landon talked every week—about classes and girls and the ways God was challenging Cole in his faith.

What would their son do without the man who was everything to him?

And then there was Devin. Their firstborn as a married couple was only twelve. He needed his father with every breath. Same with Janessa. At eight, she would barely remember Landon if something happened to him.

Amy's sweet face filled Ashley's mind. What about her? She had already lost her entire birth family in that horrific accident. Could she survive losing Landon, too? Ashley didn't think so.

She swallowed. *Help me, Lord. Take away this terrible fear. It's suffocating me.*

Even with his cough, Landon was too healthy to die anytime soon. Hadn't the doctor just told them Landon's tissues looked healthy? *Yes, exactly.* Ashley was letting herself worry about diseases and diagnoses that didn't yet exist. A story filled her heart, one that Jesus had told.

The parable of the sower, the one who threw seeds of faith into his field. Some landed on hard ground and the birds ate it. Other seeds fell on shallow soil and sprouted, but with no root systems, quickly died. And still others landed on fertile soil, where they grew and flourished.

It was the other seed condition that always concerned Ashley. The one where the seeds of faith were choked out by the weeds of worry. The worries of the world. Was that happening to her? Could her faith be suffocated by worry? Ashley wouldn't let that happen. *I trust You, Lord. I do. Whatever happens today, You hold the moon and stars and earth. So You can hold me and my family. I believe that.*

Ashley took a deep breath and did what she often did in situations like this. She began to recite everything she was thankful for. Her faith and Landon, of course. And each of her children by name. Then every gift her children brought to her and to the world. Their kindness and intelligence and laughter.

Next she thanked God for her extended family, each person by name.

With every passing minute she felt more relaxed, more sure that she wasn't invisible here on the forty-third floor in one of a hundred skyscrapers in Lower Manhattan.

She was seen by the God of the Universe and she was loved. She kept her prayer of thanksgiving going until Landon and Dr. Berg walked through the door. Landon was grinning. That was Ashley's first sign that maybe . . . just maybe everything was going to be okay.

Dr. Berg folded his arms and looked at Ashley. "Your husband needs some good allergy medicine." He grinned. "Otherwise he looks perfectly healthy. For now, anyway. His organs look perfect. Like he never spent a day at Ground Zero."

Ashley was on her feet and in Landon's arms before Dr. Berg could say another word. "Is this real?" She looked from her husband to the doctor. "Are you serious?"

"Very much so." Dr. Berg laughed. "I'll leave you two alone. You can check out down the hall."

When he was gone, Ashley searched Landon's face, his eyes. "You're . . . you're okay?"

"Yes." He touched his lips to her cheek.

Tears stung her eyes again but she couldn't stop smiling. "Landon, you're not sick!"

"I told you." His hands were on her face and in her hair, and he kissed her in a way that took her breath.

Then he whispered close to her skin. "I'm not leaving you. Not ever." He found her eyes again. "I want to grow old with you, Ashley Baxter Blake."

She clung to him until she had her breath and composure. Everything was different now. The blue sky outside the office window and the joy in Ashley's heart. "We need to meet up with the others." She kissed him again.

"Yes." His smile fell off a little. He didn't have to say anything. She could read his eyes. Landon might have a clean bill of health, but there were countless others who did not. Others, like Jalen, who never stood a chance. Landon sighed. "Thank you for making me do this."

He wasn't talking about the doctor appointment, Ashley could tell. He meant the time they would spend today at the 9/11 Memorial Museum, thinking back on all that happened nearly two decades ago. The time with Dr. Berg was behind them.

Now it was a time to remember.

THEY MET UP with Luke and Reagan and Tommy in the shaded courtyard just outside the doors to the 9/11 Museum. Ashley and Landon had decided to tell their family later about the doctor appointment and Landon's incredible results.

For now they had other things to think about.

Ashley hadn't known how she would feel about being back here, seeing the spot where the Twin Towers had stood and visiting the museum with Landon. Reagan had said as much on their walk yesterday.

Reagan's father had died here, before she had time to tell him goodbye.

Other than Tommy, they all had chapters in their stories that were marked by the events of 9/11. And being here was bound to take them all back one way or another.

After a thirty-minute wait, they entered through the double glass doors. The first wall held dramatic images of a passenger plane tearing through the North Tower. Ashley felt Landon's arm come around her. They didn't move, didn't look away.

And Ashley was back there again, in Bloomington, working at Sunset Hills Adult Care Home in the blur of hours after the terrorist attacks. Her favorite residents, Irvil and Helen, were concerned because a scary movie was on television. Only it wasn't a movie, it was real live footage of the most unimaginable horror anyone had ever seen.

Then Landon was at the front door of Sunset Hills and he was asking her to step outside. And he was telling her he had to go to Manhattan. Where he'd been hired months before. If it hadn't been for his injury on the job in Bloomington, he would've been there in the same tower as his best friend, Jalen, when it collapsed. Instead Jalen was there and already Landon knew his buddy was missing. Landon had to go. Had to head for the remains of the buildings and work around the clock until he found his friend.

Like it was happening all over again, Ashley didn't want Landon to go. And she remembered knowing something with a certainty that took her breath. Because on that awful Tuesday—for the first time—Ashley had known she wasn't only Landon's friend.

She was in love with him.

The memory broke.

Luke and his family moved up ahead, but Ashley and Landon remained, anchored in place. A somber quiet filled the museum. No matter how many people walked through the doors today, no matter how crowded the hallways, each person was alone with their memories. Alone with whatever the terrorists had stolen from them that September morning.

Landon leaned close and his voice fell to barely a whisper. "I was like a different person here. Looking for Jalen. Almost like a machine. Hungry . . . exhausted . . . it didn't matter. I just kept looking."

Ashley nodded. "I remember." She felt the fear again, how she had worried Landon would never come back to Bloomington.

"So much loss." Landon stared at the wall. "I miss Jalen. I miss him still."

Ashley had never met Landon's college buddy. The one who had convinced him to be a firefighter. When Landon's pursuit of Ashley wasn't working, Jalen had talked him into moving to New York City. *Come to the action*, he had told Landon.

And so Landon had put in his notice with the

Bloomington Fire Department and made plans to move to Manhattan. Only he got hurt in an Indiana house fire first. The one where he saved the life of a little boy. A few weeks later Landon was still nursing a broken leg when he should've been moving to New York City.

Otherwise . . .

Ashley couldn't finish the thought.

But for the next hour, the story played out on the walls around them. Yes, in a different set of circumstances, Landon definitely would've been running into the Twin Towers right next to Jalen. The terrorist attacks would've trapped him beneath hundreds of tons of steel and cement and glass. Landon's arm wouldn't be around her now. Rather, his name would be engraved on the memorial wall.

One more person they would be remembering today at Ground Zero.

8

The visit to New York City and Lower Manhattan was turning out to be harder than Reagan had expected. After a day at the museum, she was more aware of the truth. Her father wasn't here. Of course not. He had been a believer in Jesus, a man with a heart after God's heart. He was in heaven, and maybe he had a window to this day.

So he could pray for Reagan and Luke and Tommy as they woke up today—on the anniversary of 9/11—and as they did what they had come to do. As they remembered and honored Reagan's dad. The grandfather Tommy had never known.

Luke and Tommy were still getting ready, so Reagan took the elevator to the lobby. She found a quiet chair and phoned her mother. It was something she did often, but the call each year on September 11 was different.

"Hello, dear." Her mom sounded tired. "How is it?"

"New. Nothing looks the same. Where the towers stood."

"Hmm." Her mother hesitated. "One of these years I'll have to come with you." She sounded doubtful. As if the memories were hard enough from far away. "What's it like?"

Reagan thought about yesterday's tour. "The time line at the museum doesn't leave anything out. It was like . . . like watching it happen all over again."

There were personal reasons why 9/11 was hard for Reagan. Her mother knew that, same as Luke knew. But Reagan and her mother didn't talk about that now. Her mom took her time. "Reagan . . . I was going to call you. I . . . have new information. About your father."

"New information?" What more could there possibly be to know? Her father had been working at the top of the World Trade Center when the plane tore through the building.

And he'd never been heard from again.

What could her mother mean? Reagan pinched the bridge of her nose. "Mom . . . new information?"

"Yes." She took a deep breath. "I heard from the widow of one of your father's coworkers. She's looked for me since the attacks that day."

Reagan stood and walked to the front door of the hotel. She needed air. "Why? What for?"

"Because . . ." Her mother hesitated. "This woman's husband called her before the North Tower collapsed. They stayed on the phone together."

And then Reagan's mother told her the story of how her father had spent his final minutes. It was a story they hadn't known before this, and it made Reagan both sick and beyond proud.

As the story came to an end, Luke and Tommy stepped off the elevator.

"I have to go, Mom." Reagan didn't cry. The news her mother had just shared was too profound, too unbelievable. "I'll call you later."

The conversation ended and Reagan met up with her husband and son. She didn't say a word about what she had just learned. She could barely get her mind around it herself. She would tell Luke and Tommy later. For now they needed to connect with Ashley and Landon at the memorial.

Traffic was terrible around Ground Zero so they walked the last few blocks. Today there were twice as many people wandering the parklike area as yesterday. They met up with Ashley and Landon and all five of them headed to the four-sided waterfall, rimmed by a memorial pool.

Ashley and Landon split off to find Jalen's name on the other memorial wall, and Reagan, Luke and Tommy made their way to where her father's name was engraved. It didn't take long to find it and as they did Reagan was overcome by the truth.

They were in the exact spot where the North Tower once stood.

In the very place where her father had been working high above them that Tuesday morning, the three of them huddled and stared at his name in the stone wall.

THOMAS DOUGLAS DECKER.

Reagan's eyes blurred with tears and she put her hand on the cold letters. All around her people were doing the same thing. Remembering the ones they lost, finding some sort of solace in touching a piece of the wall.

Tommy pulled a slip of paper and a pencil from his backpack. This part had been his idea. A way to take home the memory from today. Reagan watched their son position the paper over her father's name. Then with quick gentle strokes, Tommy ran the side of his pencil over the paper so that the name came through.

A permanent keepsake.

There was an open bench nearby, and the three of them sat down. The sun shone through the trees here, which Reagan appreciated. She'd been freezing since they reached the reflecting pool. Here on the bench Luke sat on one side of her, Tommy on the other. Reagan stared up where the tower used to stand. A hundred times she had come here to visit her dad. Her mother would bring her when she was little, and as she got older she would stop by on visits from college.

"You came here to see Grandpa, right, Dad?" Tommy's voice was soft. Appropriate for the moment. "When you and Mom were dating?"

This was something Reagan and Tommy had talked about last night. Tommy knew he was born before his parents married. And he knew they'd been apart for a year after his birth. But he'd never seemed to want more information than that. Reagan and Luke both wondered if today he might have more questions. If he did, they planned to answer him.

Luke grabbed a quick breath. "Yes. I came here with your mom." He lifted his eyes to the sky, as if he were looking to the spot where the eighty-ninth floor used to be. "His office was beautiful."

Reagan's eyes followed the same path. "He liked you so much, Luke." She linked arms with her husband. "You told him you could picture having an office down the hall from his. Both of you businessmen at the top of your game."

"I remember. He had an infectious personality." Luke turned to Tommy. "You're a lot like him, Son."

They were quiet for a moment. Tommy looked up, too, but he couldn't possibly know what it used to be like here, how it had felt to stand at ground level between two hundred-floor buildings. As impressive as the new World Trade Center was, nothing would replace the way the Twin Towers had looked.

Especially from this close.

"You said you didn't get to say goodbye to him." Tommy turned to her. "You mean . . . you didn't talk to him? In the days leading up to . . . that morning?"

Reagan shot a look at Luke.

"Your mother and I"—Luke faced Tommy—"we had every intention of honoring God with our relationship. We had guidelines."

Tommy didn't look like he was quite tracking. "You mean you weren't going to have sex before getting married?"

"Right." Reagan hesitated. Reliving this part of her life story was always painful. "That was the plan."

Luke explained how on the night of September 10 they were in Bloomington at school.

"We had a deal. We didn't hang out in our apartments alone. But that Monday night we broke our own rule." She looked off. "We wound up watching the New York Giants on the couch at my apartment."

"Your mom and I . . . well, we got caught up in the single moment we had tried to avoid. That's where we were when the phone rang." Luke sighed. Again his eyes found the invisible spot in the sky.

"It was your grandpa." Reagan could still hear her dad's voice as he left a message that night. "He loved the Giants and he had called to celebrate with me." She looked down. "I didn't take the call. I . . . I missed the chance."

"And the next morning . . . ?" Tommy looked from Reagan to Luke.

"I was in class when I heard about the attacks." Luke stared off. "I ran to find your mother."

A sad understanding darkened Tommy's expression. "So . . . Mom, you never got to talk to him?"

"No." Reagan felt the sting of sorrow in her eyes. "By the time your dad came to my apartment, I was already packing. I had to get home." Tears trickled down Reagan's face as she finished the story. In the devastation and horror of the morning, communication broke down between Reagan and Luke. Reagan boarded a bus from her college apartment in Bloomington to her home in New York City.

"The whole time I told myself he was alive." Reagan dabbed at her cheeks. "If anyone had found a way to make it out, my dad would have." She looked up again. "He would've done anything to get out of there."

Of course, now she knew different. But that story could wait.

Tommy was quiet for a long moment. He stood and moved to the edge of the rimmed waterfall again, the spot where his grandfather's name was engraved. Five minutes passed before he finally returned to his spot on the bench. He looked at Reagan. "What happened next?"

"I wouldn't talk to your father." She turned to Luke. "Something I still regret."

Then she told Tommy how she went home and learned the terrible truth. Her father had not made it out. He had been killed with thousands of others when the towers collapsed. In the days and weeks that followed, no matter how many times Luke tried to reach her, Reagan refused him.

She paused. "A month later I learned I was pregnant. With you."

Again the realization seemed to come over Tommy. "From that night . . . ?" He drew a sharp breath. "The night before the attacks?"

"Yes." Luke put his arm around Reagan, but his eyes locked on Tommy's. "Your aunt Ashley brought us back together. Months after you were born." He paused. "I didn't know about you until then."

Reagan needed Tommy to understand something. "You were always proof of Romans 8:28." She put her hand on Tommy's knee. "God works all things to the good for those who love Him."

Tommy nodded slowly. "Such a . . . crazy story." He turned and after a few seconds, he hugged them both. "I'm sorry. For all you had to go through back then." He kissed Reagan's cheek. "Sorry you didn't get to talk to Grandpa one more time."

Peace and sorrow mixed like a healing balm in Reagan's soul. "He would've been so proud of you, Tommy." She leaned her forehead against her son's. "I know you'll meet him one day."

Sitting there on the bench with two of the people she loved most in the world, Reagan could almost forget what it felt like that long-ago Tuesday morning. She hadn't only been upset with herself and Luke for what they'd done the night before.

She'd been destroyed.

Back then, every time she thought about Luke she could hear her father's voice on the message machine, the kindness and light, the way he had sounded leaving the message that evening. After that, the idea of ever seeing Luke again was preposterous. She hated him and she hated herself.

Those parts of the story she spared their son.

After a few minutes, the three of them wandered around the perimeter of the reflecting pool, pointing out details and avoiding other mourners.

They met up with Ashley and Landon, and the five of them moved toward the new Memorial Glade adjacent to Ground Zero. Tommy walked beside Reagan, quiet, pensive. Clearly more keenly aware of all 9/11 had cost them. Not just Reagan. But Luke and even Tommy, himself. He slid his hands into his sweatshirt pockets. "I wish I would've had the chance to visit him here. On the eighty-ninth floor."

"Mmm." Reagan smiled. "You would've loved the view."

Later today they planned to take the elevator to the top of the new World Trade Center. Just so Tommy could get an idea of how high up his grandfather had worked.

They slowed their pace as they reached the new garden. It was built to honor those still dying from diseases caused by 9/11. A quiet somberness hung over the pristine grounds and the giant pieces of granite that jutted up from the edges of the path.

Reagan found a bench and Ashley took the seat beside her. "So many memories."

"Yes." Reagan turned to her sister-in-law. "How's Landon? His cough . . . I've noticed." It wasn't something Reagan had wanted to ask about before. But here at the Memorial Glade, the question seemed appropriate.

"Well . . ." Ashley glanced toward her husband, a few yards away. "We were going to tell you all later. Landon saw a specialist yesterday morning. When we first got to the city." She grinned at Reagan. "He has allergies. Nothing more."

"Really?" Reagan felt a wave of relief. "Thank God. That's incredible."

"Yes." Ashley looked at Landon again. "His health doesn't make sense. God alone."

Again silence fell over them. Most people walking or sitting in the memorial garden complex didn't speak. Each caught up in a story known only to them. The strange thing was, everyone here was connected in some way. Because on a page nineteen years ago, their stories had all intersected.

They had that in common.

Reagan breathed deep and gratitude filled her heart. Yes, she had lost her father on 9/11, but look at how far God had brought them since then. Nineteen years ago, Reagan never could have pictured a day like this. Sitting here on a beautiful September morning, walking and remembering in the exact place where the towers had once stood. Here with Luke, the love of her life. And with their son.

God's mercies really were new every morning like the Bible said. And God had a way of taking the very worst situation and bringing good out of it. Hope from horror. Mercy from madness. And something God proved when He gave her Tommy.

Beauty from brokenness.

And now Reagan had something else, a treasure she

would keep forever. The story her mother had told her earlier that morning. In a few days, when they were back home and the time was right, Reagan would share the story with her family. It was too sacred to share here with strangers milling about. For now, holding the truth deep in her heart was enough for Reagan. The fact was this: Her father hadn't only been a businessman on the eighty-ninth floor of the North Tower that Tuesday morning.

He had been a hero.

9

The experience at Ground Zero was changing Tommy. He could feel it.

From the moment he stepped out of the Uber and set foot on the sacred sidewalks surrounding the new One World Trade Center, Tommy had been struck by one thing: 9/11 had really happened.

This tragedy was part of the past for him, of course. Same with his friends at school and his cousins. At school, some teachers glossed over 9/11 as part of a sociology lesson. But it was history. As much as Bunker Hill or Pearl Harbor.

Every year on this date Tommy's family hung an American flag, and most of their neighbors did the same. But in the back of Tommy's mind the idea that terrorists had actually flown commercial airliners into the Twin Towers seemed inconceivable.

It had happened, of course. Occasionally he and his family would watch an old movie set in Manhattan and a panoramic shot would include the Twin Towers. They were real. They had stood on this very spot and they had housed thousands of workers.

Tommy had also known that his parents' story was intrinsically connected to what happened on 9/11. But until today he hadn't understood the very grave scope of the matter. How his mother had missed the chance to have a final conversation with her father and how what had happened that Monday night had resulted in his own birth. And at the same time, had nearly separated his parents forever.

But the part that hit him hardest today, the aspect of this real-life 9/11 that was still sending shock waves through Tommy, was the heroic actions of the first responders. The numbers lost that day were mind-blowing.

Tommy wandered back to the display detailing how many firefighters and police officers had died on 9/11 or because of it. Not only the 343 firemen and 71 police officers when the towers collapsed, but since then another 204 firefighters and an additional 241 NYPD men and women.

He was still trying to grasp the loss when a man walked up to him. A quick glance and Tommy spotted the FDNY patch on the shoulder of his uniform. He was Hispanic, maybe in his late forties, and he looked a million miles away.

If the guy wanted privacy, Tommy wasn't going to interrupt him.

After a minute or so the man breathed deep. "Seems like yesterday."

There was no one else around. Tommy shifted so he could see the man better. "My grandfather worked on the eighty-ninth floor of the North Tower." He squinted. "This is my first time here."

The man nodded. "Only three of us from my station made it out alive that day." He gazed toward the place where the North Tower once stood. Then he turned to Tommy. "Javier Sanchez."

"Tommy Baxter." He could hardly believe it. Javier had actually been here that long-ago September 11. "They . . . don't teach us much about the attacks in school." Tommy didn't want to push. But if the man was willing to talk he would listen.

"My son's in high school. Tenth grade." Javier looked at him. "He says the same thing. No one talks about it. Even here in New York."

A hundred questions filled Tommy's mind, but he didn't dare ask them. Instead he stared at the memorial plaque again. "The numbers are . . . more than I can get my mind around. Hundreds and hundreds of first responders. All killed." He looked at Javier. "It's hard to believe."

The man folded his arms. "It was hard to believe back then." He looked across the grounds, like he was seeing it all again. "The call came in. Fire at the top of the North Tower. Plane crash." He blinked a few times. "We thought it was a small plane. Some sort of crazy accident." His eyes met Tommy's. "Because who would've thought hijackers would crash a plane on purpose?"

Tommy hadn't thought of that. How back then no one would've expected such a thing.

"Bad guys used to ask for money. They cared about living." Javier had a heavy New York accent. Probably born and raised here. He narrowed his eyes. "Well, Tommy Baxter. Since they don't tell you what happened, I'll tell you." His eyes welled up. "It happened. I was here."

And then as if Javier had known Tommy all his life, he began to tell the story. By the time Javier and his buddies arrived on the scene, the entire World Trade Center block was madness. "The roar of the fire was like a living, breathing dragon high above us." His voice cracked. It took a while before he spoke again. "People were running in every direction, screaming and tripping over each other. Terrified. Because men and women were burning alive up there." A single tear slid down his cheek. "That's when I saw people hitting the ground."

Video accounts of 9/11 came up every now and then in documentaries or in YouTube clips. Tommy had heard about people falling from the highest floors. "They were pushed out . . . when the plane hit?"

"No." Javier's answer was quick. "They *looked* like they were falling. But I stared up at the burning floors and I saw what was really happening. . . . A lot of them were jumping, Tommy. The inferno must've been more than they could bear. Because I watched them climb out onto the window ledges . . . and jump." He looked up again. "One after another."

This was something else Tommy hadn't considered. Had his grandfather been one of those who jumped?

Were his final moments surrounded by suffocating fire and indescribable terror? The possibility made Tommy sick.

His office would've been just below where the plane hit, a few floors beneath the all-consuming, towering flames.

"Chaos. That's what it was. We thought it was the end of the world." Javier looked toward the memorial pool again. "Hundreds more firefighters were dispatched while the Port Authority began evacuating the damaged North Tower. Instructions were to keep people in the South Tower in place. So they'd be safe." He clenched his jaw. "No one knew another plane was headed straight for us."

Javier talked in detail about running up five flights of stairs in the North Tower helping people get to the stairwells, administering first aid to men and women who had fallen. "The elevators weren't working, of course." He shook his head. "I came across an old guy collapsed near the stairwell. Chest pain. Short of breath."

Tommy could only imagine the panic.

"Looked like a heart attack." Javier shrugged. "My buddies were still running up the stairs. One flight after another. Fifty pounds of gear on their backs. But that guy . . . I had to help him. That's why we were there." His voice trailed off.

A breeze moved through the trees that lined the memorial. Leaves still summer green rustled overhead as Javier nodded. "I saved that guy. Threw him over my back and got him down to ground level. Took him to a waiting ambulance."

By then the Port Authority was ordering a mandatory evacuation of both towers. "But it was too late." Pain deepened the lines on Javier's face. "A minute later another jet tore into the South Tower."

Javier was still loading the heart attack victim into an ambulance when the second airliner hit. "Now we got two infernos, two buildings with more people jumping." He shook his head. "I knew my buddies needed me. We had to get people out of there."

Tommy didn't move, didn't speak. The man's story breathed life into everything he'd seen at the memorial. Javier sucked in a quick breath. "I remember running back to the North Tower. Thousands of people were running from the buildings, pouring out onto the street. And I was thinking, *Good . . . get out of here. Be safe!* But me and my brothers, the FDNY and NYPD, we had just one place to go. . . . Straight up."

Javier made it up twenty-one floors of the North Tower before coming across a woman bleeding from her head. "She had run down from the forty-fifth floor and somewhere along the way she'd fallen. Maybe she got knocked down. Whatever . . . she was bleeding out and she needed help."

Like before, Javier heaved the victim over his shoulder and carried her down to ground level and yet another ambulance took her away. Javier began to tremble, the memory taking a physical toll on his body. "It started with a rumble. A low growl." Javier looked up to the empty sky. "Like a beast had been unleashed over Lower Manhattan."

The sound became a roar, Javier said. "Like an EF5 tornado. Like the end of the world." He looked at Tommy. "I was planning to run back into the North Tower when it happened. The ground shook and the other flaming building began to sway and then . . . the South Tower . . ."

He didn't have to finish his sentence. Everyone alive knew what happened next, whether they talked about it in history class or not. The South Tower collapsed like a monstrous burning house of cards. "I was still assisting the woman, still helping the paramedic get her hooked up to an IV."

The ambulance driver ordered Javier to get inside and shut the door and then he sped off. The guy raced as fast and far away from the explosion of debris as he could get. Not till they reached a hospital many blocks north did the driver stop.

"I was still in work mode, still helping the woman. Her pulse was weak. She needed blood." He rubbed his hands together, his gaze distant. "She lived. The heart at-tack victim lived, too."

Javier put his hand on the memorial plaque, the one with the names of every first responder. "I kept thinking my buddies were in the North Tower, and that building was still standing. But half an hour later . . ."

Tommy knew. The North Tower collapsed also. "Your friends?"

"Twelve of them died that day. Twelve firefighters. My best guys." Again Javier's eyes filled. "Sons and husbands. Fathers." He swiped at a tear on his cheek. "I don't think about it." He shook his head. "Can't think about it . . . except today. On the anniversary."

Tommy let that sit for a full minute. "I'm sorry. I . . ." He looked at the ground and shook his head. "I'm sorry."

"God saved me for a reason." Javier sniffed. "I'm a captain now. I have a wife and kids." He pointed to the other uniformed firefighters and police officers milling about. "We work together, the NYPD and Port Authority, the FBI and us. Making sure it doesn't happen again." He pointed at Tommy. "Keeping people like you safe."

Tommy breathed deep, the cool air filling his lungs. "Thank you. For that." He faced Javier. "I've been thinking about joining the military. But since I've been here . . . I wonder if I'm supposed to be a firefighter . . . or maybe a police officer."

"Mmm." Javier's anguish gradually lifted. "I knew God brought me over to you for a reason." He nodded to a distant bench. "I was sitting there reliving that day . . . smelling the smoke and hearing the screams and sirens, the roar of the flames. Feeling the ground shake beneath my feet again. And I sensed God was talking to me. He said, *Go share with that young man.*" Javier locked eyes with Tommy. "Now I know why."

Chills ran down Tommy's arms and legs. "You think because . . . because I'm supposed to do this kind of work?"

Javier raised one eyebrow. "That's between you and Him." He pointed up. "But I'll tell you this, Tommy Baxter. Young people like you are often destined. Destined to serve." He paused. "Today . . . if I had it to do over again, I'd be a police officer. So I could come against the bad guys. Every day of my life." He shook his head. "There are more bad guys today, Tommy. And we need good cops, people like you."

"Yes, sir." Tommy hung on every word.

"We need people who rush toward a burning building. But we also need men and women who run into danger on a night of crime and killing . . . that type of person has a calling. Especially today." He sighed and one final time his eyes found the spot where the Twin Towers once stood. "That's my only regret . . . that in those final minutes before the towers fell I wasn't there. I wasn't running toward the fire."

Tommy wanted to correct the man. Javier had helped save two people. He had run toward the inferno at Ground Zero not once but twice. But Tommy stopped himself. No matter how Javier's story had played out and even though the man knew the Lord had spared him for a reason, his regret remained. Javier should've gone down with his fellow firefighters. That's what he still thought, however wrong.

"I used to take Christmas gifts to the kids, children of my buddies who died that day. Now I take presents to some of *their* kids." Javier stood a little straighter. "We help each other. It's a brotherhood that way. No one who lost a daddy or a brother or a husband or a son that day is ever really alone. Not with the FDNY." He sighed and after a minute he took a deep breath. "Nice talking to you, Tommy."

Tommy shook the man's hand. "Thank you. For sharing."

Javier pointed at him. "Keep telling the stories, Tommy. Learn more about your grandfather. Leave a message for the survivors." He smiled, and his countenance lifted a little. "It happened. Don't ever forget."

And then as if he'd done what he'd come to do, Javier nodded at Tommy and walked off. Tommy watched him until the man reached the busy street and turned down the sidewalk. Off on whatever mission God might give him next.

Tommy spotted his parents and his aunt and uncle. He couldn't wait to tell them about his conversation with Javier Sanchez. But first Tommy put his hand on the memorial plaque and closed his eyes.

Welling within him was a desire he hadn't known before today, an urgency so strong it took his breath. He could fight fires, definitely. But he felt God calling him to the other part of first responder work. The one Javier would choose if he had it to do over again. And the words echoing in the hallways of his soul came like a directive straight from heaven.

Tommy Baxter, you will be a police officer.

The words were almost audible. *Yes, God. Yes, that's what I'll do. I'll be a police officer.*

Determination like a living force built within him. He would get the training and wear the badge and uniform, and he would prove to everyone that most cops were good. He would stop traffickers in Indianapolis and keep bad guys from infiltrating the streets. And he would put an end to drugs that destroyed so many families. He would run toward danger when everyone else ran the other way. Yes, he wanted to be a police officer, Tommy was sure. And he wanted something else, something that had been in the back of his mind every minute since he left Indiana.

Annalee's test results.

10

The doctor's call came in that Monday half an hour after Annalee got home from school. Tommy had a shoot-around with his basketball team, and Annalee had chosen to skip choir practice.

Mostly because she wanted to be home when the news hit. Good or bad.

She was sitting with her mother on the living room sofa, each of them sipping a cup of green tea. *I'm not that tired,* she told herself. *It's just a virus.* Already the doctor had given them her blood results. Whatever was making Annalee tired, it wasn't mononucleosis.

By now they knew it was something, though. Because an email had come through Friday stating that her blood count was off. The white count was too high . . . or maybe the platelets were low. Something.

Annalee had tried not to think about it. She and her mom were watching a rerun of *Touched by an Angel* when her mother's cell phone lit up. Annalee had asked the doctor to talk to her mother about the results. So immediately her mom took the phone to the next room. As if she knew. "It's the doctor." She looked over her shoulder at Annalee. Then she was gone.

Five long minutes passed and her mom returned. As soon as Annalee saw her face, her heart sank. Her mother shook her head, tears already spilling onto her cheeks. "Annalee. I'm sorry, honey. It isn't good."

She sat on the sofa and pulled Annalee into her arms. Then for more than a minute the two clung to each other. Finally, Annalee eased back. She locked eyes with her mom. "Tell me. What . . . what is it?"

Her mother shook her head. "They . . . found a mass on your . . . chest wall, baby."

No. Annalee released her mother's hand. She wouldn't sit here and listen to this. How could the doctor tell her mom that? She had a . . . what was it? A mass on her chest wall? "My chest feels fine."

"It isn't." Her mother's tears fell harder. "With your blood results and the scan . . . they think it might be non—" She put her hand to her face.

"Mom . . . they think what?" Annalee's heart was racing now. "Tell me."

Her mother took hold of both her hands. "Lymphoma." The word was barely loud enough to hear. "Non-Hodgkin's lymphoma. Stage 4."

If it was *non*, then it couldn't be that bad, right? Annalee stood. She could feel herself getting faint. But stage 4? "Is . . . that serious?"

"Yes." Her mom was on her feet, too. "Annalee . . . it's cancer."

But before Annalee could hear another word or draw another breath, she ran to the stairs. This wasn't possible. She was tired, not dealing with . . . She couldn't think it. Couldn't say it. She was halfway up the stairs when she heard her mom call to her. It wasn't her mother's fault, but Annalee couldn't stand there and talk about this.

Not when it felt like the worst possible nightmare.

She reached the top of the stairs, darted into her room and slammed the door behind her. How could this be happening? Annalee flung herself on her bed and buried her face in the pillow. How could she have cancer? All of life was laid out before Tommy and her.

They were going to college and then they were going to help rescue trafficked children. She was going to make an app and market it till all the world used it to stop crimes against kids. And Tommy was going to help lock up the worst of the worst in society. That was his plan, the one he had told her about after he returned home from New York City.

And somewhere in the middle of that he wanted to marry her.

So she couldn't be sick with . . . whatever the doctor said. She was tired, that's all. A little rest and she'd be fine.

Her mother opened the door and stepped into her room. "Annalee . . ."

"Don't. Please, Mom." She rolled over and stared at her. "Don't tell me anything bad."

"Honey." Her mother's voice cracked. "I'm so . . . so sorry."

And in that moment Annalee felt her world begin to collapse around her. Not because she fully believed the things the doctor had told her mother, and not because she really thought she was sick. But because her mom was white as a sheet. She looked like she might pass out.

Suddenly Annalee knew. The doctor's words must have made sense to her mother. Because her mother clearly believed the news.

She crossed the room and sat on the edge of Annalee's bed. Her mom wasn't crying now. She looked too scared for tears. "Come here, sweetheart. Please."

All Annalee wanted was to run. Leave the house and get in her car and drive to the airport, maybe. She would take the next flight to Thailand. And Tommy would meet her there and they would get married at the little church in Phuket and no one . . . no one would ever mention her being sick again.

Instead she sat up and slid her legs over the edge of the mattress. As she did her mother wrapped her arms around her. For a long time they stayed there, her mom hugging her the way she used to when Annalee was little. A minute or so into the hug, Annalee understood why her mother wasn't saying anything.

She was crying again.

Her mom finally released her. Then she stood and pulled three tissues from the box on the dresser. With her back to Annalee, her mother dried her eyes. She might've thought she looked more composed when she turned around, but she didn't. Annalee had never seen her mom look so upset.

"What else?" Annalee wanted to know everything now. If it was real and it was serious, she needed answers. "Tell me."

And then in words and ways Annalee understood, her mother told her. How her cancer was serious and she'd have more tests tomorrow, and how treatment had to begin right away. Wednesday. Two days from now.

When it was all said and when Annalee and her mother had held on to each other again, and when her mom had begged God for perfect healing . . . Annalee had one question.

"Please . . . can I see Tommy?"

"Yes. Of course." Her mother dried her eyes again. "You're going to beat this, honey. We'll pray. Everyone will pray."

Annalee's eyes were still dry. She was too shocked to cry. A strange calm came over her. If she was sick, then it was time to get better. "God won't leave me."

"Never. Not ever." Her mother kissed her forehead. "I need to call your father. He'll be home in a few days but . . . he needs to know."

"Okay." When her mom left, Annalee walked to the

window and pulled her phone from her sweater pocket. Tommy's practice was over by now. Normally she would text him but today demanded more than that.

He answered on the first ring. "Annalee. I just got to my car."

She couldn't find her voice, couldn't make herself say the words.

"You got your results?" Tommy knew. He always knew.

"Can . . . can you come here, Tommy?" She didn't want to cry. Not now. "Please . . . hurry."

"I'm on my way."

Annalee waited for him on the front porch. In happier times, she and Tommy would sit out here and talk about politics or Bible stories or funny conversations they'd had that week. She slipped into her jacket and pulled it tight around her. The air was cooler, autumn barely holding its line against the coming winter.

It didn't matter how thick the jacket was, Annalee couldn't get warm.

Not until she was in Tommy's arms again.

ANNALEE WAITED TILL they were at their bench, the one at White River Park with the best view of Indianapolis. It sat at the foot of the prettiest tree in the city. She used to say time stood still here.

Tommy sat close to her and took her hands. "Are you cold?"

"Not now." She lifted her face to the setting sun. "Can we just sit here? For a minute?"

"Sure." Tommy's face was pale, same as Annalee's mother's. And he didn't even know the truth yet. His hands were warm against hers. "We don't have to talk."

Annalee nodded. She needed a minute. The truth was still a terrible nightmare, nothing real or possible. How could she put into words something she was only beginning to grasp? She pressed in closer to Tommy, her knees against his. The sun moved lower in the sky. In an hour it would disappear behind the buildings and night would come.

Which would lead to tomorrow. And tomorrow would lead to Wednesday.

She could do nothing to stop the ticking of the clock. And with that certainty Annalee drew a steadying breath and looked straight at Tommy. As much as she wanted to sit here and pretend it was yesterday, here was the truth. "I have cancer. It's bad."

There. She had said it.

Tommy searched her eyes, her expression. He stared down at the place where their hands were joined and then he turned his face to hers again. "No." He shook his head. "You're . . . you're perfect." He released one hand and placed his fingers against her cheek. "Who told you this?"

"My doctor talked to my mom." She didn't blame Tommy for not believing the news. She didn't believe it, either. "It feels like . . . it's all happening to someone else."

But it wasn't. And now that she'd told him the hardest part, she filled in the details. "I go in tomorrow for more tests." She leaned her head on his shoulder. "And on Wednesday they'll admit me to Indiana University Health Medical Center for treatment."

Tommy didn't stand or pace or look like he wanted to run. He put his arm around her and held her closer than before. "I . . . I don't understand."

She told him what she knew. The tumor in her chest was the size of an orange. Stage 4. Which was why the tumor was too big to be removed. Her doctor would give her six rounds of treatment to eliminate the mass and kill the cancer in her lymphatic system. "Several days in the hospital . . . then time at home for a couple weeks. Again and again. Six rounds."

The sharp exhale that came from Tommy sounded like he'd been punched. She could feel him looking up, turning his face to the sky. "Why the hospital? For the treatment?"

That had been one of her questions, too. "The medicine is strong." She started to shiver again. "Too strong for me to be home."

Tommy eased back enough to look into her eyes. "We'll fight this. Together." He didn't blink, didn't look away. "I'll be with you every day." Panic darkened his face, but he didn't waver. He shivered a bit. "God isn't done with you, Annalee. He . . . isn't done with us."

She leaned her forehead against his. "I don't want tomorrow to come."

He put his arms around her and held her again, his cheek alongside hers. After a minute or so he looked at her once more. "Tomorrow has to come." He brushed her hair from her face. "That's when you're going to start beating this."

His words were supposed to encourage her. She knew that. Instead they scared her. "What if . . . I'm not strong enough, Tommy?" She clung to him again. "I'm so afraid."

He put his hands on her shoulders. "Annie Oakley . . . you're the toughest girl I know." His teeth were chattering now. "You will beat this!"

Annalee nodded. *Annie Oakley.* The sun still shone on them, but the air was cooling. She couldn't sit here another minute, couldn't stand the sadness. "Walk with me." She stood and held her hand out to Tommy. "Please."

He looked like he wanted to cry, but he didn't. He fought it, the way she had known he would. Since she gave him no choice, Tommy stood and drew her to his side. As they started along the canal Annalee felt the strange feeling again.

It was something she'd noticed lately. The fact that she couldn't breathe right. When she was lying down or sitting or moving too fast, her lungs didn't seem able to get a full breath. She had told herself her energy was to blame. Too little sleep or not enough vitamin B. Changing that should help and then she'd feel normal again.

But now Annalee knew better. Every strange thing

she'd been feeling was probably related to her cancer. She shuddered. *Relax, Annalee. Breathe.* A few more steps and she settled down. *There.* She was breathing better now.

With Tommy's arm warm around her shoulders.

Another couple was walking toward them. A guy and girl maybe in their mid-twenties. As they came closer Annalee could see their wedding rings. They laughed and talked and before they reached Annalee and Tommy they stopped and kissed.

Nothing too long or inappropriate for being in public. They were in their own world. Too in love to notice anyone else. Living out their very own happily ever after.

As the couple passed, the man smiled at the woman. "I'm ready to go home."

She smiled. "Me, too."

Home. Together. Annalee slipped her arm around Tommy's waist as they kept walking. Would that ever be the two of them? Married and able to go home together? What would that be like? Annalee set her gaze straight ahead. Why did they have to wait till then?

After today she'd be in and out of the hospital. The details her mom had shared were horrible. Her doctor had apparently said Annalee would lose her hair and she'd lose weight. Even her eyelashes and eyebrows would disappear. Chemo and radiation would overtake her and she'd be fortunate if she ever felt normal again.

If she ever felt as good as she did right now. She slowed her pace.

Tommy looked at her. "You want to go back?"

"No." A grove of trees stood just off the path ahead. She led him there and she leaned against one of the trunks. He faced her, inches away, and Annalee brought her hand to his cheek. "I love you, Tommy. Do I tell you that enough?"

"Yes." He looked concerned. "You always tell me. I love you, too." He hesitated. "You're going to get better, Annalee. You need to believe that."

"I do." She didn't hesitate. But they both knew there were no guarantees. Not with cancer. She studied his handsome face, the line of his jaw. "Hold me. Please." Her voice fell to a whisper. "Don't let go."

"Annalee." He drew her into his arms and cradled her head to his chest. "I'm here." This moment was entirely different than the one on Karon Beach last summer. Rather than passion and possibilities, this embrace was wrapped in worry. Desperation. "I'll help you through it. Every day," Tommy whispered into her hair. "I won't ever leave."

His words meant everything to her. Not only that he wouldn't leave her here, now. At the starting line of the most terrifying fight of her life. But he wouldn't *leave* her. Not ever. She understood that from his tone.

The sun was setting and she had to get back. Tomorrow everything would change. She would be busy with doctor appointments and whatever medications they might start her on in anticipation of her hospital stay. And the next morning after that . . .

Annalee didn't want to think about it. She breathed in the smell of Tommy's cologne and memorized the sound of the water moving through the canal. The feel of his arms around her. And all she wanted was to stay this way with him forever.

She moved just enough to see his face. "I wish you could come home with me. Stay with me. Overnight." She didn't have to spell it out. "You know?"

The look in his eyes was the same one he'd had on the beach of Phuket. Even with the vastly different reasons. He touched her face. "Do you mean . . . ?"

"Yes." Annalee took a slow breath. "Everything's different now." Her heart beat faster. "So what if . . . what if we never get the chance." Her breath mingled with his. "Kiss me, Tommy. Would you?" She took gentle hold of his face. "Please."

He searched her eyes. "We'll get the chance, Annalee. One day." He wove his fingers into her hair.

And like something from a dream, his lips were on hers. Never mind that they couldn't spend the night together. Tommy's kiss was the sweetest thing Annalee had ever known. The sun was setting, shadows falling, and time stopped as he kissed her again. Like they weren't in the park and she wasn't sick.

Tommy searched her eyes. "That . . . was amazing."

"Yes." A thrill of soft laughter quieted every concern in Annalee's heart. "All I want is you." She slid the side of her face against his. The feel of him this close made her forget everything else.

"Me, too." Tommy looked straight through to her soul. "But I want so much more, Annalee. I want you well." He kissed her once more and then, breathless, he stepped back. "I need to get you home."

"I know." Leaving here was the last thing she wanted to do. She wanted to stop the sun in the sky and keep darkness from falling. So they could stand here a little longer. Kiss and laugh and talk about the day when they wouldn't have to say goodbye. When they could stay like this till morning and let passion have its way. Maybe dreaming would keep the dark away. Anything to outrun tomorrow. Because in this beautiful unforgettable moment, Tommy's next kiss said all she needed to know.

And cancer couldn't get a word in edgewise.

11

Tommy took the day off school Wednesday, and watched the poison enter Annalee's body one drip at a time. He couldn't remember the name of the drug or the kind of medication the doctor had inserted into her chest port before this one.

All that mattered was Annalee.

Hours passed and it was just the two of them in her hospital room now. Annalee's mother was down in the cafeteria, but Tommy wouldn't move from her side. He couldn't.

"How do you feel?" He sat in the chair beside her bed and held her hand. The one without the IV needle.

"Tired." The light in her eyes had never dimmed. Not once. And she hadn't complained since treatment began. She looked deep into his eyes. "How about you, Tommy? Are . . . you afraid?"

"Of what?" Tommy didn't dare let her see his fear. "God's using this to make you better. That's what we both want."

He stared at the bag above her bed. Getting cancer treatment at the hospital was a whole lot more complicated than he had known. And there were a dozen known side effects for her type of chemo. But this morning even as the doctor went over the list of probabilities, Annalee's peace never wavered.

Tommy kissed her hand and kept eye contact with her. "So you don't feel sick?"

"No." A soft laugh came from her. "The side effects don't hit for a long time. Days even."

Tommy nodded. "I . . . hate that you have to go through this." He gritted his teeth and locked eyes with her again. She didn't look good. Her skin was gray and her face seemed thinner than a week ago.

"Hey." She pressed her fingers between his. "We prayed about this . . . remember?"

"Yes." He sighed.

Prayer. That's what he needed more of today. Prayer would make a difference. He believed that. But not once since he'd gotten to the hospital had he prayed, and now his thoughts raced a thousand miles an hour in every possible scary direction.

"What is it?" She searched his face.

"It's just . . ."

"You're scared." Annalee lifted her head. "It's going to be okay, Tommy. We have to believe that." She settled back into the bed. "I have this . . . I don't know. A peace, I guess. It's like I can hear God saying I'm going to get through this."

With all his heart he wanted to share her peace. But the facts flew in the face of his faith. Especially today, when her diagnosis had never been more real. He couldn't say any of that, so he just nodded.

"I know." A grin tugged at her mouth. "Let's talk about you. Have you told your parents yet? About being a police officer?"

"No." He raked his fingers through his hair. "I'll tell them tonight." Maybe that was it. First Annalee's treatment, and then the fact that he had to go home after this and tell his parents his decision. He didn't want to be a lawyer or a doctor the way his family expected.

He wanted to be a cop.

"Tommy . . . talk to me." She was the picture of calm. "Tell me again why you want this? Especially now, when things are so crazy. Being a police officer . . . it's never been more dangerous." She was quiet for a moment. "Then maybe you'll know what to say to your parents tonight."

One of her machines began to beep. The sound was incessant and loud and Tommy's anxiety doubled. Now what? Was her body rejecting the chemo? "I'll be right back." Tommy stood and went to the door. He stuck his head out and flagged down a nurse at the station across the hall. "She's having a problem in here! Please hurry."

As Tommy returned to his spot he noticed Annalee's raised eyebrows. "I'm fine." She shook her head. "My IV bag needs replacing."

A male nurse entered the room and checked her monitors and the other machines at the head of her bed. He swapped out the IV bag and tapped a few buttons. "Should be good."

Tommy exhaled. He winced at Annalee. "Sorry. I just . . . it's hard enough to watch you go through this. If anything went wrong . . . if—" He couldn't finish his sentence. "I had to be sure."

Her smile warmed his heart. "Where were we?"

Was it his imagination or did her voice sound weaker? "Why . . . I want to be a police officer."

"Yes." If she was troubled by his new career choice, she didn't let on. "All the reasons, Tommy. Come on."

They'd gone over some of these, but he could see what she was doing. If he talked about becoming a cop then maybe he wouldn't worry about her. He clung to her hand and leaned forward. As close as he could get to her. "I want to do something good. Something that matters."

She nodded. "I'll always remember you running toward that burning car." Her eyes held his for a long beat. "Who does that?"

He ran his thumb over the top of her hand. "Kids being trafficked, drug dealers destroying lives for a pocketful of cash, gangs terrorizing inner-city neighborhoods." He looked straight at her. "Someone has to defend our city, the people who live here."

"Who else but you?" Annalee didn't look away. "Glad you're telling your parents tonight."

"Yeah." Tommy felt an ache in the pit of his stomach. "I think they'll take it okay. I hope so." He looked at the area on her upper chest where the port was sewn into her skin. "How do you feel now?"

"I'm fine." She yawned. "You need to go home. Do your homework."

She was right. He released the bed rail so nothing separated them. Then he leaned close and hugged her, best he could with the tubes and blood pressure cuff and IV. "All I want . . . is to be back at the park, kissing you by the canal."

Their faces were inches apart. She looked deep into his eyes. "I'll remember everything about it. As long as I live."

Which would be a very long time, Tommy thought. He leaned closer still and kissed her forehead. "I'd kiss you now." He looked over his shoulder. "But your nurse might not like it."

"My mom, either." Annalee smiled. "At least not here, in the hospital. You know."

Tommy straightened, his hand still wrapped around hers. Before he could ask Annalee one last time how she was feeling, there was a sound at the door. Annalee's mom walked in with a water bottle and a small coffee.

"I got this for you." She set it down beside Annalee. "Breve latte."

"Mmm." Annalee hit a button and raised the bed. Then she released Tommy's hand and took the coffee. "You know me so well."

Tommy really did have to go. He kissed Annalee's cheek and then hugged her mother. "Thanks for letting me be here."

Her mother's smile did nothing to hide the worry in

her eyes. "It means the world to Annalee that you're here. To me, too."

Annalee's parents truly were two of Tommy's favorite people. He looked deep into her mom's eyes. "Please. Call me if anything changes." He grabbed his backpack. "I'll be here tomorrow after school."

Not until Tommy pulled in the driveway twenty minutes later did he remember about the conversation he needed to have with his parents. He had researched the Indianapolis Metropolitan Police Department. They had a ride-along program Tommy wanted to take part in as soon as possible.

The talk couldn't wait.

Especially when his parents were asking every other day about his acceptance to a handful of top schools. Which was he going to attend and when was he going to make his decision. "Registration happens early spring," his mom had told him last night. "The sooner you let the school know, the better."

Tommy parked his car in the garage and cut the engine. Yes, he was interested in a number of universities. The plan had always been that if Tommy didn't become a doctor, he'd be a lawyer, like his father. Everything about his high school courses, his ACT and SAT test scores suggested one of those careers was the logical path.

He stepped out of his Jeep, took his backpack from the passenger seat and headed inside. At the top of the stairs from the garage into the house, Tommy heard his parents in the kitchen with Malin and Johnny. They were laughing about some YouTube clip. A dancing dog, from what Tommy could see on the computer.

"Hey." His dad motioned for Malin to turn the volume down. A hush fell over the room. "How's Annalee?"

Tommy set his backpack down against the wall and slipped his hands in his jeans pockets. "She's tired, that's all I can tell for now. Otherwise . . . she's so positive." He shrugged. "You wouldn't know she was getting chemo at all."

Malin walked up and gave Tommy a side hug. "I prayed for her."

"Me, too." Johnny was eight years old, but he had a wisdom that made him seem much older. He joined Tommy and Malin. "She's going to get better. Right?"

Tommy shared a look with his parents, who stood a few feet away. "Yes." Tommy patted the top of his little brother's blond head. "She is, Johnny. I believe that."

Later, after Malin and Johnny went to bed, Tommy asked his parents to join him in the living room. His mom and dad took the sofa and Tommy sat in the chair opposite them. His mother frowned. "Is . . . she worse than what you said?" She leaned forward, studying Tommy. "Tell us."

"It's not that." He shook his head. "The worst side effects don't happen until a few days from now."

"And they get worse with each treatment." His dad took his mother's hand. "I researched it."

Tommy held his breath. *Give me the words, Lord. Let them understand what I'm about to tell them. Please.*

His dad's smile was easy. "So . . . you want to talk about something else?" He sat back and crossed his legs. "Have you decided which school?"

"Every day my friends at the gym ask me." His mom's eyes lit up. "We all have graduating seniors and their kids have all decided."

Tommy slid to the edge of his chair and planted his elbows on his knees. "Actually . . . that is what I want to talk about." He hesitated. "My plans for next year."

"The best thing about Duke is it's closer than Harvard. Not even a ten-hour drive." His dad grinned. "But who's counting?"

"I . . . didn't pick Duke, Dad." He looked to his mom and back to his father. "I didn't choose any of them." He straightened. "Actually . . . I've decided to skip school— for now, anyway." He watched the shock begin to hit. "Because I want to be a police officer. That's what I want to do. . . . I figured we needed to talk about it."

The disbelief on his parents' faces began to morph. His father stayed quiet, calm. But his mom . . . Her brows formed a V and lines appeared across her forehead. She stood and put her hands to her face. Then she lowered them and sat down again. "Are you kidding?" The question was rhetorical. "You must be."

"I'm not." *Oh, boy.* Tommy felt his heart begin to race. "Why . . . would I joke about something like this?"

"Reagan." His father's tone was suddenly sharp. "Please. Let's listen to him."

"Listen?" His mother uttered a sound that was more

cry than laugh. "Tommy . . . you're the A student, the one who always wanted *eight* years of college. Remember?"

"She has a point." Tommy's dad looked confused.

"Of course, Mom has a point." Tommy stood and paced a few feet toward the window. When he turned back he worked to keep his voice level. "I was supposed to do big things at school, I know that. Be a doctor like Papa or a lawyer." He looked at his father. "Like you, Dad. That's all we've ever talked about." He didn't want to sound rude. "But I changed my mind. I don't know how else to say it."

His mother crossed her arms. "You can't just . . . change your mind. You can't—" She seemed to hear her harsh tone for the first time. She looked away and when she turned to Tommy again, her eyes were damp. "A police officer? Tommy . . . do you know how dangerous that is? With how things are?"

"Yes." Tommy felt an angry chill run down his spine. "That's the price of defending the streets, Mom. So that you and Dad and Malin and Johnny can be safe."

"Okay. We . . . want to help." Tommy's father sounded almost desperate to restore peace. "I know an officer at the downtown precinct. I could ask him about their ride-along program."

Light burst through Tommy's heart. "Really?"

"Sure." His dad looked at his mom and then back at Tommy. "I mean . . . I'm assuming you want to do that. Before making up your mind."

"I've made up my mind." Tommy had to be clear about that. "This isn't . . . some tangent. It's what I plan to do. Kids are out there being trafficked right now." He returned to his chair. "But yes. I'd love if you could connect me with your friend."

His mom stared at his dad. "What are you saying?" Her voice sounded shrill. "That you'd . . . help him make this decision?"

"He said he's already made the decision, Reagan." His dad looked down. "We can talk about it later."

"We need to talk now." A tear fell onto her cheek. "He's throwing away his future, Luke. We can't let that happen."

Tommy couldn't believe this conversation was happening right in front of him. He stood. "I'm going to bed. I can't do this."

He hugged his dad and then stopped short in front of his mother. "I was worried about how you'd take this." His own eyes felt damp. "But I never thought . . . you'd react like this."

"Tommy . . ." His mom called after him as he walked away. "I'm sorry. It's just . . . you can't be a police officer right out of high school!"

That last line stopped Tommy cold. He turned and stared at his mother. "I'm not going to respond to that. Mom, I . . . I've never seen this side of you."

"Reagan." His father sounded disappointed. "Please." He looked at Tommy. "Son, we'll talk more later. Your mother . . . she needs time."

"Okay." Tommy nodded at his dad and gave his mom a final look. "I hope you're better tomorrow."

Once he was in his room, Tommy exhaled. He trudged across the floor and dropped to his knees at the foot of his bed. Only rarely did he do this when he prayed. Most recently during Annalee's scan. And now, in light of his aching heart.

He had no choice tonight.

With his head bowed, he asked God to help his mom understand and he thanked Him for his father's response. Then he prayed for the real reason he was on his knees. Annalee's health, her survival. And he promised God this wasn't the only time he'd be here begging for help. He'd be here every night.

Until Annalee was well.

12

Luke's head was spinning. He called in to the office that morning and told his secretary he wouldn't be in. "Reschedule my meetings and cancel my calls," he told her. "Something's come up."

Something Luke had never imagined. That his son who had aced school all his life would change his mind about attending college and choose a career in law enforcement. Reagan had gotten up earlier than usual and left him a note on her pillow.

> *Gone to workout.*
> *I'll shower there.*
> *I have work at school all day.*
> *I love you, but Luke . . . we need to talk later.*

At least she'd told him she loved him. Last night when they went to bed Reagan hadn't said a word to him. Not a single word. He understood. She was angry because he'd brought up the Indianapolis ride-along program. But that was only because Luke had wanted to help somehow. Reagan's reaction had been so negative. Their son clearly needed an ally.

Even after taking a night to process their new reality, Luke could barely draw a full breath. Tommy wanted to be a cop? He wanted to skip school when Ivy League universities were offering him full-ride scholarships because of his grades?

Reagan's reaction had been so quick, so biting, Tommy never had the chance to tell them the most important part: why he wanted to do this.

Why would the son of a lawyer—the grandson of a doctor—with grades and test scores better than anyone in the state, suddenly change his mind and want to be a police officer? At a time when some people want to defund police?

But that morning as Luke scrambled a few eggs and made a spinach smoothie, his shock and disbelief gave way to the slightest hint of something else. An emotion he hadn't expected.

Pride.

Tommy had always been an exceptional son. Never mind his grades and scholastic accolades. What stood out about their oldest child was the way he cared for people. First day of third grade, a new kid arrived with braces on his legs. Kevin was his name. The child limped and kept to himself and until he met Tommy, the boy had no friends.

According to the teacher, Tommy welcomed Kevin to hang out with him and the guys during recess. When a fourth grader came running across the yard and tripped the boy, Tommy fought back.

So much that he wound up in the principal's office.

Luke and Reagan had met him there and Luke would never forget what the woman told them. "Tommy will have to miss recess for a week because he fought back. But off the record, it was the exact right thing to do. Kevin needed a defender and Tommy stepped up."

Tommy stepped up.

It was the same thing Luke and Reagan had heard about their son in middle school when a couple kids threatened a girl on the bus. Tommy put himself between her and them and told the pair never to speak to her again. If they did, they'd have to get through him first.

Luke glanced at the framed pictures of his kids on the fireplace mantel. Tommy was six-three and muscled from his time in the weight room and on the basketball team. But he was wiry. Never the intimidating lineman type. No, it wasn't Tommy's physical presence that allowed him to speak up for someone being bullied. It was his heart. His concern for others.

Last year it had been an incident on the basketball court. Tommy's team had been visitors at a nearby school, and the opposing team had an attitude bigger than the gym. Just before halftime, their point guard pushed Tommy's teammate. Hard and on purpose. Three additional Northside guys jumped off the bench and rushed the floor to teach the kid a lesson.

This time Tommy didn't throw a punch or retaliate. He put himself between the offender and his own angry players and somehow he defused the moment. Entirely.

Later his coach told Luke, "Your son has this innate ability. He knows when to get in someone's face, and he knows when to talk the same person off a ledge."

And Luke remembered what the elementary school principal had said. *Tommy stepped up.* He stood for what was right and true and he looked for a peaceful resolution, whenever possible. He was born with a strong sense of protecting those around him, looking out for those who couldn't look out for themselves.

And wasn't that what being a cop was all about? What it was supposed to be about, anyway?

Luke knew exactly how he was going to spend this day. The situation with Tommy was too important to put action off even a single day. He made himself a cup of coffee for the road and set out for the downtown precinct of the Indianapolis Metropolitan Police Department.

His friend was expecting him.

Detective Mike Lockwood had married one of the lawyers at Luke's firm six years ago. Not long after, Mike joined Luke's monthly prayer breakfast. Luke and Mike hit it off and sometimes they'd catch up over coffee after the breakfast was over.

Today the plan was to meet at the park across the street from the police station. Luke took a bench in the shade of a hundred-year-old oak. Ribbons of warm sunshine shone through the branches.

Luke saw Mike exit the station and head his way. Mike had played running back for Indiana University's football team a decade ago and he'd gotten stronger and faster since then. He was a friend to the community and a presence at every call he answered. Black and bald with warm brown eyes and a keen perception. The sort of cop who could see right through you. Which was why the IMPD had promoted him to detective.

The two shook hands and Mike sat down. Luke didn't waste time getting to the point. "Tommy rocked our world last night." He shrugged. "He wants to join the police force."

Mike squinted. "Tommy who?"

A ripple of laughter caught Luke by surprise. "That pretty much sums up our reaction."

"Your Tommy?" Mike leaned forward. "The one bound for Harvard or Duke?"

"The very same." Luke sighed. "I've been thinking all day how I should've seen the signs. Tommy's always had the heart of a cop."

"Hmm." Mike crossed his arms. "How did Reagan take the news?"

"Terrible. We haven't talked about it since." He hesitated. "It was my fault. I brought you into it. Told Tommy he could maybe do the ride-along program with you."

A flash of understanding filled Mike's eyes. "Not the best timing."

"Right." Luke nodded. "Definitely."

Mike thought for a moment. "You think he's serious? About applying to the department?"

"As serious as I've ever seen him." Luke paused. "I just thought your ride-along program could help him know."

"I agree." Mike leaned back against the bench. "Things can get pretty intense out there."

Mike went over the specifics of the program. "Tommy's eighteen, right?"

"He is."

"He'd need to be 21 before we'd hire him. " Mike blinked. "Does he know that?"

"Hmm." Luke imagined Reagan's relief at the news. "I don't think so."

"There are a few states that'll take him at eighteen. But it'd be a move for sure."

What would Reagan think about that? Tommy becoming an officer and moving away all at the end of this school year. Luke put the thought out of his mind.

Mike ran his hand over his head. "As for the ride-along program, there are risks." Mike raised his brow. "We had a deputy from another department do a ride-along last month. The officer he was with got ambushed, and both men were shot in the hail of bullets." Mike paused. "They both lived, but it was touch and go for a few weeks."

The news hit Luke hard. He hadn't considered the possibility that Tommy could get shot on a ride-along. Somehow he had thought the program would be more informative than dangerous. Like when law school interns from IU shadowed Luke in the courtroom for a day. But of course spending a day with a police officer would be risky. Criminals didn't care if a kid was along for the ride. To them, a cop was a cop.

Luke clenched his jaw. Reagan wasn't going to like this news. He sighed. "If it's what Tommy wants to do, I think a ride-along is the best thing. Even with the risks."

Mike gave Luke a light slap on the shoulder. "Your boy will be okay. And maybe he'll find out it isn't for him." Mike smiled. "Then he can get on with college."

Luke weighed his friend's words on the drive to his next stop. A visit with his father. After all, many years ago Luke had thrown his parents a curveball far worse than what Tommy had tossed them last night.

If anyone could help him process Tommy's announcement and what should happen next it was his dad.

Dr. John Baxter.

REAGAN SPENT THE day running from Tommy's news. How was it possible that her Ivy League son was choosing a life of law enforcement? Putting himself in harm's way when he was supposed to be helping people in some medical office or courtroom?

After her workout she drove straight to Indiana University Health Center. She met Annalee's mother, Donna, in the lobby. The woman had dark circles under her eyes and her smile didn't last long.

"Annalee's struggling." Donna led Reagan to the bank of elevators. "The nausea is kicking in . . . a couple days early according to her doctor."

They made their way up to the fourth floor and down a hallway to Annalee's room. She was asleep when they walked in, but it was all Reagan could do to hide her shock. The girl who had always been so vibrant and full of life had seemingly overnight become small and frail. Her face was sunken and her cheekbones stuck out in a way they hadn't before.

"She's lost weight." Donna whispered as she took the chair beside her daughter's bed. "I think that's been happening gradually."

Reagan pulled up a second chair and positioned it next to Donna. "What's the plan? For her treatment?"

"Her doctor is taking it very seriously." Donna didn't look away from Annalee. "Six rounds of chemo, every couple weeks. Three days in the hospital with each session."

A few years ago, one of the teachers at Northside had been diagnosed with lymphoma, but her treatment was very different. Outpatient, one day a week off and on for six months. Reagan didn't bring that up. "I'm sure every patient's plan is different."

"Yes." Donna glanced at her and then back at Annalee. "Same with the side effects."

Tommy's announcement suddenly didn't seem that important. Reagan couldn't imagine being in Donna's chair, watching her child suffer through chemo and having no idea how things would turn out. Silence fell between them and for a moment, Reagan closed her eyes. *Lord, heal her. Please get her through this and let her live.*

She put her hand on Donna's shoulder. "What about the side effects?"

"Well . . ." Donna kept her voice low since Annalee was still asleep. "She'll have steroids in the coming week and antinausea medicine." She looked back at Reagan. "It could take two weeks for her hair to start falling out. It varies."

Reagan felt her heart sink. Annalee was a beautiful girl by any standard. But she was known for her long blond hair. Hair that other girls longed for and no beauty salon could produce from a bottle. Reagan had assumed Annalee might lose her hair, but now it was certain. The loss would be one more thing the girl would suffer through.

Annalee stirred, and Donna moved to her side. "It's okay, sweetie. I'm here."

"Mom." She moaned and turned her head one way then the other. After a few seconds she blinked her eyes open. "I . . . don't feel good."

"I know, honey." Donna set her shoulders. As if she was determined to find some untapped personal strength, anything to help bear her daughter's burden. "The doctor's getting you medicine for that."

"Okay." Annalee looked at Reagan and smiled. "Mrs. Baxter . . . you didn't have to come."

"I wanted to." Reagan stayed in her chair, but she leaned closer. "We're all praying for you. That you'll be better soon."

"Yes." Annalee nodded. "Me and Tommy are praying . . . that same thing." She closed her eyes and in no time she was asleep again.

"They're giving her something to make her sleep."

Donna sat back down. Her eyes never left Annalee. "I'm just . . . I can't . . ." She hung her head and her body began to shake.

Reagan slid her chair closer and put her arm around Donna's shoulders. "You and Dan will not walk this alone." Emotion tightened her throat and she took a few seconds to find the words. "Today I'll tell the school. At the assembly, like you asked." Reagan hugged her friend close. "The whole Northside community will be with you. Every day. Every hour."

Donna turned to her. "Dan will be here after lunch. It's a lot for him, balancing work and visits to the hospital. He wants to be by her side through it all."

"Annalee knows that." Reagan paused. "There's no easy way to get through something like this." She checked the time on her watch. "I need to go. Please . . . tell me if I can do anything."

"I will." Donna stood and walked Reagan to the door. "Tommy has been amazing. He was here all day yesterday. He'll be here this afternoon, too. When school lets out." She managed the slightest smile. "He's a great young man. You must be . . . very proud of him."

Very proud. Reagan felt the words like a cut to her heart. "Yes. We are." She didn't let her deeper concerns show as she hugged Donna. "I'm here for you."

Reagan walked down the hall and took the first elevator. *You must be very proud of him.* She squeezed her eyes shut for a few seconds. Did Donna know Tommy was considering police work? No, that wasn't possible.

He wouldn't have told Annalee's parents before he told his own.

The truth was, Reagan had so much to be proud of when it came to her oldest son. So why had she treated him so terribly in the face of his news? She should've reacted like Luke. *Sure, Son,* she could've said. *That's wonderful. When do you think you'll apply to the department?*

Instead she had alienated him and let him go to bed hurt and angry.

Reagan reached her car and slid behind the wheel. Of course she was proud of Tommy. But a police officer? The idea was still sending shock waves through her soul. Even so . . . what kind of mother was she to treat her son that way? Tommy had been happy, after all. Excited to share his announcement. The thought stayed with her. Why couldn't she have been more like her husband—suggesting ways Tommy could get into police work more quickly? More efficiently? She had no answers for herself on the drive to Northside High and none when she joined with other teachers in the auditorium minutes ahead of the assembly.

Reagan headed up the Northside PTSA. She worked in the high school office, and managed all parent volunteer duties. It was a paid position, and one she loved. Now, surrounded by the high school staff, Reagan waited till each class had filed into the building. There were nearly five hundred students in grades nine through twelve. When all of them were seated, she took the microphone at center stage.

"Some of you may know that Annalee Miller is sick."
Reagan felt a catch in her breath. Her eyes met Tommy's
in the audience.

But her son looked away.

Reagan didn't blame him. She took a slow breath.
"Annalee has non-Hodgkin's lymphoma. She's very ill,
and she'll miss the rest of this semester. Probably much
of the spring, as well." She kept her eyes away from
Tommy this time. Her announcement held enough
heartache without her being constantly reminded of the
trouble with her son.

The announcement didn't last long. Reagan told
them that the school would be doing fundraisers to help
the Miller family with expenses while her parents cared
for her. "We'll send something home from school soon,
letting you know how you can help. Until then we'll do
what we can right now." She looked around. "Please
stand. Principal Larson is going to pray for Annalee. For a
miracle."

It was all Reagan could do to keep her composure as
she turned the microphone over to the principal. Larry
Larson had been the head administrator at Northside for
more than a decade. When one of their own was sick or
injured, he took the news personally. Mr. Larson was a
praying man, like much of the community. The school's
student body and parent community were grateful for
the fact.

With teary eyes, the man asked the students to bow
their heads. As he began to pray, Reagan watched the

students form circles, their arms around each other. A group of a dozen or so surrounded Tommy. And of course. Everyone knew he and Annalee were inseparable. If Annalee was sick, then Tommy was suffering, too.

The show of love and friendship was striking.

On the way home that afternoon Reagan realized something that made her sick. The students at Northside were clearly determined to give Tommy the utmost level of support. Reagan blinked back tears as she pulled into her driveway. Whatever the situation, whatever he needed, his friends would have his back.

She pulled into the garage and gripped the steering wheel. If Tommy's friends and classmates had known about his decision to skip college and be a police officer, every one of them would've stood by him. Cheering for him. Excited for him.

So then the real question was this.

Why couldn't she?

13

The idyllic world Tommy had known just a few weeks ago was gone. Forever, it felt like. Annalee was worse every hour, weaker and sicker no matter how much he prayed. And things were just as bad at home.

Tension was still growing between Tommy and his mother. Not only that, but things seemed strained between his parents. They were barely speaking to each other. All in the days that had passed since Tommy had told them his decision.

Malin and Johnny hadn't noticed. They were busy with school and homework and after-school teams. But Tommy knew. He could see the way his mom and dad looked at each other these past few evenings, and it wasn't good.

Despite that, they must have come to some agreement. Because yesterday after he returned from the hospital, his dad had pulled him aside. "Detective Mike Lockwood called. You can do a ride-along tomorrow, if that works. I told him you didn't have basketball on Saturdays till the season begins."

"Really?" The thrill that ran through Tommy had only confirmed his desire to be a cop. That's when he told Tommy about the age requirement. Tommy had to be twenty-one before he could work for the IMPD. But there were other states where he could work first. Right after graduation. Then he had glanced toward the next room, where his mom was helping Malin with a math assignment. "What about Mom?"

"She's okay." His dad hadn't sounded totally convincing. "She wants you to see what it's like."

But at Johnny's soccer game this morning, Tommy didn't think his mom was okay at all. She barely made eye contact with him. After lunch, as Tommy was headed downtown to the police station, he found her in the kitchen making cookies.

"Want help?" He still had fifteen minutes before he had to leave. "I can clean up. Dishes are my favorite." He tried to keep his tone light. "You know me. King of the kitchen."

His mother's smile fell flat. "Thank you." She set down her dishrag and looked at him. Straight at him for the first time since his announcement. "Tommy . . . I'm sorry. For how I've been acting."

He nodded. "Dad says you're good . . . with the ride-along today?"

"I am." She exhaled. Like she was carrying a ton of bricks on her shoulders. "You've seen your grandpa John at work in the hospital, and you've been with your father in the courtroom." Her expression was tight. Dark with what was obvious worry. "You need to do this. So you can see if . . ." She stopped herself.

"If what?" Tommy felt a rush of frustration. "Mom. I'm not going to change my mind. If that's what you think."

She didn't say anything in response. Instead she hugged him—longer than usual. "I'm sorry. That's all." She looked at him. "Be careful, Tommy. Please."

Now Tommy was doing the ride-along paperwork at the downtown station. He wore dress pants, a white button-down shirt and loafers. No jeans. No tennis shoes. The department took the ride-along program seriously.

At least his mother had been kind to him on the way out the door. But now he understood why she'd agreed to this. Because she thought he would get in a police car and see . . . what? The danger of it? The frustration? Clearly she thought riding alongside an officer would change his mind about being a policeman.

They would have to talk about that later.

Tommy finished filling out the forms and turned them in at the front desk. The next four hours would be spent in a police car. Then he'd go to the hospital to see Annalee. To see how she wasn't improving and how God wasn't answering their prayers. At least it seemed that way.

In the meantime, being with Detective Lockwood was going to be a great diversion. The man met Tommy in the lobby a few minutes later. He shook Tommy's hand. "You look just like your dad."

"Thank you." Tommy had heard that before. It was always a compliment.

The detective nodded for Tommy to follow him.

"You'll ride with me this afternoon. I don't get out on patrol very often, so this will be good for both of us. After today, I'll assign you to one of our other officers."

"Yes, sir." Tommy could barely breathe as they walked to the man's squad car. Along the way Detective Lockwood told him what to expect. "Anything can happen out there. We're working to take down a couple of very dangerous gangs and a group of our officers is closing in on a sex-trafficking ring. Beyond that there's the 9-1-1 calls. And they come in just about constantly."

Tommy remembered something Annalee's dad had said when they were in Thailand. The crime they'd seen on the streets there was just as bad in Indianapolis. And most major cities across the United States. Some of it might be more hidden, but it was out there.

Detective Lockwood was still running through the possibilities. "The most dangerous calls are the ones that take us by surprise. The routine traffic stop where an officer is shot before he or she can say a word. Or the calls that lead us on a chase—by car and then by foot. Always the goal is to get the suspect safely in custody. Whether they have a weapon or not."

Already Tommy's heart was beating harder. "I've watched just about every episode of *Cops*. The chases seem pretty dangerous. Especially at night."

"They are. Other bad guys could be waiting for us, hiding in the shadows, ready to shoot. The truth is, every call is a risk." Detective Lockwood paused as they reached the squad car. A new-looking Ford Explorer. "But it's a risk we're all willing to take. Because honestly . . . we want to be part of the solution on how people see cops. We could walk away, get a different job. But for most of us, this is a calling. Someone has to help the people. My wife and daughters understand that."

Of course they do, Tommy wanted to say. Why couldn't his mother be like them? Maybe she just needed time to get used to the idea. Tommy hoped so.

Once they were inside the squad car, the man explained that the vehicle's floor was made entirely of rubber. No carpet at all. "Nothing to slow us down if we need to enter or exit quickly."

Detective Lockwood then pointed out the brake pedal. "It's larger than normal. Easier for us to stop in a hurry if a crime is in progress."

In the door there were white envelopes. "For tickets," the detective explained. "And you'll see hand sanitizer there. Which we need more than you'd think."

On the center console was a laptop on a swivel. "The computer gives us options police officers didn't have in the old days. It's loaded with programs that help us run plates, check IDs on suspects and write reports."

Beneath that was a built-in radio with a microphone and a series of switches. "The microphone is constantly connected to dispatch. Same with the one on our uniform." He tapped the receiver unit near his shoulder. Then he pointed to a switch on the console. "Flip this and everything's on. Lights, sirens. Back lights. And the wall of light for a traffic stop. All of it ready for action."

Tommy was mesmerized. He'd never been inside a police car before, and what he'd seen on *Cops* couldn't compare to being here in person.

"And of course our spotlight." Detective Lockwood put his left hand on a shiny knob near the windshield frame. "This helps us see addresses or people we're looking for."

Tommy looked over his shoulder to the backseat. "The containment area is only on one side of the car?"

"Not for all police vehicles, but for this one, yes." The detective nodded to the open seat. "Once in a while we need to transport a citizen for noncriminal reasons. An elderly person, or someone lost. That sort of thing. Obviously we don't use the containment area for those situations."

Every detail made Tommy more thrilled about being out on the road.

Detective Lockwood pointed to the other side of the backseat. "This suspect containment area is pretty typical. Hard plastic. Nowhere to hide anything—drugs or weapons. Plexiglass all the way around the top. That way we can see whoever's back there, but they can't spit on us or harm us in any way."

Tommy noticed the bars on the window. "Are those new? I haven't seen that before."

"You'd be surprised how easily a suspect can kick out a window. The bars protect us and the suspect."

At the top of the inside roofline, the detective pointed

out a compact printer. "We run off tickets right here in the vehicle. That keeps the simple traffic infractions legible and quick. Much nicer than a handwritten ticket."

The ride-along started with basic patrol time. "We check out the city's most crime-ridden areas, looking for victims in need of assistance. Sometimes we pick up a drug dealer or two. But as soon as we get a call, that takes precedence."

Detective Lockwood cruised from the station to Haughville, one of the most crime-ridden neighborhoods in Indianapolis, he told Tommy. "We have an epidemic of drugs and gang activity in this area. A police presence here is critical."

In recent weeks, Tommy had done his research about the IMPD. The last officer killed in the line of duty had been in 2014, and a number of others had lost their lives in the decade before that. Beyond that were a number of high profile cases from around the country where police officers were convicted of murder because their wrongful actions resulted in the death of a suspect.

The job was incredibly tough, and not all cops were good. Tommy knew that.

But considering the way many big-city communities had turned on their police departments, the IMPD still had a fairly good relationship with its citizens.

Even in the toughest areas.

A few years ago the department hosted a lip-sync challenge to a Justin Timberlake song, and nearly a hundred community members took part in the video. The resulting YouTube clip only further improved relations with the city.

But here in Haughville, Tommy couldn't imagine many of the residents were thrilled to see a police car coming their way. Sure enough, a few minutes later Detective Lockwood radioed for backup. "See that." He nodded to a trio of old-model sedans in a parking lot overrun with weeds. "Drug deal going down for sure."

Tommy had read the rules for a ride-along with the IMPD. If a dangerous situation presented itself, the officer conducting the ride-along was encouraged to take their citizen passenger to a safe location, if possible. Tommy doubted there was such a thing in Haughville.

"We'll come at them from a side street and keep a low profile. You'll stay in the car." The detective had his radio in his hand. He was in constant contact with dispatch and after a few minutes, three patrol cars joined them. In letters and number codes Tommy didn't know or understand, a plan was made. Two other officers took the lead and surprised the drug deal, and in a rush of action three men were in custody.

"We've been looking for two of those guys all year." Detective Lockwood smiled when he was back in the car. His forehead was damp with sweat. "Someone's daughter . . . someone's son. They won't get a drug buy tonight. Might save a life."

If he could, Tommy would've given all four officers involved in the bust a round of applause. A year ago one of his basketball buddies lost an older brother to a heroin overdose. Tommy had a theory about drug dealers and users. The dealers should serve a decade minimum. Maybe more. Something severe enough to make people think twice about selling drugs for a living.

The users should get a mandatory three years in a lockdown rehab facility.

Tommy had written a paper on it after the death of his teammate's brother. Hard prison time for the dealers to cut off supply, and forced help for the user—to remove the demand. He got an A on the paper, but if he got a job with the police department, he could work to see his ideas become reality.

After the arrests in Haughville, an emergency call came in. Children in danger at a home near East Thirty-fourth and Sutherland Avenue. Another area Tommy and his friends avoided—especially after dark.

Tommy watched from the passenger seat of the squad car as Detective Lockwood approached a shirtless man stumbling near the front porch of a dilapidated house. "Them are my children!" No question the man was drunk. Or maybe on drugs.

Again backup had been called, and another two cars appeared on the scene at the same time as the angry citizen noticed Detective Lockwood.

"No!" The shirtless man was losing his shorts, but he didn't seem to notice. He pulled a knife from his pocket and waved it at the detective. With his other hand he made something that looked like a gang sign. Tommy couldn't tell. Then without warning the man began running down the street.

Other officers were out of their cars by then and suddenly a chase was under way. Tommy couldn't believe it. The action was playing out on the sidewalk right in front of him. Detective Lockwood might've been in his forties, but he was faster than lightning. During the chase, even from the police car Tommy could see the man shove a small plastic bag into his mouth. He rolled down the window so he could hear better.

At the same time, Detective Lockwood reached the suspect and handcuff him.

Tommy wasn't sure what had happened to the knife.

"Spit it out, man." Detective Lockwood shouted. "That stuff will kill you."

Another officer reached the scene and Detective Lockwood shouted. "He has the drugs in his mouth." He turned to the suspect again. "I said spit it out! I'm begging you, man. Don't kill yourself."

Finally the man spit the plastic bag from between his teeth. The other two officers took the suspect to one of the waiting patrol cars. Tommy watched the detective jog back to the house and up the steps. He knocked on the door. "Police. Open up."

Tommy was gripped by the scene. What had happened inside the house? Detective Lockwood knocked a few more times, announcing himself again and again. Finally he tried the door. It must've been unlocked because the detective hurried inside.

A minute later, on the radio, Tommy heard Detective Lockwood call for an ambulance. Maybe two minutes after that, the detective walked out of the house. He had a little boy on his hip and a baby cradled in his other arm. He handed the infant to a female officer who had just arrived on the scene, but the toddler stayed with him.

The child was sobbing, crying so hard Tommy could easily hear him. But the detective—one of the toughest men in the precinct according to Tommy's father—held the child to his chest and whispered to him until the boy stopped crying. An ambulance showed up and paramedics rushed into the house and then back out with a woman on a stretcher.

Not long after, another car joined the scene. Tommy could hear from the radio that the people who approached the house next were from social services. The children were headed for foster care. Tommy didn't need training to understand that much.

For ten minutes Detective Lockwood held the little boy, while the toddler clung to his neck. After he passed the child to one of the social workers, the detective jogged back to the squad car. From a box on his backseat, the detective pulled a teddy bear and ran it to the child. Tommy couldn't hear Detective Lockwood, but his actions said it all.

Detective Lockwood cared about the child. As if the boy were his own.

Something else. The fact that here, on one of the worst nights in the toddler's life, the detective was ready.

Not with a sharp word or a mere callous arrest. But with a teddy bear. A toy so the little boy wouldn't feel so sad and alone.

Back in the car, Detective Lockwood explained the situation to Tommy. "The suspect hit the mother of the children. Square in the face. Knocked her out. Then he called police as if he were the victim." The detective sighed. "They were both doing meth. Poor kids."

Before the ride-along was finished that afternoon, Detective Lockwood answered a call about a confused man. They found the older gentleman wandering in the middle of a busy intersection. As soon as they stopped and parked, the detective was out of the car. He put his hand on the man's shoulder and coaxed him into the squad car.

"You trying to get home?" Detective Lockwood checked the rearview mirror. "Your daughter called in. She's looking for you."

"That's good." The man tried to laugh. But fear filled his voice. "I'm looking for her, too."

Tommy shifted so he could see the gentleman. He was in his eighties, at least. His eyes were wide, and he clutched a worn hat in his hands.

The detective entered an address in his GPS and took off toward the man's home. "Tell me about yourself, Abraham."

"Well . . . I'm married to a good one. Fifty-three years now."

Detective Lockwood smiled. "You're a blessed man."

"I am." The man's fear eased. "That I am."

Abraham's daughter was waiting for him outside her house. She helped her father inside and then thanked the detective. "My mother died three years ago. Dad hasn't been the same since."

On the way back to the station, Tommy let the ordeal sink in. He had expected to see a string of arrests and traffic tickets, maybe a few foot chases. But he had forgotten one obvious aspect of the streets.

Just like in Thailand, people needed help. Trafficked kids, and old folks like Abraham. Police officers were often the only people willing and able to help.

Tommy was still thinking about all he'd seen on the ride-along when he arrived at the hospital. Annalee wasn't doing well. Her parents went home to shower, and Tommy stayed. He held a cool cloth to her head and grabbed a basin when she needed to throw up. None of it helped. She fell asleep looking sicker and weaker than she had yesterday.

Can't you hear us, God? Everyone's praying for her, so why is she so sick? Tommy stared at Annalee. *What did she do to deserve this?*

The babies in the drug house and the old man wandering the street—police could do something to help them. But not so Annalee. Only God could stop the side effects of chemo or the deadly power of cancer left untreated.

And for some reason God wasn't answering.

When her parents returned, Annalee was still sleeping, so Tommy left. Tears clouded his eyes all the way home. *Please, God, hear me. Help Annalee.* He couldn't stand seeing her so sick. *I believe in You, Lord. You can get her through this. Please.*

Tommy wanted to turn his car around and take Annalee from her hospital bed, drive her as far away from here as a tank of gas could get him. But it wouldn't matter. The disease would follow them. There was no outrunning it. And until God decided to help them, things would only get worse.

Darkness had long since fallen over Indiana by the time he pulled into the driveway at ten o'clock that night. He could see his parents in the living room, so Tommy took the back stairs. He didn't want to talk with them. Didn't want to visit or share about the ride-along or give them an update on Annalee.

Besides, the ride-along hadn't made him afraid of being an officer. It made him want to apply tomorrow. He'd be nineteen soon, so maybe he'd start his law enforcement career in Florida. Where age restrictions weren't as tough. Of course, that would only make his mother more upset.

Malin and Johnny were in bed, so Tommy was quiet as he changed into shorts and a T-shirt. He strapped on his boxing gloves and slipped down the back stairs, all the way to the garage. A punching bag had hung from the far bay since Tommy was sixteen.

For the next thirty minutes Tommy tore into the bag without taking a single break. Over and over and over again he hit the bag, lit into it with everything he had. Even with the gloves he could feel his fingers bruising, feel his tendons stretching. But he didn't care.

Punch. Punch. Punch.

He was exhausted but for these few minutes Tommy was at least doing something. *Make it go away, God. Make her well again. Please fight for her.* Silence echoed through the garage. *Fine.* If God wouldn't get rid of it, then Tommy would.

Punch. Punch. Punch.

Yes. This was what he needed to do. One jab after another and another. His breathing came harder and faster, but he kept hitting the bag, kept fighting. Destroying Annalee's enemy one sharp jolt at a time. Until he was too tired and broken to hit the bag one more time.

Tommy stepped back, his sides heaving, and he crumpled to the floor. There on the cool cement, the tears came. An ocean of them.

Sobs seized him and he covered his face. "No! Not Annalee. Please, God." The words seethed inside him and filled the air around him. And then Tommy wept like he'd never done in all his life.

At that instant, the garage door opened and his dad saw him. From his place on the cement floor, Tommy could see the shock on his father's face. The fear. "Tommy!" In a rush his dad was beside him, helping him up. "Son . . . we didn't even know you were home. What . . . what are you doing?"

Tommy was still gasping for breath. "Beat . . . beating

it!" They were the only words he could say. The only thing he wanted to do.

His father pulled him into his arms and held him. For a long time.

And even though he was exhausted and hurting and brokenhearted, Tommy had the sense he had done good here tonight. Gone twelve rounds with his invisible enemy, the opponent that had haunted him since the doctor called with the news. The one he alone would never defeat, no matter how many times he ripped into the punching bag.

Annalee's cancer.

14

Her hair was everywhere, and Annalee couldn't stand it.

She didn't want another morning of finding blond silk clumps on the pillow or watching her pretty hair fall to the floor when she crossed the room. She didn't want to see it scattered on her bathroom sink or dropping in sections at the dining room table.

This was Day 10 since her chemo began and it was time.

Annalee had made the plan with her mother yesterday, and now—Saturday afternoon—she was ready to see it acted out. Gathered in her family's great room was everyone Annalee loved. Her parents and her brother. Her aunt and uncle from Bloomington and Tommy's parents. Also two of her closest friends from school.

And Tommy.

She had planned what to say, so she walked to the front of the room, where a sheet was spread out over the carpet. Every step was like trudging through knee-deep snow and her nausea was like a fog. Pressing in around her.

When she turned and faced the group, her eyes found Tommy's. For a long time she only looked at him.

His handsome face and clear blue eyes. How kind he had been to her these past two weeks, standing at her side, sitting at her hospital bed. Praying for her. And believing she would get through this. That most of all.

She cleared her throat. "My hair . . . it has to go." What remained of it was in a ponytail. Annalee removed the pink scrunchie and slipped it onto her wrist. If she'd thought of this a week ago, she could've donated it or had a wig made from her hair.

But she didn't have enough left for that now.

For the last time in a long time, Annalee felt her hair spill over her shoulders and around her face. The feeling was all she'd ever known. She breathed deep and took a pair of orange scissors from the barstool next to her. "I asked you here to help make me bald." She smiled, but there was nothing funny about the moment.

At the back of the room she saw tears gather in her mother's eyes. Same with her aunt and Mrs. Baxter. *Be strong*, she told herself. *Jesus, give me strength, I beg You.* A calm came over Annalee. "Rather than seeing my hair fall out piece by piece, I would like each of you to cut a section from my head."

The room was silent.

Annalee swallowed. *Don't turn and run to your room. You can do this. God, help me do this.* "Last, I'd like Aunt Lily to shave my head." Lily owned a beauty salon in Bloomington. She would be best able to shave Annalee's head when the cutting was over.

Annalee had saved the best part for last. "What will

make today different, is that as you each cut a part of my hair, I'd like you to pray for me. Out loud. So that this"— she ran her hand through her hair and came out with a knot of blond—"this isn't something happening to me against my will. But something I release . . . to God . . . while each of you prays."

"Like a holy time." Her dad added his voice like a coda. "I think we're each honored that you asked us to be here, to take part in this, sweetheart."

Everyone in the room nodded. Some had tears, but a few of them smiled. Not because there was anything happy about this moment, but as if they were trying to comfort her. Agree with her plan.

"Are you ready?" Her mom came to her side. "And are you sure?"

"Yes." Annalee hoisted herself onto the stool. She used her phone to start a playlist of worship music. Songs she had chosen yesterday, specifically for this time. "Way Maker" by Leeland came on first. It was one of Annalee's favorites. She slipped the phone into her sweater pocket.

Before anyone moved or started cutting, Tommy took another barstool from the kitchen and brought it alongside Annalee. Then he reached for her hands and locked eyes with her. "Right here, Annalee," he whispered. "Keep looking at me. I won't let you fall."

Only then did tears fill her eyes. But they weren't tears of sorrow or defeat. They came from the overflow of her heart, from the place that belonged to Tommy

Baxter alone. He was struggling with this. Wondering why God wasn't helping her. But he did his best to hide his frustration from her, especially now. Of course he wasn't going to let her fall. She squeezed his hands and faced him.

In the background the first song played on. It sang of God being the way maker, the miracle worker, the promise keeper and the light in the darkness. It was true. God was with her. He held her life and the number of her days and He would make a way for her. He would work a miracle out of this nightmare. And He would keep His promises because He was the light both in and around her.

He was good. Even if she didn't survive this cancer.

Her mom took the scissors first, and stood next to Tommy. She looked straight into Annalee's eyes. "It will grow back, sweet daughter. The hair I've combed and braided and curled since you were a little girl . . . it will grow back." She kissed Annalee's forehead. "I believe that."

Annalee nodded. Her throat was too tight to speak. Her mom lifted the scissors to her hair and cut a section. But she didn't let it fall to the ground. Instead she kept it wrapped tight in her hand.

"Father, we come to You in acceptance of Your will, Your plan." Her mother's voice was soft, broken. But it grew steadier with each word. "At the same time, we thank You for the healing You are giving our girl." She cut another small section. "Like trees pruned each autumn, we believe you will restore Annalee's body and energy and health. And yes . . . even her beautiful hair."

Then, her mother stooped down and set the pieces of Annalee's hair on the sheet. Like they were too precious to just let drop. The song was reaching Annalee's favorite part and all around the room the people she loved began to sing along.

These were the lyrics Annalee clung to, the ones that sang about God working even when they couldn't see Him or feel Him. The sound of their soft voices breathed peace through Annalee. The same way Tommy's hands around hers did.

Next came her dad. "Hi, honey." He put his hand alongside her face and looked long into her eyes. "You probably don't remember when you were a little girl. Three or four years old." He laughed, blinking back tears. "At bath time you absolutely hated having your hair washed." He ran his thumb over her eyebrow.

"I do remember." Annalee felt two tears spill down her cheeks. "I was afraid the soap would sting my eyes." A quiet laugh came from deep inside her. For a few seconds she was that same little girl again. "You remember what you would do?"

"Yes." Her dad put one hand on his hip and raised the other out to the side. "I'm a little teapot, short and stout. Here is my handle . . . here is my spout."

Soft laughter came from others in the room as they watched Annalee's dad bend at the waist. "Something about that song always made you laugh. And I would take that light blue plastic cup and we would pretend it was a teapot." He brushed at a tear on his cheek. "Only then would you let me rinse out the shampoo." His smile faded. "I always loved washing your hair, honey."

He took a deep breath and paused for a minute. Then he lifted the scissors to a section of Annalee's still soft blond strands. "Father, this is the hardest thing I've ever done. Watching my little girl go through this. Seeing her lose a part of her she's loved since she was a toddler." His voice broke and it took half a minute before he could speak again. "We trust You, God. Please . . . heal our girl. Heal Annalee for us, Lord. Only You can help us."

Annalee squeezed her eyes shut. She hadn't cried once since being admitted to the hospital. But now her tears came in a flood, quiet streams of sadness and release running down her face. Her mother brought her a tissue and Annalee let go of Tommy's fingers long enough to press it to her eyes. Then she tucked the tissue into her other pocket and held his hands again.

Tommy was so close, their knees touched. She could feel his heartbeat in his fingers, smell the minty fresh of his breath on her face. He was holding her up, making good on his promise.

The song changed and this time it was "Lord, I Need You." And every word mixed with Annalee's deepest thoughts. *I do need you, Lord. I need you every hour of this journey. Stay with me, please, Lord. Help me.*

Her dad cut one section—same as her mother. Then he too laid it on the floor. Once more he touched her face. "I love you, baby girl."

Annalee could barely see through her tears. "Love you, Daddy."

Austin was next. Her younger brother looked uncomfortable, like he was sick to his stomach at the thought of taking scissors to Annalee's hair. But he came, anyway. This was what Annalee wanted and Austin wasn't going to back down from that. Clearly.

He stood next to Tommy and grinned at her. "I keep thinking of the time we went camping. Just the family. You were, I don't know, maybe eight years old." His eyes were dry, but the sadness there could fill an ocean. "We found that stick covered in sap. Like . . . dripping with sap, remember?"

Annalee's own laugh caught her off guard. She nodded. "What were we thinking?"

"You wanted to be a forest princess. Something like that." He shrugged. "I did what you asked. I wrapped your hair round the stick until it was poking out from either side of the top of your head." His laughter faded. "Dad had to take his pocketknife and cut the stick out. Right?" He looked at their parents, standing together a few feet away..

"It was like doing surgery." A faraway look came over her father's face. "You thought you'd have to stay home from school for a year."

Annalee could still see herself looking in the mirror once the stick was finally out. "I lost a lot of hair. But just from one side. No one ever noticed."

Austin took the scissors from their dad. Then he lowered his voice so only Annalee and maybe Tommy could hear. "It kills me to cut your hair, Annalee. You have the prettiest hair of any girl I know."

Again Annalee's tears came. She closed her eyes. The strength she needed couldn't come from any human. Not in light of her brother's words. *Help me, Lord. So much love around me, but so much sadness. Please, help me.*

Everyone sang as the song changed. This one was about God being the king of everything. Even the hearts of His people. Austin breathed in sharp through his nose. Like he was trying to find the strength to voice his prayer. "Dear Jesus, I know You love my sister. Even more than I do." He sniffed. "God, she's the nicest person I know. And I believe with everything in me that she has much to do on this earth for the next hundred years. At least."

Annalee felt a smile tug at her lips. She loved her brother so much.

"So please"—Austin gritted his teeth—"kill off this cancer. Every cell of it. So that Annalee never, ever has to go through this again." He cut one section of her hair and set it on the ground. Then he handed the scissors to their uncle Roger, Lily's husband.

The music continued to fill the room, reminding them with one song after another that God was sovereign. He was here and He was carrying Annalee. Holding her, no matter what happened. While Uncle Roger cut three areas from Annalee's hair, he told a story about getting together for a day at Lake Monroe, and how Annalee and her friends had used sticks to make Pippi Longstocking braids. "Those sticks stuck straight out to the sides of your head." He chuckled. "And even then your hair was beautiful."

"Sticks again." Annalee laughed. The respite from crying felt wonderful. "Seems to be a theme."

The sadness lifted and against the backdrop of a song about healing from heaven, Annalee took a deep breath. She looked into Tommy's eyes and felt hope fill her heart. Yes. She could get through this. No girl had ever been surrounded by so much love.

Tommy whispered close to her face. "Remind me to get you a box of sticks later."

Bit by bit, section by section, her head felt lighter. Colder. Next came Tommy's parents. His dad did a few cuts and prayed the entire time for God to bring good out of this situation. "We believe in Romans 8:28, Father. You make all things work to the good for those who love You."

Tommy's mom took the scissors and with great care she cut a section from the side of Annalee's face. "Your beauty, Annalee, comes from inside you. God has made you one in a million, and so your beauty will continue to shine till you're old and gray." She paused. "But your hair matters. I'm honored you would ask me to be here today. And one day—when you're better and your hair grows back—I'll be here to celebrate that, too."

Her prayer was one of gratitude, thanking God for the healing ahead and for the things Annalee had yet to do. The ways she would change the world in years to come.

Her friends were next. They worked together, reminding Annalee of the time they all used food coloring to dye their hair blue for their school's spirit day. "I thought we'd have blue hair forever." Carly laughed. "But nothing could ruin that beautiful blond color of yours."

Iris said something that touched Annalee to the core. "Your hair will still be there." She wiped at the tears on her cheeks and cut a part of what remained of Annalee's hair. "Still that same pretty color. Only now it'll be shorter. And it will live just beneath the surface. Because life is like that sometimes."

Finally it was Tommy's turn.

He released her fingers and stood just in front of her. Then with his dry eyes lost in hers, he took her face in his hands. "Remember that first day in the school's theater room?"

"Yes." Everyone else seemed to fade away. "You . . . were looking at me." Her voice was steady. "I thought you were the cutest boy I'd ever seen."

Tommy smiled. "I thought I was dreaming. Because . . . a girl as beautiful as you didn't just show up on the first day of freshman year." He paused. "And every one of my friends thought you had the prettiest hair of any girl they'd ever seen. So pretty." He ran his hands over what remained of it. "But I have to tell you something. Something I never told you before."

Annalee held her breath. She had no idea what was coming.

Tommy put his hands on her face again. "For me, it was never your hair, Annalee." He looked all the way to her soul. "It was your eyes." He kissed her forehead. "It was always your eyes."

And suddenly—for the first time since the haircutting began—Annalee felt the sadness lift. Yes, she was losing her hair. The image she'd come to expect every morning in the mirror would be different now. Maybe forever.

But nothing could touch the thing Tommy loved most about her. The eyes that showed her family and friends and all the world her love and joy, her peace and patience. Her kindness, gentleness, thoughtfulness and faithfulness. Cancer could make her sick and tired and broken. It could even leave her bald.

But it couldn't touch her eyes—the windows to her soul.

As the hour played out, as Aunt Lily shaved Annalee's head and as her hair was taken to a waiting trash bag . . . as the music stopped and the praying ended and people left the house, Annalee knew two things with all her heart. She was going to fight this cancer.

And she had never loved Tommy Baxter more.

The one who—from the beginning—had looked right past her hair and straight to her heart.

From the very first time their eyes met.

15

For Reagan, life outside Northside High felt like it was crumbling a little more each day. But here inside the brick walls of her favorite campus, Reagan felt peace. Especially this afternoon.

The last hour of school today would be the student clothing drive—the one Annalee had set up at the start of the school year. The items would be donated to an Indianapolis safe house for sex-trafficking victims. Donna Miller was going to be here, too—since Annalee couldn't.

It was the middle of October and Annalee was in the hospital again. But she was supposed to come home soon. Her doctor had said this time she would need a few weeks to recoup from the chemo and steroids. Which was why in addition to clothing, today the students at Northside were each bringing letters or cards for Annalee. Something to encourage her.

The clothing drive figured to be the one bright light today, at least for Reagan.

Things at home were still strained, with Tommy doing IMPD ride-alongs every Saturday afternoon. So great was the tension, that when school got out today

Reagan was going to meet Luke for coffee. So they could talk through what they hadn't been able to work out at home regarding the situation.

Until then, Reagan was more than happy to be here at Northside, setting up for the event. None of the Millers knew about the cards and letters. Reagan could hardly wait to see Donna's reaction. Yes, the Northside community was loving the Miller family through Annalee's cancer. Reagan had passed a sign-up sheet around for students and their parents to bring the Millers meals throughout the week.

On top of that, Reagan had helped the school set up a GoFundMe account and already families at Northside had donated twenty thousand dollars toward Annalee's medical expenses.

Reagan was setting up the last of six tables when Donna walked up and set her purse against the wall. "I'm ready." She smiled, but her eyes still looked weary. "Annalee's so glad I'm here."

An ache cut through Reagan as she hugged her friend. Tommy's sweet girlfriend would've done anything to be here for the clothing drive she had arranged. Her absence was further proof of how sick she was. Reagan sat down in one of the folding chairs behind the long table. "How's she feeling?"

"She's still vomiting." Donna took the seat beside her. "Her nausea is crippling. She can barely open her eyes some days. And she's lost more weight. Every day she looks a little thinner. But for the past hour she's been holding down liquids." Donna folded her hands on the table. "We're praying for victories along the way. That is for sure one of them."

The bell rang and Reagan smiled to herself. Donna was about to experience another victory. Before a minute passed, the doors pushed open and a stream of students entered the auditorium. Each of them carried a bag of clothes and a few dragged overfull black bags behind them.

This message from the Northside students was clear—if Annalee wanted used clothing to support victims of sex trafficking, then that's what she would get. The students would do anything to help her feel better. To let her know they cared.

The teens dropped the clothes off at one of the six tables, then they made their way to Donna Miller.

"Here." A senior girl handed a pale yellow envelope to Donna. "This is for Annalee. Tell her I'm praying for her every day. And tell her we miss her."

"Thank you." Donna smiled. "This is the nicest thing. She'll love it."

The stream of students bearing encouragement for Annalee had only just begun. Next came three freshman boys. Each of them had a folded piece of paper for Donna. "We don't know her that well. But we are believing she'll get better superfast," one of them said.

By then, students were lined up for the chance to talk to Donna. A look of astonishment shone on her face. She cast a quick glance at Reagan. "You . . . you knew about this?"

"It was their idea." Reagan grinned.

TRULY, MADLY, DEEPLY 175

And still the stream continued. One after another the students approached Donna and gave her something for Annalee. At the end of the hour, more than a hundred bags of clothes sat piled high on the tables. And someone had run to get Donna a box for the cards and letters. When the final bell rang, encouragements for Annalee spilled over the cardboard edges.

Each of the parent volunteers greeted Donna and wished Annalee the best. "We're praying at our house," one of the women said. "Every evening before bed."

When the room was empty, Donna sat back down and pulled the box close. Almost like she was hugging it. She turned teary eyes to Reagan. "I don't know what to say."

"I told you . . . it was the students. A few of Annalee's friends spread the word and everyone was on board." She reached out and covered Donna's hand with her own. "They love her. We all do."

"And the clothes . . ." Donna shook her head. "So many bags."

The drive had netted ten times what they had hoped to collect. Already Principal Larson had asked the parent volunteers if they'd come back to sort through the bags. Some clothing could then be set apart for the safe house. The rest could be sold and the proceeds given to supply other needs for the residents.

"Annalee won't believe it." Donna shook her head. She ran her hand over the letters and cards. "The coming week will be hard. She's so tired and her immune system is low. She can't go to school."

"But she'll have all week to read words from her classmates."

"Exactly." Donna lifted the box and walked with Reagan to the door. "She'll have a scan in the next few weeks. To see if the treatment is working." A shadow fell over Donna's eyes. "So much depends on the results."

"I'll come by the house this next week to see her." Reagan tried not to think about Annalee having another scan. "Things will be better. They will."

"I pray for that every hour."

Reagan helped Donna get the box into the backseat of her car. Then Reagan headed to the coffee shop.

Luke was waiting for her.

This was the first time they'd taken a moment away from home to talk since Tommy brought up the idea of being a police officer. Luke had already ordered Reagan her favorite vanilla latte. He smiled and Reagan felt herself relax. Maybe he was seeing things her way, after all. They spent the first few minutes talking about his current case, and then Reagan updated him on Annalee and the school clothing drive.

Finally, Luke exhaled and leveled kind eyes at her. "We can't keep on like this. Passing in the kitchen, going to sleep at different times." He gave a slight shrug. "You're blaming me for something Tommy has decided. This . . . change of direction. It's all him."

Her frustration rose quickly, and Reagan didn't think to keep her tone in check. "You *told* him about the ride-along program, Luke. You set it up for him."

He folded his hands on the table and leaned closer. "Please . . . talk quieter."

"I'm sorry." She sighed. "Don't you see, Luke? You met with Mike Lockwood and a few days later Tommy was in the passenger seat of a cop car."

"Yes. I did." Luke worked the muscles in his jaw. "But Tommy had already looked into the department's ride-along program. He told me that."

"Oh. He . . . didn't tell me." Reagan needed a minute. She took a sip of her coffee. "Thanks for the latte, by the way."

"Of course." Luke's expression softened. "This isn't a battle between me and you." He hesitated. "Have you talked to Tommy? Really talked to him? Since he told us?"

"No." A ribbon of guilt wrapped itself around Reagan's heart. "Have you?"

"Yes." Luke leaned back. "I asked him why he wanted to be a police officer. Something he didn't tell us that first night."

Guilt mixed with her fear. "What . . . did he tell you?"

"Remember that boy in third grade? The one with braces on his legs?"

Of course she remembered. "Tommy stuck up for him at recess. Took down the bully who tripped the poor boy."

"Exactly." Luke crossed his arms. "Has it ever occurred to you that just maybe Tommy was born to do police work?"

She held her breath. Tommy was too young to know what he wanted. He hadn't finished with a 4.0 GPA and the highest test scores in the city so that after graduation he could go to one of the nation's top universities. God clearly wanted him to pursue higher education. The doctor and lawyer route. Also being a cop was dangerous and—

A dozen more rebuttals fought for position in Reagan's mind. But she couldn't say any of them.

Instead she could see Tommy sitting in the principal's office that third-grade year explaining his position. His little voice and big conviction. "I'm sorry, sir," Tommy had said. "But someone had to help Kevin."

And suddenly the truth came over her like rain. How come she hadn't remembered that before? Not just the time in third grade, but a line of memories took their place in her mind. Each of them involving Tommy standing up for someone.

Reagan covered her eyes with both hands. Luke was right. Tommy *had* always helped people. He was wired that way from the time he was a child. With the realization came a regret like nothing Reagan had felt in a long time. She lowered her hands and looked at Luke. "You're right." She shook her head. "I . . . forgot about that."

"I wondered." He reached across the table and took her hand. "You're not really angry at him, anyway."

The feel of his skin against hers was something she had missed. More than she knew. Luke was right about this, too. Of course she wasn't angry at Tommy. How could she be upset with him for wanting to be a police officer? That didn't even make sense. "I can't believe how I treated him."

Luke studied her. "You two need to talk. That's all."

"But I still feel . . ." She was shaking now. "Couldn't he help people in a hospital? Or in a court of law?"

"You're scared." Compassion filled Luke's expression. "You're afraid, Reagan. That's all."

Of course that was it. Ever since Tommy had told them his decision, fear had practically suffocated her. "You think that's it? Fear made me get angry with him?"

Luke waited a moment before responding. "Tell me, sweetheart. How have you spent your free time these last few weeks?" His smile was gentle. "I think I know . . . but tell me."

Reagan withdrew her hand and sat back in the wooden chair. "I knew you caught me that one day." She felt sick again. "Every Google search led to another. I . . . came across a fallen officers page. All the fallen police as far back as you could go. Men and women who had been shot to death or killed in pursuit of a suspect. Guys in their forties who had dropped dead of a heart attack in the middle of training. Officers dying from 9/11-related illnesses—like Ashley told us about."

"So . . . you've spent hours there." Luke wasn't asking. Somehow he knew. "All that time on that site. Seeing how cops die?"

Reagan took a long sip of her latte. She shook her head. "No. That was just part of it." Her Google search had only fueled her fear. No question. Sometimes she had searched police officer dangers until her chest was too tight to take a full breath. She felt ashamed of herself. "I also looked up police risks and police ambushes. I googled the photos of spouses and kids left behind when an officer had died. And I researched what happens to a cop who sees too much violence."

Luke didn't blink, didn't look away. His tone was rich with understanding. "Did that help?"

Her frustration bubbled up again. "Maybe it did." She leaned her forearms on the table. "Luke, being a police officer is dangerous. It is. The more I researched it, the more true that became for me."

"And Tommy knows that." Luke took both her hands this time. "Honey, life is dangerous. Doctors have heart attacks and lawyers sometimes get stalked by the suspects they prosecute." He paused. "Look at your dad. No one would've thought being a businessman would be dangerous."

He was right. Reagan had shared with Luke the story about her father, the one her mom had told her on the anniversary of 9/11. "The thing is . . ." Reagan searched Luke's eyes. "I don't know how I can live through it. Every day . . . not knowing whether he'll come home."

They finished their coffees and Luke moved to the chair beside her. The shop was nearly empty except for the two of them. "Come here." Luke took her in his arms. "Faith in God, Reagan. That's how we'll both get through it."

Reagan still couldn't believe it. Were they really talking about this? Really coming to agreement that their Tommy was going to be a police officer? Shouldn't there be more discussion, at least? Did Tommy really know the risks of being a cop? She dropped her voice to a whisper. "The average life expectancy of a police officer is just fifty-seven years."

"Reagan." His eyes were kinder still. "Only God knows the number of our days."

"But that's nearly twenty-two years less than—" She stopped herself. "Only God knows."

"Yes."

A sigh slipped from the deepest place in Reagan's soul. If Tommy wanted to fight crime with his one precious life, that was his choice. Not hers.

Luke had to leave. He had a meeting back at the office. They stood and Reagan leaned her head against his for a few seconds. "I'm sorry again. For how I've been."

"You do know that most police officers are heroes." He moved a strand of hair from her eyes. "Imagine life without them."

"Of course." Reagan was horrified that she had come across as if she believed anything else. "I have the highest respect for everyone wearing a badge, Luke. You know that."

"I do." He raised his brow, his expression gentle. "As long as it's not your son." He didn't wait for a response. "Just think about that, Reagan. When you talk to Tommy."

Reagan thanked him for the talk and when Luke was gone she sat down and stared at her empty coffee cup. A different kind of sick came over her. Had she come across that way to Tommy? Like she thought police work was something less than being a doctor or a lawyer? That wasn't how she felt at all.

Police officers . . . firefighters . . . first responders. All of them put their lives on the line every day. Their job description was simple—help people, help society.

Another coffee. That's what she needed. She got in line behind a trio of teenage girls and at the same time a pair of police officers entered the coffee shop. A man and a woman. Both black. They were chatting, smiling as they got in line behind Reagan.

Probably somebody's husband . . . someone's wife. The son and daughter of parents who likely supported them. People who were proud of them. Did they have children, little ones hoping their daddy or mommy would come home at the end of the day? Every day?

Reagan wanted to hug them. Instead she turned and smiled. "Thank you. For your service."

"Of course." The male officer was quick to respond. "It's our pleasure."

Our pleasure. The words stayed with Reagan as she stepped up and ordered another coffee. She paid for her drink and slid her card forward. "I want to pay for whatever the officers are having."

"Okay." The guy behind the counter took her card and grinned. "I love when people do that. It's only right."

"Yes." Reagan took her drink to her table and waited while the police officers ordered. Both of them looked back at her and waved.

"Thank you." The woman smiled and held up her coffee. "Means a lot."

After they left, Reagan collected her credit card and

went to her car. For a long while she sat behind the wheel, staring at the bushes in front of her. The next call could cost the officers their lives. Yet here they were, smiling between tasks. Doing the job they were called to do.

"Lord, You see my heart." She whispered even as tears filled her eyes. An image came to mind. The same two officers coming to her door with somber faces. Middle of the night. She shook her head. "No, Father. I can't lose Tommy. I cannot." She squeezed her eyes shut and leaned back against the headrest. "Change his mind, God. Please. Give him another passion so—"

The male officer's words hit her again.

It's our pleasure.

In a single moment, her fear faded. She still had questions, still desperately wanted Tommy to change his mind. But for the first time since Tommy had told them about his decision, Reagan understood why her son wanted to be a cop. It wasn't merely that he felt a duty or obligation to serve his community. Being an officer was something he truly wanted to do.

The job would be Tommy's pleasure, too. Reagan could feel that now with all her soul. And if that's how Tommy felt, how could she be anything but supportive? If spending his life in a police uniform was what Tommy wanted, Reagan had to find a way to feel the same. For Tommy's sake.

Even if the struggle lasted the rest of her life.

16

The cracking sound split through the air and Tommy stopped, the wind cold on his face. He was walking with Annalee across the frozen Eagle Creek Reservoir just northwest of Indianapolis. But now . . . now all around them came the sound of cracking ice.

"Annalee!" He shouted her name. What was happening? They'd done this before and the ice never gave way.

But then, it was way too warm for the reservoir to be frozen. Also neither of them had fishing gear.

"Why are we doing this?" Annalee looked up at him. They were holding hands, walking farther out to the center of the water. "Maybe we should go back!"

Tommy's teeth chattered. And suddenly he realized what was happening. The ice wasn't thick enough. It had to be four inches thick before it was safe for ice fishing.

More cracking. Louder, and coming from all around them. Then Tommy saw something that stopped his heart. Lines were appearing in the ice. Faster and deeper. "Annalee!" He shouted her name and pushed her toward shore. "Run!"

But the moment they took their first steps back to

land, freezing water bubbled up between the cracks and the ice beneath them began to sink. "Annalee! Get down!"

She dropped to her knees and he did the same. The only way to keep from falling through the ice was to disperse their weight. Tommy knew that. But it wasn't helping. The water was rising, the ice cracking faster, louder.

And then just as they made a few feet progress toward land, the ice supporting Annalee gave way. "Tommy . . . help!"

He lunged for her, but before he could grab her boot, she slipped into the frigid water. "No!" Tommy's scream echoed across the frozen lake. "Someone help!"

But no one came, no one heard. And Annalee was sinking, flailing in the freezing reservoir, and then with a final scream . . . she disappeared.

Tommy could see her dropping, falling far, far below the surface. He moved toward her, flung his body in her direction and before he could draw another breath he was underwater, too. The cold stung and dragged him down, and no matter how hard he tried he couldn't reach Annalee.

She was sinking toward the sandy floor faster, and faster, headed to the bottom. Tommy couldn't scream, couldn't call out, couldn't move. This was it. They were going to die here in the ice-cold waters of Eagle Creek Reservoir and no one would find them till spring. He pushed toward her, arched his back and reached out for her. But the distance between them only grew.

He was dying, desperate for air. And before Tommy could stop himself, he opened his mouth and breathed. Freezing water filled his lungs and his body writhed in pain. The sunlight faded to shadows and the last thing Tommy saw was Annalee. Her motionless body on the floor of the lake.

And then came a darkness like Tommy had never known before.

He squirmed and fought it, pushed through it and suddenly, miraculously he gasped and this time his lungs filled with precious, life-giving air. Warm air. And he wasn't trapped in the frozen water beneath the ice of Eagle Creek Reservoir.

His feet kicked their way free of the sheets and blankets and he sat straight up, breathing hard, grabbing as much air as he could. What had happened? He blinked. Where was he? Sweat ran down his forehead and he looked around. What was this?

He was in bed.

The clock on his nightstand read 3:03 a.m.

Tommy leaned back against his padded headboard and closed his eyes. He ran his hands over his arms and felt his hair. Everything was dry. He wasn't with Annalee and they weren't falling through the ice.

The entire, terrible ordeal had only been a dream. A nightmare.

Eventually Tommy caught his breath. He eased himself back down and turned on his side. Even then the images stayed with him. The awful way he hadn't been able to help Annalee. The impossibility of reaching her and pulling her to the surface.

His heart raced. The dream was just like his life.

Annalee was going back to the hospital for another round of chemo. Two days from now. She was getting sicker and weaker and sinking to the bottom of the lake. God still wasn't answering their prayers, and there was nothing Tommy could do about it.

Sleep wouldn't come, so he did what he'd learned to do long ago in these situations. He closed his eyes and started with Matthew 11:28–30.

Come to me, all you who are weary and burdened and I will give you rest. Take my yoke upon you and learn from me, for I am gentle and humble in heart, and you will find rest for your souls. For my yoke is easy and my burden is light.

Over and over Tommy silently repeated the words. *Come to me, all you who are weary and burdened . . .*

Peace began to ease the tension in his muscles. Annalee wasn't getting better, no matter how much they prayed. But God was here, now. Tommy could feel His familiar presence. *If You're here, Lord, then help Annalee. Don't let her drown.* He exhaled. *Come to me, all you who are weary and burdened and I will give you rest . . .*

Eventually Tommy fell asleep.

When he woke it was nearly nine o'clock. Which meant his family would be downstairs having pancakes. A Saturday morning tradition in the Baxter family. Tommy dragged himself from bed and looked out the window. No snow or ice. Only blue skies as far as he could see.

He got dressed and joined his mother in the kitchen. She had just started with the scrambled eggs. "I'll help." He took the pancake mix and poured it in a bowl. "Where's Dad?"

"He'll be back soon. He got up early to help plant trees in Grandpa John's backyard."

"Sounds like Dad. He's always helping someone." Tommy grinned at his mother. "And you wonder where I get it?"

Malin and Johnny helped set the table and their dad arrived just as breakfast was served. Tommy waited till his siblings finished eating and went out back before telling his parents about the dream. "I get it. I mean . . . with all Annalee is going through."

"Of course." His dad put his fork down. "I'm sorry, Son. What a horrible night."

"Yeah." He took another bite of his eggs and stared out the window that overlooked their backyard. "It wasn't even winter, but we were walking on ice . . . and the water was freezing cold. Which didn't make sense. But it was as real as us sitting here."

For a minute no one said anything. His dad broke the silence first. "How is she?"

"She has her scan Monday." Tommy pushed his fork through his eggs. They didn't look as good now. "A lot will depend on that. It's complicated."

"But . . . how *is* she?" His mom asked the question this time. "You've been gone so much with school and visiting Annalee . . . we haven't really talked about how she's handling all this."

Tommy appreciated that his mom didn't make a dig about the time he'd spent with the ride-along program. During breakfast she'd been more relaxed. As if something had happened since yesterday to soften her.

He pushed back his plate. "Honestly . . . she looks terrible." It felt good to talk about this. "Her mom bought her a wig—which she's wearing at home. But it doesn't hide how thin she is . . . or how weak."

Last night at her house Annalee had collapsed on the way back from the bathroom. Tommy had been there to help her, but even then she couldn't seem to make her legs work. More side effects from the chemo, her mother told Tommy. "I don't get what God is doing." He pushed his plate back. "We keep praying, but nothing. Like . . . is He even listening? Does He care?"

No wonder he'd had the crazy nightmare.

His dad took the question first. "Disease . . . sickness. It's part of a fallen world, Tommy."

"Sure, I know." His tone sounded sharper than he meant it. "I've heard that. But God's supposed to love us, right? And Annalee hasn't done anything to deserve this. She's the most faithful girl I know."

"He does love her, Tommy. He loves you both." His mom's voice was gentle. Kinder than it had been in a while. "Still . . . I'm sorry." She hesitated. "Tommy . . . I have to tell you something."

He wasn't sure where this was going.

His mother folded her hands on the table. "I've had . . . a very bad attitude toward your decision to do police work and the ride-along sessions. Even toward you." Her voice grew softer still. "Your dad and I . . . we talked yesterday."

"About what?"

"You being an officer." She didn't break eye contact with him.

"Okay." The slightest hope lifted Tommy's spirits. "How do you feel now?"

"Scared to death." His mom didn't blink, didn't smile. "I don't want to worry about you heading to work every day or wonder if your wife and kids might have to live without you." She looked down at her hands for a long moment.

"Mom's still working through it." His father put his arm around her and looked at Tommy. "I think you can understand how she might feel."

Actually, Tommy hadn't thought about the danger. He faced his mother. "I guess . . . I thought you were upset because you wanted me to be successful." He shrugged. "Make more money."

"No." His mom looked up. "That was never it." She shook her head. "Police officers are some of the most successful people I know. Smart, courageous."

Tommy waited, letting her finish.

"It was always this . . . this raging fear. Like a monster breathing down my neck. What if something happens to you, Tommy?" She sighed. "I don't think I could take it."

Wow. Tommy shifted his gaze back to the window and the orange and red leaves on the trees outside. All this time, here was why his mother had been so upset. Because she was afraid something was going to happen to him. The news made Tommy feel better. Her attitude had been so bad since he'd told them his decision, Tommy could only think she cared about the money he was walking away from.

Which hadn't seemed like her at all. Plus, his mom had always been grateful for cops.

Tommy could remember times when their family had been out shopping or at a restaurant and his mom had gone out of her way to thank an officer. Why hadn't this hit him before? Of course she was afraid. Danger was part of life for everyone who wore a police uniform. For any first responder, for that matter.

"Thank you for telling me." He met his mother's eyes. "Fear . . . it isn't from the Lord, Mom. That's what you always told us when we were growing up." He thought for a moment. "Of course, I'm scared about Annalee. So I get it."

"Trust God." She looked off, as if she were seeing those old days again. Back when fear was about not getting hurt in a basketball game or making the right friends at school. "I don't know how many times I told you that."

"And you believe it." His dad still had his arm around Mom. "You just have to remember how to let go."

His mom nodded.

Tommy was still a little confused. "So . . . you're not mad at me. But you still don't want me to be a cop?"

"Yes." His mom's expression looked weary. "I'm sorry. I'll work on it, but . . . yes, that's where I'm at."

"She's trying." His dad seemed to want to encourage Tommy.

Despite his mother's troubled spirit, the conversation helped. Tommy felt more at peace as he headed off for his Saturday ride-along. Today—like the last few Saturdays—Tommy was riding with Officer Raul Garcia. He was tall with the build of an NFL linebacker.

"Call me Raul," the officer had told Tommy their first time out together. "By the way, Lockwood's superhigh on you." Raul grinned. "Says you'll probably run the place someday."

"Oh yeah?" Tommy liked Raul. The guy was young like him.

"But first"—Raul winked—"you have to get by me. I'm twenty-four and that's been my goal since I was hired."

This afternoon they were out on Post Road and East Forty-second, an area known for gang violence and drug sales. Raul was a talker, and as they patrolled the area he chatted about his parents. "Salt of the earth, Tommy." He smiled. Raul was always smiling. "Raised me and my four brothers to love the Lord first, family second, and everything else after that."

Tommy already knew he and Raul shared the same faith. But this was the first time the guy had talked about his family. The conversation had mostly been about police work until now. "Four brothers. Sounds like my friends the Flanigans. They have six kids."

"I love a big family. I want one of my own someday."

Raul kept his eyes on the road. "And I love being the old-est. You're the oldest, too, right?"

"Yes." Tommy shifted so he could see Raul better.

"We're the exception, us oldest. Most cops are mid-dle kids. Peacemakers. Social justice advocates in the sense of wanting safer streets. A little rebellious." Raul squinted at a group of guys gathered on the sidewalk up ahead. "Bet you didn't know that."

Tommy hadn't known. But he was more concerned with the activity in front of them. Now that they were closer he could see that there were three guys. "Drug deal?" Tommy felt comfortable asking Raul.

"It's not a family reunion. I can tell you that." Raul honed in on the guys, never speeding or using his lights. "Time to have a little talk."

But before he could reach them, the guys must've spotted the squad car because they took off running in different directions. "Party's over, boys," Raul muttered under his breath. He called for backup, and sped toward the one guy running straight ahead of him. He slammed the squad car into park. "Don't leave," he told Tommy.

As Raul exited the car, Tommy saw the runner reach in his pocket and grab a large gun. "He's armed," Tommy shouted after Raul. Of course, the officer would've seen the weapon. Tommy didn't have much experience in identifying guns, but this one looked like a 9-millimeter.

Raul had already told him that the dealers in the area

were using armor-piercing ammo. The sort of weapon that didn't give cops a chance.

"Drop the gun!" Raul shouted. He had his own weapon drawn now, too.

Tommy wanted to run from the squad car and help his new friend, but he couldn't. He was strictly forbidden and he wasn't armed. So he did all he could do. *God, please stop that guy. Protect Raul, please.*

The suspect ran a few more yards and then before Raul caught him, the guy did an about-face and sprinted toward where Tommy was sitting. He was younger than Tommy had guessed. A teenager, most likely. No telling what was going to happen. Was the runner going to jump in the squad car or turn down an alley? Tommy's heart pounded. If the suspect tried to steal the vehicle, Tommy would have to jump out.

Instead, a few feet from the car, the suspect tossed his pistol and stopped. His sides were heaving and clearly he couldn't catch his breath. Something else, too. The kid's eyes were only half open.

"Why you running from me, huh?" Raul was out of breath, too, as he reached the guy. But he was recovering fast.

"I ain't running." Anger spewed from the kid. He wore an oversized gray hoodie and baggie sweatpants. He had a blue bandanna wrapped around his head. "You profiled, man. Why you gotta profile?"

"Anything sharp in your pockets, any other weapons?" Raul pulled his cuffs from his back pocket. "Shouldn't have run, man. No reason to make me chase you."

The suspect jerked his shoulder, but he didn't resist or try to run again. "I ain't going in. Not this time."

Raul cuffed the kid. "You're under arrest."

Two additional officers approached as Raul searched the suspect's pockets. Tommy had a front-row seat to the whole thing. From the radio he heard dispatch report that the other two suspects had also been apprehended.

Raul must've found the guy's wallet because Raul knew the guy's name now. "You're just sixteen, Wallace. What you doing out here on the streets?"

The kid didn't talk. Tommy searched the guy's face. He looked hard and sick and broken. Like he'd lived three lifetimes out here. *Sad*, Tommy thought. In a different world, Wallace could've been an athlete or a scholar. Anything but whatever he was doing out here on Post Road.

A quick check of Wallace's pockets netted a bag of heroin, two pain pills and a container with needles and a syringe. "You on heroin, Wallace?"

At first Wallace didn't say anything. But then he hung his head. "I don't wanna be, man. I don't know how. I'm drug sick."

"You're new out here." Raul positioned himself in front of the suspect. He put his hand on the kid's shoulder. "You dealing, Wallace?"

"No, man. Just using. I swear." The kid hung his head so far down his neck looked broken. "I can't . . . live like this. I need help."

"Okay." Raul's tone softened. "We'll get you help.

Possession of a firearm's gonna hurt you and you can't be down here buying heroin, but I'll do what I can." He waited till Wallace looked him in the eye. "This is your first offense, that right?"

"Yeah, man. I . . . I didn't mean it. I don't deal. I'm being straight with you."

From what Tommy had seen, almost every suspect who talked about being honest was, in fact, lying through their teeth. But Wallace seemed different. Raul must've thought so, too, because he was talking to the kid about getting into rehab. Doing community service. Something to keep him out of jail.

When Raul was back in the car and after he had filed a report, Tommy leaned against his seat and exhaled. "I thought the kid was going to steal your car."

"He could've." Raul glanced at him. "What would you have done?"

"Gotten out."

"Good answer." Raul breathed deep. "Kids like Wallace . . . they've been raised to hate us. But the thing is, they need us. If we can get Wallace clean, get him into a community service program . . . someday he might be one of us."

Tommy set his eyes straight ahead. He had long been a Marvel fan, loving the way Captain America and Iron Man laid down their lives to help people. But right now there was no hero he'd rather be like than the one sitting beside him.

Officer Raul Garcia.

17

Luke could barely concentrate.

He rose from his leather chair and walked to the wall of windows that rimmed two sides of his law office. From his spot on the eighteenth floor, clouds hung low over Indianapolis, but they were nothing to the turmoil in Luke's spirit. He was working a case that involved a store owner attacked by members of a new gang, a group of particularly vicious criminals whose only goal was to terrorize the city.

For the past month, since Tommy told them about wanting to be a police officer, Luke had worked hard to convince Reagan. No reason to discourage their son, he had told her. And he, himself, leaned on truth. *Do not be anxious about anything . . . Do not worry about tomorrow, for tomorrow will worry about itself.* Those and a dozen other Scriptures Luke had shared with Reagan or texted her from work.

But today he had learned a lot about this new gang.

He and Mike Lockwood had met for lunch and the detective had never looked more serious. "These guys are big trouble." He set his jaw. "We'll need a lot more officers to take them down." The new group was into robbery mainly. "They wear hoodies and gloves and masks. Eight or ten of them pile in a van and go to their location. A tech store or a jewelry shop. Someplace with high-end goods." He paused. "Then they storm the place."

What Lockwood had said next made Luke's blood run cold.

"Every one of them is armed and the groups are organized. Two stand lookout at the door while the other six or eight grab goods. If anyone gets in their way they take them down." He hesitated. "Last time they killed all three employees. They leave no witnesses.

"They're hard to find, hard to identify." Lockwood added that the gang had one simple motto when it came to police. "Shoot to kill."

Now Luke was sorting through his firm's case—a civil suit running concurrently with the criminal one. At least two members from the gang were going to prison, by the looks of it. But like his friend said, the gang was growing faster than the police force could handle.

Lightning shot straight down onto the city and a chill ran along Luke's arms. What was he really advocating for Tommy? He walked back to his desk and sat down. Not only that but Annalee's scan results were in. Her chest tumor was only slightly smaller, not nearly as much as her doctor had hoped. Over the next several rounds, they would have to increase her chemo.

Something her parents weren't sure she could handle.

Every minute Tommy wasn't doing homework or at

the gym or on a ride-along, he was with her. Praying for her. Helping her to the bathroom. Reading to her. Worrying about her—no matter how positive he tried to stay. But it was taking its toll on Tommy . . . and on his faith.

Luke couldn't imagine a more difficult season for any two young people. And Tommy and Annalee were two of the best.

His phone lit up. Luke checked it and saw a text from Lockwood. Probably just thanking him for lunch.

Typically Luke wouldn't check messages during the workday. But something made him open this one. The text was short:

Luke, we have an officer down. He's critical—in the hospital on life support. I wanted you to know before Tommy sees it on Twitter.

Then Luke read the officer's name.

No. Please, God, no!

Luke grabbed his briefcase and ran from his office. He called Reagan in the elevator and for the entire twenty-minute drive to his house he kept the radio off and prayed. *Please, Lord, let him live. This one has to pull through. Please, Father.* His heart pounded. He drove as fast as he could without breaking the law.

Reagan was waiting. Her face was pale, but she wasn't crying and the whole ride to Northside High she said just five words. "Thank you. For calling me."

This was why she didn't want Tommy to be a police officer, of course. It was just after three o'clock, which meant Tommy would be in the gym practicing with his team.

Luke had no idea how his son would take the news.

He and Reagan held hands as they walked to the gym. Reagan stayed outside. "I can't." She looked at Luke. "I can't do it."

How could he blame her? Given the situation, he had no idea how he was going to tell Tommy the news. But he had no choice. Luke entered through the gym's side door and walked right up to the coach. "I need to talk to Tommy." He explained the situation and the coach blew the whistle.

Tommy dropped the ball midcourt and jogged over. "Dad?"

"Come outside, Son. We need to talk." He led Tommy outside, twenty yards from where Reagan sat on a short brick wall.

Tommy seemed to notice her. He looked from Reagan back to Luke. "Dad . . . talk to me."

"Son . . . there's been a shooting. A police officer."

The news hit Tommy like a punch to the gut. He was still sweating from practice, and now he leaned over his knees. "No." His eyes never left Luke's. "Is he . . . is he okay?"

Luke put his hands on his son's shoulders. "He's . . . in critical."

Suddenly the question seemed to come over Tommy, the way Luke knew it would. Even before he could tell him the rest of the news. Tommy straightened and shot a desperate look at Luke. "Who . . . who was it?"

This was the hardest part, the reason Luke had to get Reagan and come here in person. The name of the officer. And now he held Tommy's shoulders as he told him the terrible news.

"It was your friend, Tommy." He pulled his son close. "Raul Garcia."

TOMMY COULDN'T GET to the hospital fast enough.

Coach let him leave practice, and his dad went with him in his car. Before they left, Tommy met his mom near his parents' car and hugged her tight. "Pray. Please, Mom."

"I am." She released him. "Go, Tommy. You need to be there."

Now Tommy and his dad hurried through the emergency room doors of Indiana University Health Medical Center in Indianapolis and checked in at the front desk. They were told to wait in a nearby room.

Five minutes later, a woman with wide eyes and a tearstained face came up to him. "You're Tommy Baxter." She held out both hands. "I'm Raul's mother. Elena."

"Yes, ma'am." He took her hands and stood. "And this is my dad, Luke Baxter."

The woman hugged Tommy. "He loves his Saturdays . . . with you, Tommy."

No words could possibly express what Tommy was feeling. He put his head on the woman's shoulder as he held her. "I'm so sorry, Mrs. Garcia. So sorry."

"He's going to make it." She stepped back and wiped her eyes. "We have to believe he'll make it."

Then Raul's mother brought them to another waiting room, where three other officers and family members waited for word. Tommy sat next to his dad and leaned over his knees. Then he shaded his face with his hand.

God, it doesn't seem like it lately . . . but I know You can hear me. Help Raul. He can't die. Please.

How could this happen? Five days ago they'd been in Raul's patrol car talking about family. Just five days ago. Tommy had just watched Raul chase down an armed teenager and talk him into getting help for his drug addiction. So why? What had happened?

He could hear Raul's words like he was sitting next to him again. *If we can get Wallace clean, get him into a community service program . . . someday he might be one of us.*

One of us.

And Tommy thought about something else Raul had told him. How they were dealing with one of the toughest gangs the city had seen and how they needed more officers. More men and women committed to doing what was right. Removing crime from the streets so citizens could live in safety.

A certainty grew from his heart to his soul and filled every part of his being. Suddenly his purpose became clearer than air. After what happened to Raul, Tommy was no longer thinking about being a police officer.

He was convinced.

18

Annalee let herself sink back into the hospital bed. She'd been waiting all morning and afternoon and now he was here. Tommy walked through the door and set his things down near her bed.

He wore a Northside sweatshirt and dark jeans, but his handsome face was troubled. More than usual. "Hi." He came to her. He hugged her despite the tubes and wires and machines. He held her longer this time. "You look good." He whispered the words near her face. "I mean it. So good."

He always said that and she always believed him. Because his words helped her get through another day. And today—the last day of this chemo round—had been especially tough.

Annalee's mother was in a chair in the corner of the room. Often she left when Tommy came to visit. So they could have their privacy. But this time she stayed. She was too worried about Annalee to leave.

"I just left Raul's waiting room." He hovered over her, their faces inches apart. "He's showing some improvement."

"Good. I'm praying for a miracle." Annalee lifted her thin arm and put her hand alongside his face. "God has him."

No question the shooting had rocked Tommy. But it had done something else. It had shaken his faith. Something Annalee hadn't thought possible. Yesterday before he left her hospital room he'd told her something that terrified her.

His expression had hardened. "If God isn't going to help you . . . if He isn't going to save Raul, then I'll do what I can without Him."

Annalee hadn't known what to say. Tommy's faith had never wavered before all this.

And so she had asked him something. "Bring your Bible tomorrow, Tommy? Please? I miss you reading it to me."

Now—despite whatever battle Tommy was waging with God—at least Raul was a little better. Annalee watched Tommy pull his Bible from his backpack. He took the chair beside her bed. "I brought it. Like you asked."

"Thank you." Annalee settled into her pillow. A wave of nausea came over her, but she hid it. Whenever she was in the hospital, Tommy read to her. Some books were the perfect distractions. The Bible was perfect peace. And today, maybe reading it would help him, too.

Tommy opened the book. "Philippians, chapter four."

"Perfect." Annalee loved this section. "Go ahead."

"Okay." He cleared his throat. "Rejoice in the Lord

always. I will say it again: Rejoice! Let your gentleness be evident to all. The Lord is near."

A physical peace warmed Annalee's heart. These verses were truth and right now she needed them more than medicine.

Tommy's voice was soft, soothing. "Do not be anxious about anything, but in everything, by prayer and petition, with thanksgiving, make your requests to God. And the peace of God, which transcends all understanding, will guard your hearts and your minds in Christ Jesus."

He brought her hand to his lips and kissed her fingers. "I love you, Annalee."

"I love you." Her voice was a whisper, her nausea fading. She opened her eyes and watched Tommy find his place.

"Finally . . . whatever is true, whatever is noble, whatever is right, whatever is pure, whatever is lovely, whatever is admirable—if anything is excellent or praiseworthy—think about such things. Whatever you have learned or received or heard from me—or seen in me, put it into practice. And the God of peace will be with you."

Tommy kept reading, and toward the end of the passage, Annalee closed her eyes. She knew the lines by heart, but they seemed more impactful coming from Tommy. "I know what it is to be in need, and I know what it is to have plenty. I have learned the secret of being content in any and every situation . . ."

She opened her eyes and looked at him. They said

the last line together, their voices blending in a chorus of hope and faith, trust and belief. "I can do all this through Him who gives me strength."

Tommy didn't move. She didn't, either. They only looked deep into the desperate places of their hearts. After a while, Tommy closed his Bible. "I needed that."

"Me, too."

Annalee's mother came to Tommy and gave his shoulder a gentle touch. "That was beautiful." She sighed. "Sometimes I forget that help is so close."

"Yes." Annalee loved her mother so much. The hours she had spent here, the support she had given. "You're so strong, Mom. But you can't be brave all the time."

"I know." She bent down and kissed Annalee's cheek. "I'm glad I was here for this. And now"—a smile lifted her face—"I'm going to get coffee."

When her mother was gone, Annalee looked at Tommy. "Okay . . . so how is he really? Officer Garcia? You said he's a bit better?"

"He's still in a coma. But . . . he's breathing on his own."

"What?" This was definitely a breakthrough. "His mother must be so happy. How is she?"

"You'd love her." A single laugh came from Tommy, and he shook his head. "There are always four or five officers in the waiting room and today she brought chicken sandwiches for everyone."

Annalee wasn't sure how to ask the next question. But she hadn't watched the news and she wanted to know. "How did it happen, Tommy?"

"It was back at the same area, the place where Raul helped that kid. Remember? Wallace?"

"The guy on heroin."

"Right." Tommy took a deep breath and told her how Officer Garcia had come upon another drug deal going down in the same spot. Only this one involved the main dealer.

Annalee tried not to imagine Tommy answering that call. Pulling up to a drug deal, his life on the line.

"So Raul approached the guys and one of them turned around and shot him. Six times." Tommy shook his head, clearly disgusted. "The bullets are the kind that go through police protective vests. Four of them hit Raul in the chest."

Annalee looked toward the window. *God, help that man. Please.* "That . . . should never happen."

"I know. Raul shouldn't be alive."

"Exactly." Annalee found his eyes again. "But God . . ."

Tommy took a deep breath. "His mother . . . she prays constantly. She said she knew Raul would come off life support today." He looked straight at her. "One of the guys told me she was thanking God for that early this morning. An hour before it happened."

"Incredible." Annalee rolled onto her side so she could see Tommy better. "I want us to have that kind of faith."

"I did. At the beginning." Tommy looked at the tubes and machinery surrounding her. "So why aren't you feeling better?"

"I'm getting better. The process is tough, but He's healing me, Tommy." Her voice fell to little more than a whisper. "Remember? At the beginning . . . you believed that, too."

"I want to believe." He leaned over the bed and put his hands on either side of her face. "Your faith that all this is just a passing storm . . . it's beautiful, Annalee."

"Thank you." The feel of his breath against her face was intoxicating. "What about you?"

"Don't worry about me."

"Okay." She searched his eyes. "You know what I want?"

"What?" He came closer and brushed his cheek against hers. "Anything, love. Just tell me."

The moment was sweet, pure. She and Tommy so close that the hospital bed and tubes and wires all faded away. "Pretend with me . . . please, Tommy."

"Pretend?" It took just a few seconds for understanding to fill his eyes. "Okay. Where are we, Annalee? Take me there."

"Hear it?" She spoke soft against his cheek. "The ocean . . . just behind us?"

"Mmm." He paused. "Yes. I hear it. It's calm today. The waves are . . . gentle."

"They are." The soft breeze against her face was so real she was sure they were at the beach. "Smell the ocean? Feel the sand . . . beneath our feet?"

"It's wonderful." He didn't kiss her, but his lips were that close. "No hospital gray . . . no sickness. You're healthy and whole . . . and you're here. In my arms." He stayed there, his breath mingled with hers. "The sun's setting . . . do you see it?"

"I do." She closed her eyes. "A hundred beautiful colors. Painted across the sky . . . just for us."

"It's not as beautiful as you, love." His eyes locked on hers again. "You're all I want, Annalee. And you are getting better. I want to believe that."

She nodded. "I . . . think I'll sleep . . . for a bit."

"Okay." He kissed her cheek, slow and tender. "Fun being at the beach with you, love."

"Fun being with you."

There was the sound of Tommy taking his hospital chair again and the feel of his fingers intertwined with hers. Then the sounds of the machines began to fade and a different noise surrounded her. The slow lap of ocean waves against the white pristine shore of Karon Beach, the occasional seagull calling out as it swooped over the water.

Annalee felt herself smile. The warmth of the setting sun, the sand silky soft against her toes and the sound of Tommy breathing beside her. A warm wave washed over their feet and the sea breeze stirred their hair. Tommy leaned close and kissed her. The sweetest kiss.

And then Annalee fell asleep.

19

In the pitch dark of her bedroom, Reagan stared at the ceiling and tried to slow her breathing. Her heart raced, pounding against her chest. She grabbed her phone from her nightstand and checked the time.

2:17.

Morning was getting closer with every minute and still Reagan couldn't sleep. Couldn't catch her breath. *What if Tommy really does become a police officer right out of school?* What if he moved somewhere like Florida and worked far away from home until he turned twenty-one. And what if he was giving someone a ticket on the side of the road and a car flew by and hit him? Someone texting . . . or drunk . . . drugged, maybe?

Police officers stood too close to traffic every time they wrote a ticket.

Or what if he takes a domestic violence call and someone ambushes him? That happened all the time. For years Reagan had watched *Cops* with Tommy and Luke on summer nights when the little kids were in bed.

Before she had the slightest thought that Tommy might actually become a police officer.

The show had taught her every kind of danger a cop faced. Every day. Every hour on the job. *What if he pursues a suspect and a chase happens?* And what if Tommy was speeding to catch the guy and he had to run a red light?

Or what if someone coming the other way didn't hear the sirens or see the flashing lights, and what if they drove straight into Tommy's police car and . . .

Stop! she ordered herself. Her anxiety was getting worse. She tried to think about the past. Tommy as a little boy . . . Tommy playing his first basketball game at eight years old. Tommy learning to ride his bike.

But what if some other little boy is learning to ride his bike and he gets hit by a car? And Tommy had to respond to the call and . . . and see the unthinkable? What would that do to her son? How might he change after a year of working on the streets as a cop?

Don't do this! She shook her head. If she didn't stop breathing so hard she would wake up Luke. And what about her heartbeat? Surely he could hear that, even in the deepest sleep.

Luke rolled over and opened his eyes. "Reagan? Are you . . . are you okay?"

She turned on her side and looked at him. Her eyes had long since adjusted to the darkness. "It's happening again."

"Honey," he whispered. "Don't do this to yourself."

"I'm sorry." She put her hand on his shoulder. But that only made her heart beat harder. "I . . . can't breathe right." She flipped onto her back. "My mind won't shut off. I . . . I can't slow my heart down."

"Pray." Luke reached over and pushed her hair from her face. "Remember?" He hesitated. "God, you are the Prince of Peace. Please . . . stand guard over our bed. Right next to Reagan." His voice held an unwavering love.

"Yes, please, God." Reagan closed her eyes. Her breathing slowed just a little.

"And breathe Your spirit through this place. Surround Reagan with the truth of Your presence." Every word from her husband was like balm to her soul. "In Jesus' name, amen."

"Amen." Reagan felt her heartbeat ease off just enough. She took her first deep breath in an hour and turned back on her side. The pillow felt cool and wonderful.

She blinked a few times. "Why does this keep happening?"

"Do you remember, honey?" He put his hand on the side of her face. "How to make the panic go away? How to fall asleep?" He studied her face. "Remember?"

And suddenly she did remember. Of course. The answer was gratitude.

Luke had come up with this a month ago, when Officer Garcia first got shot and Annalee wasn't getting better and all of life seemed to be crumbling around them. *Gratitude changes everything*, Luke had told her.

And so it had. Time and again. She breathed a little easier. "Be thankful."

"Yes." Luke smiled. "You're going to be okay."

Reagan closed her eyes. The problem was that the panic made her forget about gratitude. In the midst of the stormy hurricane of fear, she could barely recall her first name. She blinked her eyes open. "You." She put her hand on his shoulder again. "You're the best thing that ever happened to me, Luke Baxter. Have I told you that lately?"

"You have." He kissed her and eased his arms around her. "I'm here, baby. I'm not going anywhere."

What had she ever done to deserve him? Reagan would never know, but one thing was certain. She wasn't angry anymore. Not at Tommy and certainly not at Luke. His love and care were the reason she was getting through this season at all. The season of accepting the fact that Tommy was going to be a cop.

But even with all that, Reagan's heart still beat hard and she wasn't the slightest bit tired. It wasn't enough to remember how to fall asleep. She had to put the lesson into practice. "I . . . need to thank Him. If I want to fall asleep." Yes, that was it. *Be thankful. Look to the Lord and thank Him.*

"Exactly. Every time you feel afraid, Reagan. When you think about Tommy in a uniform and your heart starts to race. When you can't sleep."

"Just be thankful." Reagan felt better now. She was calming down. "For every single thing."

"Yes." Luke whispered to her. "Start at the top of the list. Don't stop thanking Him."

"Okay." Reagan had closed her eyes then and started at the beginning. Just like Luke had asked her to do. *Thank You, Lord, for my husband. Luke is everything to me, God. And thank You for my family. For Tommy and Malin and Johnny. Thank You for my Baxter sisters and brothers and their families . . . and thank You for . . .*

Peace began to work through her veins. Why did she so easily forget about this?

Thank You for Ashley and Landon, and that You brought Landon into my sister-in-law's life all those years ago and that You're still working in their lives today.

And thank You for Elaine, and that Luke's father would find someone to love after losing his first wife. And thank You for Kari and Ryan and . . .

Reagan thanked God for everything He had done, all He had given them. Every beautiful memory and wonderful truth. The list was so long that somewhere near the beginning she stopped worrying. Stopped thinking about her racing heart and her fast breathing.

The exercise worked—every time.

Her mind slowed and peace filled the air and—like the greatest gift—sleep came.

REAGAN OPENED THE oven door and pulled out the spaghetti casserole. She'd made it with zucchini noodles. Officer Garcia's favorite. This morning he had come home from the hospital, and tonight Reagan and Luke and all three kids were bringing dinner to the Garcia house.

The officer's parents and siblings and a dozen other officers would all be there. Everyone was bringing something to share, and Raul had already told Tommy he was most looking forward to Reagan's spaghetti.

"I told him about it on our first ride together," Tommy had said. "So if you could make that, he'd be through-the-roof excited."

Through the roof. Reagan set the casserole on the counter and exhaled. As if this were any other ordinary day. And the officer hadn't just cheated death in a way even his doctors said could only have been a miracle.

Raul had come off life support a few days after the shooting. Then he'd come down with a terrible case of pneumonia. Surgeons had put his abdomen back together, but infection spread through his entire body.

It was mid-November, a month since the shooting, and in that time there had been entire weeks where it didn't seem like Raul would survive.

Never once during that time did they stop praying, stop believing. And now Raul was completely healed. Yes, he would need a month at home to recover, to rebuild his energy and strength. But after that he planned to get back out on the force.

Where his life would—once again—be in danger.

Reagan understood people like Raul a little better now, maybe even people like her own son. They were wired to put themselves in harm's way. Whatever it took to help someone else.

Several hours later, Reagan carried the covered casserole as she and Luke and their kids entered Officer Raul's house. He was sitting in a big blue recliner, chatting with family and the dozen officers who surrounded him.

When he spotted Reagan and her family, he lifted his hand, a smile stretched across his face. "My favorite family . . . with my favorite dinner!"

Reagan couldn't believe it. She had heard stories from Tommy about how well the officer was doing. But seeing him now . . . She held her breath as she set down the casserole. God had done this. Only He could've brought the young man back from the brink of death time and again over the last month.

They all took chairs into the family room and joined Raul and the others.

Raul was in the middle of telling a story about a year-old foot chase. "The guy's got a gun in his hand and he finally stops running. I tell him to drop the gun and he looks at me—straight at me—and tells me, 'Hey man, I never had a gun in my life.'"

One of the officers sitting closest to him laughed. "My toddler can lie better than some of these guys."

"But that takedown last week—" One of the officers nodded to a female cop in uniform. "Guy was twice your size, Debbie. How'd you do that?"

Officer Debbie grinned. "I train with the best. What can I say?"

Reagan made eye contact with her husband. "They love this."

"They do." He leaned close. "For a lot of reasons."

Reagan already understood their desire to keep streets safe. Their calling to help people and get criminals behind bars. But she hadn't seen or considered this part of being an officer. Not until right here, witnessing it for herself.

Police officers were a family all their own.

Even Tommy joined in. "Tell them about the man stopped in the middle of the road. From my first ride-along with you." He laughed. "That was my first time to see something like that in person."

Raul seemed to be gaining energy. He chuckled. "Guy parks his car in the middle of Forty-second. Smack in the center." He shook his head. "I park next to him and approach the driver's side. 'Hey, mister. You know you're parked in the middle of the road?'"

A few of the officers chuckled and nodded. As if they'd all been there one way or another.

"So he looks right at me—sort of—and he says, 'I'm not in the middle of the road, Officer. I'm driving . . . down the highway.'" Raul's eyes got wide. "I mean his car is in park. Traffic backing up behind us."

"Not for long," Raul's mother clapped her hands. "Not with my boy out there!"

"Amen." Raul's dad gave him a thumbs-up. "Love you, Son."

"Love you, Pops." Raul winked. Then he turned to the rest of the room. "Guy had an empty bottle of vodka on the seat beside him."

"But he hadn't been drinking." Tommy cut in. "Never touched the stuff."

"Poor guy." Raul shook his head. "Connected him with a rehab center for alcoholics. I have to check in on him when I get back to work."

Story after story the hour played out until Raul announced he was hungry.

Malin looked at Reagan and Luke. "Me, too!"

"Yeah." Johnny nodded. "I'm starved."

They all laughed, and Reagan realized something. She hadn't expected to have a good time tonight. The officers were funny and sharp, kind and witty. She wasn't naïve to the fact that scattered amidst the nation's cops, some were corrupt. Some were worn out and jaded and prone to bad decisions on the force.

But here—in this room—were some of the nicest people Reagan had ever spent an evening with. And Tommy already fit right in.

They filled their plates with spaghetti and meat loaf, homemade sweet potato fries and salad, and Reagan and Luke and the younger kids took a spot at the kitchen table. Tommy joined the officers in the living room, balancing plates on their laps.

Before he sat down to eat, Raul made his way closer. He walked with slow, careful steps, and he wore a wide band around his midsection. But otherwise he looked fantastic. He introduced himself to Luke and then Reagan. "I've heard so much about you." He cast a look at Tommy, who was in a conversation in the other room. "Your boy's special. When he's old enough, he's going to make a great addition to the force."

Reagan nodded, but a rush of emotion stopped her from saying anything. Tommy . . . in a police uniform. The idea still terrified her.

"Thank you." Luke shook the officer's hand. "He sure loves working with you."

"Well . . ." Raul chuckled. "He'll have to ride along with one of the other LEOs for a few more weeks. But then we'll be back at it."

"Leo?" Reagan blinked.

"Sorry." Raul grinned. "Law enforcement officers. LEOs."

"Of course." Reagan laughed. "I should've learned that from watching *Cops*." It was one more part of the code, part of the camaraderie this group shared not just with each other.

But with everyone who wore a badge.

"Ma'am." Raul looked straight at her. He was a handsome guy, but his eyes shone with new concern. "Tommy told me . . . you're afraid of him being an officer."

"Yes." Tears stung at the corners of Reagan's eyes. "I . . . I'm working through it."

"She is." Luke put his arm around her. Then he raised his brow at Raul. "But you're proof . . . the danger is real."

"It is." Raul didn't look away from Reagan. "My mom told me something the night before my first day on the job. She told me this: 'God knows the number of your days, Raul. God knows.'" He had the hint of a smile. "I think that helped her. It definitely helped me."

Two tears slid down Reagan's cheeks and she brushed them away. Her heart was too full to cry, too thankful to do anything but smile. "That's why you're here today."

"Exactly."

Reagan stood and hugged the young man. "Thank you." She stepped back. "I'm glad your number wasn't up."

"Yes." He chuckled. "Me, too." Raul made his way back to his recliner and rattled off another story.

Reagan turned to Luke. His eyes told her he knew exactly how she was feeling. Officer Raul's words had been just what she needed. The hope she would hold on to.

Worry never made anyone live longer. Fear never kept people from dying or getting sick or being shot by a criminal. Whether you were a doctor or a lawyer . . . or a businessman like her father, the world was a dangerous place.

And at the same time it was utterly safe. Because no cancer, no bullet from a drug dealer's gun could ever take someone's life until the exact right time. One out of one of the people breathing and moving on earth would die one day. But the hope was in what Raul had told her just now.

God knew the number of their days. And that wasn't only true for her and Luke and their kids, but for every police officer in the room.

20

The scan that Monday afternoon hadn't been originally scheduled. Annalee knew that. Her doctor wanted another look just four weeks after the last test for one reason.

To see if the stronger chemo was working.

It had been four days since her last hospital stay, but the effects of the drugs kept making their way through her body. Annalee wore a blond wig and sat in a wheelchair in the waiting room with Tommy and her mom. Across her mouth she wore a mask.

Her doctor was concerned about her immune system. Any cold, any flu bug could be disastrous. Plus it was ten days till Thanksgiving. The last thing Annalee wanted was to be sicker over the holidays.

"How are you feeling?" Tommy took her hand. The way he always did when they were together. "You have more color."

"She does, doesn't she." Annalee's mom sat across from them. Her eyes looked dark with worry. "I think you're looking better."

"Thanks." Annalee felt like she could throw up at any

minute. There had been a constant ringing in her ears for days now and her feet and hands tingled like they were asleep. She hadn't felt this bad since the beginning. "I'm getting better." She nodded. "I believe that."

"So . . . you feel okay?" Tommy studied her face. "If you don't, you can tell me, love."

Annalee let herself get lost in his beautiful eyes. She'd worried him enough. Besides, the new symptoms were to be expected. Stronger chemo . . . stronger side effects. "I'm fine." She smiled, and the action took all her effort. "Anxious for the test so we can know it's working."

A nurse opened the door and stepped into the waiting room. "Annalee Miller."

"Yes." Tommy answered for her. He looked at her mother. "Is it okay? If I wheel her back?"

"Of course." Her mom stood and framed Annalee's face with her hands. "I'll be praying. The whole time." She kissed the top of her daughter's head. "I love you."

"I love you, too." Annalee reached out and took her mom's hand. "Hey, I meant to ask you . . . how's Austin? I'm worried about him." She paused. "Me being sick, it's been hard on him."

"He's okay. He's at a friend's house." Her mom took a quick breath. As if she was determined not to mention the obvious. That Annalee's cancer had been hard on all of them. "Your brother prays for you every day, honey."

Annalee smiled. "He told me." She sank into her chair. "Well . . . we'll know soon."

Her mother stepped back and sat down.

Tommy pushed her toward the door and followed the nurse down the hallway. They made a few more familiar turns before they reached the scan room. "You can wait here." The nurse was new to them. She pointed to a spot against the wall, just outside the door.

"I'd like to wait with her inside. Until the test." Tommy's voice was polite but determined. "If you don't mind."

The nurse thought for a few seconds and then she smiled. "That's not in the rules. But . . . it's fine. The tech will tell you when to leave."

Alone in the room, Tommy parked Annalee next to a single plastic chair. He sat beside her and once more took her hand. Despite how awful she felt, she grinned at him. "You're a rule breaker, Tommy Baxter."

"Only for you." He wouldn't look away, wouldn't take his eyes off her. "I'd get in that tube with you if they'd let me."

She laughed, but the sound was weaker than before. "Please don't ask."

"I like this." He put his hand alongside her cheek. "Hearing you laugh. Especially today."

"It's going to be good news." She almost forgot where she was, with Tommy so near. His presence made her dizzy—in the best possible way.

"I believe you." He sat back in his chair. "Did I tell you what Officer Raul said to my mom? At dinner last night?"

"You . . . said it was fun." She leaned her head back

against the wall. "I wish I could've been there." The talking was making her tired. "Did . . . he say something else?"

"Yes." Tommy's expression looked more serious. "Something from the Bible. He told her God knows the number of our days."

"Mmm." She let the words work their way into her heart. "I love that."

"So I'm not going to worry, Annalee Miller." He held her hand a little more tightly. "This scan is going to bring us good news. But no matter what happens today . . . God holds you." He exhaled. "What could be better than that?"

"That sounds more like the Tommy I know." She looked at him. "You're not mad at God anymore?"

"I don't understand Him." Tommy shifted so he could see her better. "But the world makes no sense without Him."

A female tech walked in and hesitated. "Uh . . . I think you're supposed to be outside, sir."

"Actually"—Tommy winked at Annalee—"I have permission this time. Annalee . . . she's a special one."

Kindness filled the woman's eyes. "Very well." She motioned to the door. "But you really do have to leave."

Tommy nodded. "Thank you." Then he looked at Annalee again. "Good news, love. Only good news."

And like that he was gone.

Once she was inside the tube, the tech gave the usual instructions. She'd hear a series of orders. The machine would be loud and if she needed help she could push the button. Annalee barely listened. Her dad had reminded her again last night, "Go someplace wonderful, Annalee. Don't stay in the scan tomorrow. Take wing."

Today she knew exactly where she wanted to go. She closed her eyes and breathed in deep. Her stomach hurt, but not for long.

Not where she was going.

Once, six years ago, she and her family had traveled to Atlantis in the Bahamas. Paradise Island, the place was called. Annalee had been only twelve, but the memory remained as clear as if they'd gone last week. That summer a millionaire donor for Each One International had provided airfare and lodging for Annalee's entire family to spend a week at the resort.

And while Karon Beach was magical with its recent memories of her time with Tommy, Annalee knew one thing. If she and Tommy ever really did get married, she wouldn't want to spend their honeymoon anywhere but Atlantis.

Since pretending was free, that's exactly where she was headed.

First, Annalee put herself in a packed church opposite Tommy. She was wearing the most beautiful gown— white lace and cap sleeves, a fitted bodice and a train that spread out behind her. Tommy looked more handsome than ever. Black tux, white shirt and a white bow tie.

Her uncle was an ordained minister, so he was officiating the ceremony, of course.

"Take a deep breath. Hold it," the machine barked at her.

Annalee obeyed, but she wasn't in the tube any longer. She was looking into Tommy's eyes and he was telling her how he'd never imagined he could love anyone as much as he loved her.

For all my life—whatever comes our way—I will love you, Annalee Miller. His vows landed deep in her heart, every word finding its place. *I will hold you when you cannot stand, and laugh with you till we cry. And when you're sad . . . I will catch your tears and take them as my own.*

Then it was her turn and she felt the crowd fade away. *I love you, Thomas Luke Baxter. When I look at you, I see myself. The best parts of me. And when you look at me I feel your very heart. I will believe in you whatever you do, and cheer for you when you win. And you will always win, Tommy. We both will. Because we have each other.*

The wedding played out before her eyes. Tommy slipped a ring on her finger and she could feel the cool gold, see the brilliant diamond. And she was slipping a ring on his finger, too, and they were kissing. Not the kiss from their walk along the canal before her treatment began. A different kiss. Longer, deeper.

A kiss that told all the world they would forever belong to each other.

And like that they were married and walking up the aisle, grinning so big they were laughing. Annalee blinked and they were at a reception, and people were talking and cheering and looking at them while they danced.

"Never My Love" played throughout the room and Tommy was singing to her. *You ask me if there'll come a time . . .*

"Exhale. Hold your breath." The machine's voice was as distant as the moon.

Which was what Annalee could see now. In the cool of night, they were walking out of the reception, hand in hand, to a waiting car. And the moon had never looked more beautiful. Full and bright overhead. Then they were boarding a plane and headed to the Bahamas.

Annalee could see it all . . . the palm trees that lined the runway and the lyrical accent of the driver who picked them up and took them to Atlantis. They were staying at the Reef, the building where Annalee and her family had stayed. Only they were checking in to an ocean-view room and then . . .

Then Tommy opened the glass door and led her out onto the balcony and heaven itself seemed to spread out before them. The pale blue water and white sand, the strip of land that separated the two beaches. And the most beautiful manicured grounds that spread as far as they could see.

Their wedding had been in the evening, but it was daytime again—because why not? And the sun was setting as they walked back into the room. The bed had a ceiling-to-floor view of the water—a privacy window no one could see into. Tommy drew the sheer curtain across the patio door. Because what was going to happen next needed privacy.

Intimacy.

And they could still hear the ocean outside, one wave after another, mixing with the lilting instrumental music that played across the resort. The surf and beach sounds were like the most romantic symphony, and Tommy turned to her.

I've dreamed about this since the day we got engaged, he told her. And she was in his arms and they were kissing. A passionate kiss that took them slowly to the bed. More than once they had talked about this moment, the time when they could finally be together the way they wanted to be.

"I can't wait to sleep with you," Annalee had said on their canal walk. "If we get married . . . being with you—all of you—that will be the most beautiful part of living."

Tommy's cheeks had turned red. "Annalee!" He chuckled and pulled her into his arms. They swayed together for a few seconds. "Listen to you!"

"You're surprised?" She stepped back, her arms still around his neck.

He thought for a second and laughed again. "I guess not."

She had started running down the path that day and he had chased her. And before they left the park he told her something that still remained with her. "You're one in a million, Annalee Miller. I *am* going to marry you one day . . . and that honeymoon will be the highlight of my life."

"Breathe. Hold your breath." A series of sledgehammer sounds echoed through the tube. But not one of them interrupted Annalee.

Because this was their honeymoon. The ocean breeze dancing in the sheer curtain, the sun setting over the horizon. They were kissing again, breathing faster than before, and Tommy was whispering to her, *We have all the time in the world, Annalee. All the time.*

And they were taking off their shirts and the way he was looking at her made her feel like the prettiest girl alive. Then he—

The machine fell silent and the table Annalee was lying on began to slide out into the open room. Standing there was the tech. "Okay, Annalee. That's all." She held out her hand and helped Annalee off the table. Then she left while Annalee got dressed again.

When Annalee was back in her wheelchair, the tech patted her shoulder. "You got through it. I'll get your boyfriend."

Her boyfriend. Two words that reminded Annalee this wasn't the Bahamas and she and Tommy weren't married. She wasn't lying on a luxurious fresh bed looking out at the ocean and she and Tommy weren't about to—

He rushed into the room. "Hey." He stooped down to her level. "How was it."

"A dream." She put her hands on his shoulders and smiled. "If you only knew."

He stayed down at her level. "You . . . fell asleep?"

"Sort of." She leaned closer and let her forehead rest on his. "It was the most beautiful dream ever."

"Well, then . . ." He took gentle hold of her face. "I believe it'll come true, love. Someday. Somewhere. Sometime away from here."

"Yes." She smiled at him. "I believe, too. With everything in me."

And so she did. As they left the scan room and headed back down the hallway, Annalee was no longer thinking about her test results or whether she'd need more chemo or steroids or antinausea medication. She was back in the Bahamas.

She could practically feel the sheets on her skin.

21

For the rest of his life, Tommy was sure he would remember this Thanksgiving Day, and the sight of Annalee and her parents and brother walking up the porch of his uncle Landon and aunt Ashley's house. She was a vision, Annalee. Her flowy skirt swished just above her ankles, and her navy sweater hid just how much weight she'd lost. She wore the blond wig, the one she loved most.

She looked too pretty to have cancer. He opened the front door as they got closer. The Baxters always gathered at the old farmhouse in Bloomington for Thanksgiving, and this year they had invited the Millers. Because the news from Annalee's scan was so good.

Her tumor was disappearing!

She didn't need a wheelchair now, even though she'd had another round of chemo since the scan. Maybe because of the great news or maybe because God was working a miracle, she felt stronger these days. Able to walk. And the color really was back in her pretty freckled cheeks.

Tommy met them at the door and resisted the urge

to let Annalee lean on him. She wanted to walk on her own, she had told him a few days ago. Like a normal person. She had missed it. Instead he shook hands with her dad and hugged her mom and brother.

"Glad you could make it!" He grinned at each of them. "Everyone's inside."

Over the last three years Annalee's family had shared other dinners here at the Baxter house, so there was no need for introductions. Tommy's dad had asked the family to avoid talking about Annalee's cancer.

Better just to enjoy the time together.

When everyone had said their hellos, Tommy walked with Annalee to the back porch, where they could be alone for a few minutes. He had promised that even he wouldn't ask how she was today. So he put his arm around her and together they stared across the back field.

"It's so pretty." She shaded her eyes. "Let's walk to the stream out back . . . next time."

"We will." He held her close, warmed by the feel of her body against his. "This spring. It's a date."

"Perfect."

They were talking in code. She would finish with her treatments in early January. Then there would be another scan weeks later. That one had to show just one result if they were actually going to take a walk to the stream in spring.

No evidence of disease. NED, her doctor had called it.

"What are you thankful for, love?" He held her closer

still. They would talk about it at dinner, go around the table so everyone could share. But he wanted to have this moment with her first. Just the two of them.

She turned to him. "So much." She paused. "I'm . . . thankful for the smell of turkey and potatoes coming from your aunt and uncle's house. And for the chill in the air reminding me that winter is coming. Time is passing. The seasons are changing."

Here was one more thing Tommy loved about her. She was a poet. Every detail of life landed on her. Moments like this he wished he could write down what she had just said. Because he never wanted to forget it.

"Okay." He faced her now. "My turn."

She put her finger softly to his lips. "Wait. I'm not done." Her eyes danced, the way they hadn't in far too long. "I'm thankful for my friendship with Jesus and my parents and my brother. And I am forever thankful . . . for you, Tommy Baxter. I don't think . . . I really don't think I could've survived all this without you."

Where they were standing couldn't be seen from the house. They hadn't kissed since the time they walked the canal. There had never been a good moment, what with her being so sick and tired.

But here . . . with the late November cold on their faces and hope flooding their hearts, Tommy couldn't take another breath until they did. He stepped closer and took her face in his hands. "Can I kiss you, Annalee?"

She answered him by touching her lips to his, by kissing him in a way that took his breath. "Didn't you know, Tommy?" Her words were breathy, little more than a whisper.

"Know what?" He kissed her again and another time.

"This . . ." She kissed him once more and the moment lasted longer than before. When it ended, her smile took up her whole face. "This . . . is why I agreed to come today."

"Oh, it is?" He kissed her a final time and then brought her back to his side, his arm around her. There were lines they didn't want to cross, which meant it was time for a break. He caught his breath. "Wow. I guess I know what I'm thankful for."

"Tommy!" She giggled. "You wouldn't dare say that in front of our families!"

"No." He laughed and ran his hand along her arm. "But I am thankful."

They were quiet for a while, until Annalee broke the silence. "What else? What are you thankful for, Tommy?"

"For today." He turned to her and took both her hands in his. "Thankful you're standing here and looking like a vision of health. I thought God wasn't hearing my prayers. But that wasn't true." He sighed. "So I'm thankful for everything He is doing. In your life and mine. And in my parents' lives. And I'm thankful for you, love. Every minute with you."

Tommy couldn't help himself. He kissed her once more and then he took her hand. "Dinner's probably ready."

"Oh, that." She laughed again and the sound stayed with him. "I almost forgot."

For now Tommy respected her wishes and didn't ask how she was feeling or if the cold was getting to her. He didn't talk about any of it. Not the remaining treatments or the fact that she would return to the hospital again in four days. He didn't mention that he was praying hourly that the chemo and every other drug would actually work. That the cancer would be gone.

Instead he had simply made a date with her. A walk to the stream. In the spring.

For now, that said it all.

NEARLY EVERYONE HAD gone home now, including the Millers. It was just Reagan and Ashley finishing the last of the pans. Their kids were outside with their grandpa John and grandma Elaine, and Luke and Landon were watching football in the family room.

Everyone had helped with the clean up, but Reagan wanted to handle the last of the dishes alone. With Ashley. They hadn't talked in person since before 9/11. Before Annalee's cancer treatment began, and before Tommy's decision to be a police officer.

"She looks wonderful." Ashley was at the sink washing.

"Yes." Reagan stood next to her, towel in hand. "So pretty." She thought about the day, how Annalee had held up through dinner and during the conversation and dessert that followed. "It was like God gave her a day's break. A respite from all she's been through."

Ashley scrubbed a pie dish. "Life is hard . . . but days like today, when we're all together . . . laughing, sharing a meal. Being thankful. The good times are so much brighter."

No one understood better than this family the meaning of hard times. Reagan took the clean dish from Ashley and dried it. "I look at Amy, growing up. All these years since losing her family." Reagan smiled. "Watching her tonight, it was like she'd never been through any of that."

"Thank you." Ashley wiped her wrist across her forehead. "Just hearing that brings me so much joy, Reagan."

For a minute, neither of them spoke. After the accident, after Ashley and Landon took Amy in, there had been seasons of sorrow. But Amy had adjusted, and new life had blossomed for all of them. The same had been true after Ashley's mother died of cancer not long after Ashley and Landon married, and when Ashley gave birth to a baby girl who barely lived long enough to be held by her family.

Every season, every tragedy God had brought them through. "God never stops loving us. I'm seeing that more and more." Reagan dried another pan and set it on the counter.

"Definitely." Ashley finished washing the last serving platter and turned to Reagan. "How are you doing? With the whole police thing?"

"I still don't like it. If I'm honest." The fear that had plagued Reagan was easing. In the daytime, at least. "But I understand his decision better. Getting to see Officer Raul with his family and friends after he came home was important. It changed things for me." She dried the platter and the two poured coffees and took them to the kitchen table.

"You texted me that Officer Raul told you something that night?" Ashley leaned back and sighed. "You never said what it was."

"He reminded me of a truth I'd forgotten. He told me God has the number of our days." She uttered a sad laugh. "Worry won't help. Being terrified about a decision Tommy might make or . . . something any of our kids might do—there's no point in that."

"I remember finding peace with that truth." Ashley leaned forward. "After Cole had that choking incident. Remember?"

Reagan nodded. "Of course." The tension that night had been terrible. Ashley was still figuring out life as a single mother to baby Cole, and she and Luke had been fighting. "Luke left a bottle cap on Cole's high chair tray, right?"

"That's it." Ashley tilted her head and looked up at the ceiling for a minute. "So terrifying." She looked at Reagan again. "If Landon hadn't been here to do the Heimlich on him, I'm pretty sure . . . I don't know."

Reagan set her coffee down. "You dealt with your fear of being a mom after that?"

Ashley laughed. "Not like it was one-and-done. Not hardly." She hesitated. "But I remember thinking a few things. First . . . I had to be more careful."

"Don't we all." Reagan remembered the way she'd come unglued that first night when Tommy told them he wanted to be a cop.

"But also, there's only so much we can do." Ashley blew on her coffee and took a sip. "The only day ever promised to any of us is . . . well, today."

It was the exact lesson Reagan had been learning. "I have a story I want to tell Tommy, something my mom shared with me on the anniversary of 9/11. About my dad's death." Reagan folded her hands in her lap. "But I'm holding back."

"How come?"

Suddenly from the other room, Luke and Landon each let out a loud cheer. "That's my Lions!" They heard Landon clap a few times. "Gotta love Thanksgiving Day football!"

Reagan and Ashley laughed. "See?" Ashley shook her head. "We have no idea what tomorrow brings. Not for Annalee or Tommy . . . or any of us. But today?" She pointed toward the family room. "Today we laugh and clap and cheer. We celebrate because this day—this one special day—will never come again." Ashley's eyes lit up. "Same with that special day coming up a few weeks from now! Sounds like everyone's joining in on the surprise."

"I can't wait." Reagan smiled. But for now they had this day. This single moment.

Again they were quiet for a long minute, catching their breath from the day. Ashley set her coffee cup down. "Why are you holding back? About the latest details of your dad's death?"

"I guess . . . I'm afraid they'll make Tommy even more sure about being a cop."

Ashley raised one eyebrow. "From the sounds of what he said at dinner, I'd say he's already pretty sure."

"I know." Reagan was still wrestling with this part, when to tell Tommy. "He deserves to know."

For the next ten minutes Reagan told Ashley what she had learned that day and how it had changed everything about the way she viewed her father's final hour. In the years since the terrorist attacks, Reagan had often wished she'd known how little time she had left with her dad. Had she known, she would've taken the semester off school so they could've made a thousand memories together.

But now—in light of what God was doing in her heart and in view of her conversations with Raul and Ashley—Reagan wasn't as sure. If she had known, she would've spent her final time with her father worrying. Terrified about what was going to happen. And she wouldn't have gotten pregnant with Tommy, so she wouldn't be married to Luke. At least it seemed that way. All of which lent credence to the truth Raul had shared with her.

God knew the number of their days.

Because Tommy was almost certain to be a police

officer one day soon, the quicker Reagan could live within Raul's truth, the better. Worry was a thief and fear was a robber. Better not to know what was coming tomorrow. Far better to spend her time on the gift in front of her. Time with her family and laughter with the ones she loved. Hours enjoying the present she was most grateful for this Thanksgiving.

The gift of today.

22

With Annalee's next round of chemo slated for Monday, Tommy had made a plan for the Friday after Thanksgiving. He had talked to Annalee's parents and they had cleared the outing with her doctor.

Even after the full day in Bloomington, Annalee was feeling more energy than since treatment began. She had called first thing that morning and told him she was still on. "I could barely sleep, thinking about our date."

Tommy picked her up just before lunch. Her dad pulled him aside before they left.

"If she starts to look tired . . . if she seems like she's slowing down . . ." Mr. Miller rarely showed any concern when Tommy took Annalee out. But here Tommy got a glimpse of how the man clearly felt. This was his little girl, and she needed all the recovery time she could get.

"Yes, sir." Tommy didn't hesitate. "If anything changes, I'll bring her straight home."

The man raked his hand over his head. "Wisdom tells me she shouldn't go out today." He stared at Tommy. "But then I see how she is when she's with you." He gave Tommy a hug. "Take care of her."

"I will." Tommy couldn't keep from smiling. Annalee's dad had noticed the same thing Tommy had seen. She was better when she was with him. When she had even a few hours to feel like a high school senior again. "Thank you. For letting us do this."

Mr. Miller nodded. "I trust you. Just as much as she does."

Tommy put her wheelchair in the back of his Jeep and they were off. Annalee had a bag of medications she needed to take throughout the day, but as long as she felt well, the fresh air might do her good. That's what her doctor had said.

The afternoon was unseasonably warm. Nearly sixty degrees. Another reason the date seemed like a good idea. Tommy held her door open and caught himself grinning as he slid behind the wheel. "Do you know how good it feels to take you out?"

"I can't believe I'm free of that hospital bed." She rolled the passenger window down and breathed deep. "Thank You, God! Thank You."

Annalee wore a white sweater, dark jeans and white tennis shoes. Her wig this time was a blond ponytail. No one would've known it wasn't her real hair. Never mind that in three days she'd be back in the hospital having more chemotherapy, more radiation. For now they both had the privilege of celebrating.

Tommy had the day all planned. They were meeting his cousin Maddie West and her boyfriend, Dawson Gage, at the Indianapolis Zoo. First stop was the zoo diner—Café on the Commons. Though the date with Annalee had been approved last week, the specifics hadn't come together till yesterday over Thanksgiving dessert. That's when Dawson had texted about a zoo day.

Funny, Tommy thought as he headed for the zoo. He and Maddie had been too many years apart in age to be very close when they were growing up. She was out of high school before he even started. But now that many of the Baxter cousins were young adults, age didn't seem to matter.

Maddie and Dawson had only been dating a few months, but already they seemed very serious. Their story was the wildest thing Tommy had ever heard. They parked close to the café and Tommy looked at Annalee. "Wheelchair?"

"No." She angled her head. "I know I'm supposed to . . . but for this part, can I just walk?"

Tommy didn't think it could hurt. He helped her from the car and inside they met up with Maddie and Dawson. Maddie had long blond hair, like Annalee used to have. But with Annalee's wig the two could've been sisters. Dawson was tall with dark hair and an outdoorsy feel about him. He had just moved to Indiana from Oregon.

They ordered crispy chicken and fries and bottled water and found a table near the window. Annalee didn't want to look frail, she had already told Tommy that. But he slid into the booth first and situated himself so she could lean on him.

Which she did.

Maddie had met Annalee before at a few of the big gatherings at the Baxter house. But they'd never talked much until yesterday. Maddie took a sip of water and started the conversation. "Tommy says you're nearly done with treatment." She hesitated. "Is it okay? If I ask that?"

A wave of frustration came over Tommy. He had forgotten to tell Maddie not to talk about Annalee's cancer.

But Annalee only smiled. Life radiated from her eyes. "Yes, just a few more rounds." She shrugged. "You can ask. It feels good to be almost done, that's for sure."

The conversation shifted to Maddie and Dawson. Tommy was sitting across from the guy, and he still had questions about how the two of them had started dating. "So . . . you two." Tommy looked from his cousin to her boyfriend. "I know some of the details. But . . . maybe you could tell us."

A sadness seemed to flash in Dawson's eyes. He folded his hands on the table and exhaled. "It's a story only God could've written." He smiled at Maddie and then turned back to Tommy and Annalee. "But it started with tragedy. The greatest tragedy in all my life." He took a breath. "My best friend—London . . . that day she and I spent the afternoon hiking."

Dawson talked about how he'd been in love with London for years but things were never right between the two of them. "We went for ice cream after the hike, and as London got out of the car, she was hit by a truck."

Tommy had never heard any of this before. Beneath

the table he took Annalee's hand and kept listening. Dawson went on to say that London eventually died from her injuries. But not before her mother mentioned something about frozen embryos. Babies that could've been London's siblings.

"I set out to find those siblings." Dawson looked at Maddie. "And that's how we met."

Never had Tommy heard anything like their story. And after lunch, when they got Annalee's wheelchair from the car and started walking around the zoo, Tommy was struck by the bond his cousin and this man shared. It was like Maddie and Dawson had been made for each other.

The way Tommy felt about Annalee.

Since Maddie worked at the zoo, she had access to all the behind-the-scenes places. With the sunshine on their shoulders, they went behind doors marked PRIVATE and got to watch trainers feed the lions. A man and a woman would put buckets of raw meat into an area covered in hay. When the trainers were safe, two lions charged into the area and immediately found their individual feeding troughs.

"You can't be too careful with lions." The woman wiped her hands on her khaki pants. "No room for error with these beautiful boys."

As they returned to the main walkway, Annalee looked up at Tommy. "I always wondered how that worked." Her eyes shone. "I like what she said. You can't be too careful."

It was that way with cancer, too, Tommy wanted to say. But he refused to bring up her sickness. Instead he kept a watchful eye on her, making sure she wasn't yawning or leaning on her chair's armrest. Any sign that she was getting tired, and he would take her home.

The moment came sooner than either of them had hoped.

They were backstage at the leopard exhibit, and Annalee was petting the zoo's newborn cub, when Tommy noticed her face getting pale. He skipped his turn to hold the animal, and instead hurried the group back out to the main path. As he did, he felt Annalee's forehead. It was burning up. "Hey. We need to get going." He shook Dawson's hand and hugged Maddie. "I loved this."

"Me, too." Dawson nodded. "I want to hear about those ride-alongs. Maddie says you're thinking about being a police officer."

"I am." Tommy turned Annalee's wheelchair toward the exit. "Let's get lunch sometime. On a weekend, maybe."

"Sounds like a plan." Dawson waved.

Maddie did the same. "Glad you're feeling better, Annalee. Nice spending the day together."

"Definitely." Annalee's teeth were starting to chatter. No one else noticed, but Tommy could tell.

His heart began to race. He had to get her home. Now.

Annalee didn't complain once about Tommy's sudden change of plans. Not when they were saying their goodbyes and not as he practically ran her back to his Jeep. When they were in the car she turned to him. "I . . . don't feel good."

"I know." He started the engine. "You have a fever."

"How can you tell?" She lifted her hand to her forehead. Her shivering was worse. "I feel cold."

"You're burning up." He focused on the road ahead of them. He needed to get her home, but he had to be safe, too.

Annalee closed her eyes and leaned her head back. She was asleep by the time they pulled into her family's driveway. Tommy threw the Jeep into park, cut the engine and ran up to the front door. *What is this, God? Why now? Are You turning Your back on her again?* He stopped himself. *Help her, Father. I trust You, please help her.*

Her dad was immediately at the door, as if he'd been waiting.

"She's sick. She has a fever." Tommy was breathless as he raced back to the car with Annalee's dad beside him.

"I was taking a nap, watching the Pacers. Something woke me up." Her dad sounded as frightened as Tommy. "I knew it was Annalee."

Her mother was at the mall with a friend, so she met Mr. Miller and Tommy and Annalee at the hospital. The cancer ward. By then, Annalee's temperature was 103 and rising. She was restless in the bed, groaning from aches that had come over her without warning.

An hour later they knew.

Annalee had pneumonia. She was put on IV antibiotics and given a series of breathing treatments. Her doctor joined them, and his concern was written in the lines on his forehead.

"It's all my fault." Tommy paced the room. "I never should've taken her out."

"No." Annalee sat partially up in bed. "It wasn't you, Tommy."

Her dad went to her. "Please, honey. Lay down. You need to rest."

Annalee did as he asked, but she shook her head. "I need you to hear me. All of you." She was wheezing now. Tommy had never seen an illness move so fast. "I felt perfect all day. Tommy"—she looked at her father—"he knew I was sick before I did. He . . . he's the reason . . . I got here in time."

Her dad put his hand on Tommy's shoulder. "We don't blame you." He looked at Annalee. "Honey, of course it isn't Tommy's fault."

Tommy still wasn't sure. The speed of this thing made him feel dizzy. How could she be making progress against Stage 4 cancer and then be fighting for her life because of pneumonia? A few minutes later he and Annalee's parents followed the doctor out into the hall. That's when they knew how serious the fight actually was.

"We're doing all we can." The doctor's face was grim. "Her life is on the line with this infection. The next two days will be critical."

"Is there some other medication, something that could help her?" Annalee's mother sounded desperate.

But the doctor only shook his head. "Since you believe in miracles, I'd ask one thing of you all." He paused. "Please . . . Pray."

23

The breakthrough in Annalee's pneumonia came late Saturday night. Until then Luke had stayed in the waiting room with Reagan, and Annalee's parents—praying and reading Scripture. Anything to storm the gates of heaven one more time for the girl they loved.

Her doctor had told them that if they'd found the right antibiotic, and if Annalee's compromised immune system responded, they should know quickly. So when her fever broke Saturday night the doctor was thrilled to share the news.

"We don't always get the answer we want," he told them. "But God is always listening."

Luke liked that. God was always listening.

Since then, Annalee had continued to improve, so on Sunday night Luke did something he hadn't done in years. He asked Reagan to go dancing. The strain between them had passed, but they needed time together. Time to rebuild the love and laughter that had been missing since mid-September.

Luke wanted the date for another reason, too.

After dancing, he and Reagan planned to meet Mike

Lockwood and his wife for dessert. Luke had talked to Mike a few weeks ago about the four of them getting together. Mike knew about Reagan's fears. "Time together might help her see." Mike had liked the idea from the beginning. "Police officers don't live with the what-ifs. We go to work and do our job the best we can. It's a job we love."

Now Luke walked to the family room mirror and adjusted his tie. Tommy was staying home to be with his siblings, and the three kids were playing Sequence on the oversized coffee table.

"Big date, huh, Dad?" Tommy grinned at him.

"It is. And overdue, for sure." Luke looked in the mirror. His hair had stayed blond all these years. A few lines at the corners of his eyes, but otherwise he was still the Luke Baxter he'd been when he married Reagan. He slipped on his dark gray suit coat, stood a little straighter, and turned to the kids.

"Well . . . how do I look?"

Johnny smiled at him. "You look ready, Dad. And you kinda look like Tommy." He shot a look toward the master bedroom just off the family room. "What about Mom?"

"Finishing touches." Luke shrugged. "You'll understand one day, Johnny boy. Waiting on a woman is part of the deal."

Johnny looked back at the game. "I'm the youngest, Dad. I'm good at waiting."

At the same time, Malin glanced up from the game

and gasped. She stood and blinked a few times. "Dad . . . you look like the most handsome prince."

Luke bowed. "Why, thank you." He smiled and held his hand out to his daughter. "Perhaps the princess would like a dance with the prince?"

Malin giggled and scampered over to him. The flouncy layers of her pink dress bounced around her bare knees. It was the dress she'd worn to church that morning. Malin would've worn it to bed if they'd let her. She took hold of his fingers and curtsied. "The princess would, indeed, like to dance."

For the slightest few seconds, Luke didn't move. He only looked at this precious daughter, brought home from China when she was a baby. Her birth country and heritage were important to all of them. But she was a Baxter girl, through and through. All ribbons and bows, smiles and giggles.

The sunbeam of their home.

Luke took her hand and began to sing, *Tale as old as time*. He twirled her again and again and then she stepped lightly on his toes. "Dance me around the room, Daddy. Like we used to do when I was little."

And Luke did just that. Plodding across the floor, mustering as much grace as he could with a twelve-year-old on his feet. The boys had stopped the game to watch, and after a minute the part of the song that Luke knew came to an end. *Beauty and the . . . Beast.*

Then he and Malin stepped back from each other, still holding hands like a bridge between them. Luke bowed again and she curtsied once more. "You're a very good singer, Prince."

"Thank you." He grinned. "As long as you're my audience."

"And us!" Johnny jumped up and clapped. "I think you sing good, too."

Luke laughed. "If that's true, I get it from my mom." Memories from long ago filled his heart. "Your grandma Elizabeth used to play the piano and the two of us . . . we'd sit together and sing. Mostly at Christmastime."

Malin hugged him. "Thanks, Dad." She leaned up and kissed his cheek. "For dancing with me. One more time."

One more time? So was this the last time she would dance on his feet? The way she had from the time she was two till . . . till whenever she grew up? "We're going to dance again, Malin. This isn't the last time."

"I know." She grinned. "Plus . . . we'll dance at my wedding one day."

"True." Luke didn't want to think about that. He put his hand on her cheek. "But that's a long time from now."

"Yep." She giggled once more and hurried back to the Sequence game. "My turn!"

Reagan came out of their room then. She wore a black dress with short sleeves and a skirt that flowed close to her high heels. Luke whistled. "Wow . . . talk about princesses." Her dark blond hair hung down past her shoulders, and her eyes had never looked more blue. Luke sucked in a quick breath. "Honey . . . you . . . you look stunning."

"Really?" She came to Luke and the two hugged.

"Yes. Really." Luke whispered near her face. "You take my breath, Reagan."

Tommy was on his feet now. "Wow, Mom! That dress!"

A smile filled Reagan's face, and her eyes looked bright. "Your dad asked me out dancing. We used to love dressing up for that."

"And now . . . it's time to go." Luke motioned the kids close. He and Reagan hugged them all. "Have fun tonight. And may the best Sequence player win."

The kids returned to their game as Luke led Reagan out to their car. "Ever have a moment you want to remember forever?" Luke held her door for her.

Once they were inside Reagan turned to him. "You and Malin?" She smiled with her eyes. The way Luke loved. "I heard you singing to her."

Luke put his hand over his heart. "I can't remember the last time she danced on my feet like that. We sort of waltzed around the room and she was laughing and looking into my eyes." He shook his head. "Our little girl."

They pulled out of the neighborhood and Luke kept his eyes on the road. "She thanked me for dancing with her like that—one more time. That's what she said." He breathed in deep. "And all I wanted was to freeze time."

Reagan leaned back into her seat. Her tone was easy, her expression young and carefree. "I can't believe she's going to be a teenager. Where did the little girl days go?"

"Exactly." Luke let another string of memories fill his

heart. Malin, the day they brought her home. The way she was the best big sister when they adopted Johnny and brought him home. "All our kids . . . they're each a miracle."

A gentle quiet filled the car. "It's the perfect night for a waltz, my dear." He reached for her hand. "I'm so glad we're doing this."

"I couldn't believe . . . when you asked." She turned to him again. "It's been what . . . four years? Five?"

"Probably." He sighed. "That's the thing about time. The more you love life, the faster it goes."

She studied him, the length of him. "I forgot about that suit."

"I probably haven't worn it since the last time we went dancing." He ran his thumb over the diamond in her wedding ring. "I love you, Reagan Baxter."

"I love you, too."

They listened to John Mayer until they reached the studio. The place was known throughout the city for its trained dance instructors and expansive ballroom. It looked newly remodeled. *Even better,* Luke thought.

The closest available parking spot was at the back of the lot, so Luke stopped the car near the door. He didn't mind the walk, but Reagan might. "You can get out. I'll meet you after I park."

"It's okay." She lifted one heeled foot. "These are more comfortable than they look." She leaned over and kissed Luke's cheek. "I'll walk with you."

Something about the dimly lit parking area or the

distance they needed to walk to get to the studio gave Luke the slightest sense of concern. They weren't in the worst part of the city, but the area wasn't exactly safe. For a moment he thought about taking her back to the front door and insisting she skip the walk.

But then he came upon a spot and he parked. "They need more light back here."

"Agreed." She looked out her side window and then through the windshield to the wooded area that lined the lot. "Let's hurry."

Luke wasn't afraid. But his concern deepened as he helped Reagan out of the car. *Lord, walk with us. Something doesn't feel right.* He pulled Reagan close and she took his arm.

They had just started walking toward the dance building when someone behind them shouted. "Hey! Turn around!"

They both pivoted and Luke felt a rush of terror. Two men were running toward them, guns drawn. Instinctively, Luke moved Reagan behind him. The men were young with masks on their faces. Clown masks. One of them was laughing.

"What do you want?" Luke thought about fleeing, but they couldn't turn their backs on the armed punks.

The guys stopped a few feet away. Their guns were real. Luke was sure. The one who was still laughing raised his weapon higher. "Your money. Throw your wallets and purse down on the ground."

Before Luke or Reagan could do as they asked, sirens

sounded near the entrance of the driveway. The lead clown shoved his gun at Luke's shoulder. "Your wallet. Now! Or I'll kill you both!"

The sirens were louder, closer.

"They found us, man." The other masked guy turned and started running the other way. "It's too late. Come on!"

Just then a police car sped up and two officers jumped out. "Stop. Police!" they shouted, and as they did, the guy with the laugh turned and ran after his buddy.

Luke couldn't breathe. What had just happened? What if they had . . . ? He turned and pulled Reagan into his arms. "Honey. It's okay."

"Luke they . . . they could've . . ." Her skin was sheet white. She buried her face in his shoulder. "We had no warning."

In the adjacent lot, the officers tackled the guys and cuffed them. Luke closed his eyes and breathed in the smell of Reagan's hair. She was right. It had happened so fast. And just like that they could've been . . . their kids would've been without—

He couldn't let himself go there. "We're safe." His voice sounded desperate with relief. "Thank God, we're safe."

They waited while the bad guys were taken to the squad car. By then a few other officers had arrived. One of the cops who had chased down the suspects took statements from Luke and then from Reagan.

Luke still felt dizzy as they told the officers what

they knew. Reagan clung to him, like she might collapse otherwise. Yes, they had guns. Yes, they had pointed their weapons at them and demanded money. Yes, they had threatened to kill them.

The cop was maybe in his late twenties. Dark skinned. Good looking, fit. Willing to put his life on the line for Luke and Reagan. The sort of officer Tommy would be. The guy shook his head. "So sorry about the scare. Those two have been on a robbery spree since midday." He tapped his pen on his clipboard. "We've been in pursuit on and off from the first call."

Luke's lawyer brain had a handful of questions about the suspects and whether the district attorney would file the most severe charges against the men. But that wasn't his job, and he still wanted to go dancing with his wife. He put his hand on the young officer's shoulder. "Thank you. If you hadn't come just then . . ."

"I know." The man clenched his jaw. "They fired shots at a few of their victims." He took a deep breath. "We'd been following them for several blocks."

Half an hour later, when the lesson portion of the ballroom dancing was over and free dance began, Luke waltzed Reagan across the floor. His heart was beating normally again. "That was awful."

"Those officers . . . they saved our lives." Reagan looked deep into Luke's eyes. "If they hadn't shown up when they did . . ."

"Anything could've happened." Luke ran his hand along the back of her head. "I can't think about it."

She stayed in time with him. No matter how many years had gone by, the two of them still shone on the dance floor. Like a single moving, breathing unit, gliding across the polished wood. His Reagan, the love of his life.

Later over dessert, they told the story to Mike and his wife, Trudy. They all agreed that if the officers hadn't already been in pursuit of the suspects, the night could've ended much differently.

Luke watched the way Reagan seemed fully engaged in the conversation with the couple. Maybe the incident at the parking lot had given her a new perspective. She looked from Luke to Mike and his wife across the booth. "For years we've watched *Cops* with Tommy. He's always wanted to be an officer, you know."

"That's what I heard. Our kids watch it, too. They love the show." Mike put his arm around his wife. "Tommy's a wonderful young man. We already love him at the department."

"I'm sure." Reagan was still fired up. "I always say high school kids should be required to watch a season of *Cops*." She looked at Mike. "So they can see what not to do . . . drugs and robbery and violence. And so they can appreciate the danger you and your fellow officers put yourselves in every day." She took a quick breath. "Police work isn't a job. I saw that tonight. It's a calling."

Luke could hardly believe what he was hearing. It had been a while since they had all watched *Cops* together, because Tommy was too busy. But Reagan was right. She absolutely used to say that. *All students should have to watch* Cops.

Reagan was still talking, still singing the praises of police officers. And all Luke could do was watch and listen, his heart full. Because here and now, in light of what had happened tonight, the most amazing change seemed to have occurred in Reagan. She no longer sounded afraid or worried or panicked about Tommy being an officer. Quite the opposite.

His beautiful wife sounded proud.

24

The last of Tommy's ride-alongs was one for the books. He spent the afternoon with Officer Nick Conway, a twenty-two-year veteran. So far Officer Conway had responded to a bank robbery in progress where it took three officers to apprehend the suspect. There had been a domestic violence arrest, a foot chase after a guy with a stolen gun and a sex-trafficking bust.

From his spot in the passenger seat, Tommy had been close enough to hear most of what had gone on.

"You sure you want to do this?" Officer Conway cast a wry smile at him on the way back to the department. "It's crazy out here."

Tommy didn't hesitate. "More sure than ever." He stared at the city streets as they drove. "Especially after that last bust. I want to see sex trafficking closed down. Completely."

"We want that, too."

For a moment Tommy thought about the kids who had been set free because of today's arrest. Social services was still finding places for them. Tommy shook his head. "Sir, you and the others. You're making a difference out here. Every hour. Every day."

Just over a week had passed since his parents had been held up at gunpoint. Tommy had talked to the officers who had arrested the suspects that night. He couldn't imagine what might've happened if police hadn't been chasing the guys. So, yes. Tommy wanted to do this.

He could hardly wait.

On the drive back, Tommy thought about Annalee. She was home from the hospital and getting stronger. Something only God could've done considering how sick she had been. And tomorrow she was going with him to the zoo again. This time for a surprise the Baxters had all been waiting for. Something big was going down, and everyone in the family was planning to be there. Tommy and Annalee, included.

Another call came across the radio. But two other officers responded. "I need to get you back." Officer Conway kept his eyes on the road. "You'll make a good officer one day, Tommy. I believe that."

"Thank you." He hadn't gotten to know Officer Conway well. The man had a wife and three teenage daughters. A family who prayed for him to come home each day. But his skill and compassion working the job helped Tommy understand the excellence required of every police officer.

A report a few years ago had ranked Indy the tenth most dangerous city in the country. After a few months riding along with the IMPD, Tommy figured Indianapolis would be in the top five if not for its diligent police force. To the core of their beings, the cops he had worked with cared about keeping the citizens and streets safe. They were the good guys in a world with a whole lot of bad.

Since this was his last day as a ride-along citizen, Tommy had an appointment later with Lieutenant Roger Gere. The lieutenant was waiting for him. Tommy took the seat across from the man. He had no idea what was coming.

"Young man." The lieutenant had a deep voice. "Thank you for coming in today."

Tommy nodded. "Thank you for taking the time."

Lieutenant Gere had immigrated to the United States from Ethiopia. He was known throughout the department for going to bat for his officers, working tireless long hours and for being a leader with integrity. His reputation with the Indiana law enforcement was sterling. The lieutenant was driven to protect Indianapolis and the United States.

One wall of his office was almost entirely taken up with an American flag.

The man folded his hands on his clean desk. "I hear from my men and women that you want to be a police officer with the IMPD."

"Yes, sir. When I turn twenty-one. I'll probably work in Florida for a few years first." Tommy felt his heart thud against his chest. Was this . . . ? Were they going to hire him right here, on the spot? Hold a spot for him when he was old enough to wear the uniform? "It's become more than a dream for me. It's a passion."

Lieutenant Gere stood and paced behind his desk. He looked at the framed photos on the wall that ran in a line all the way to the window. "Many citizens have participated in our ride-along program." He turned and looked at Tommy. "From what I hear, you're one of the best."

"Wow . . . uh, thank you. That means a lot."

The man crossed his arms. "But I'm afraid I don't have the news you want to hear, son."

Tommy's mind began to race. "Sir?"

"Police candidates don't necessarily need a college education, Tommy." He paused. "But my team tells me you have leadership skills. We wouldn't hire you without a bachelor's. Maybe even a master's or a doctorate." He looked hard at Tommy. "Do you know why?"

Tommy felt his face getting hot. This was the last thing he had expected to hear today. "No, sir?"

"Because of these." He pointed to the framed pictures. One at a time. "These are lieutenants and captains and even chiefs of police. Each of them started as an officer, young man. But they all had something you don't have."

"Higher education?" The prospect of four or more years of schooling before he could don a uniform felt beyond defeating.

"That's right." The lieutenant sat back down at his desk. "You get your education, then come back. We'll hire you with a bachelor's degree. Then you can get your postgrad education online, if you'd like. We'll pay for it."

Tommy swallowed. "That . . . feels like a long time from now."

"It isn't." For the first time the man smiled. "I have my doctorate in behavioral sciences." He paused. "The department looks favorably on all higher education. Bet you didn't know that."

"No, sir." Tommy had never thought about it. But postgraduate studies mattered at the top of most fields. Why would police work be any different? He lifted his eyes to the photos on the wall again. If each of those men and women had college degrees, well, then Lieutenant Gere was just being straight with him.

"So, here's what I want you to do." The lieutenant leaned back in his chair, his eyes never leaving Tommy's. "You finish high school and get that bachelor's degree. Whenever you're in town, you can do a ride-along. Once a week, if you want." He lowered his chin, his eyes serious. "And when you graduate, you come see me. If you're still interested, I'll have a job for you."

The man stood and Tommy followed suit. They shook hands at the door and again Tommy thanked him. "You'll see me around. I'm sure of that."

"I'm sure, too."

Not till Tommy was in his Jeep headed home did he try to make sense of what had just happened. The highs and lows of the conversation mixed together. There would be no police job right out of high school, if he wanted to work for the IMPD. Which would make his mom happy. But the lieutenant definitely liked him. There was no denying that, or the fact that he wanted to hire Tommy. Someday. He definitely did. Tommy rolled down the window and took a deep breath. He would be a police officer in time. He would.

Just not yet.

REAGAN HAD LOOKED forward to this night since last Christmas.

The kids were in bed and Luke was working in his office at the back of the house. So this Saturday night was the perfect moment. Since their first year of marriage, each Christmas Reagan had found a quiet evening to decorate their family tree.

Their decorations were not fancy or elegant. Rather, every one of them contained a family photo. Some were handmade when the kids were little. Others had small pretty frames.

Reagan carried the third and final box from the Christmas closet. The house had been decorated in reds and greens and garlands since Thanksgiving weekend. But with Reagan's work at school, and Annalee's sickness, the ornaments had stayed in their boxes.

Until tonight.

Yes, hanging these precious memories on the tree was one of Reagan's favorite moments of the season. A time to remember the kids' sweet faces from years gone by. *A time to remember.* Reagan smiled at the first box. Christmas, itself, was like this. A mix of the happy times from Decembers gone by. Hope for those yet to come.

Reagan used her phone to start a quiet instrumental Christmas album through the house. "I'll Be Home for Christmas" played first.

"Perfect," Reagan whispered. She opened the box, and there at the top was the large cardboard star, covered in glitter. Tommy had made it when he was just two. Back then he'd had one request as he gave it to her. "Keep it on our tree forever, Mommy? Okay?" Reagan could still hear his young singsong voice.

Her answer had been immediate. "Of course, Tommy. This will be our family star forever." And so it had been.

She lifted it from the box and as she did the front door opened. Tommy walked in, and from the moment their eyes met Reagan knew.

Something was wrong.

He stopped, then he came and sank into the chair nearest her. He nodded at the yellow cardboard cutout in her hand. "My old star."

"Yes." She set it down and came to him. "I'm doing the tree tonight."

Tommy nodded. He leaned forward, his forearms on his knees. "I talked to Lieutenant Gere. Since my ride-alongs are done."

"Okay." Reagan had no idea where this was going. Had he taken a job? Already? She sat in the chair beside him. The ornaments could wait. "What did he say?"

Tommy looked at the floor. "He won't hire me." His eyes lifted to hers. "Not until I have my degree."

Reagan forced herself not to move. Not to speak.

Tommy wasn't going to work as a cop right out of high school! Her heart soared with relief.

"I know." Tommy linked his fingers behind his head and looked up at the tree. "You're thrilled." He looked at her again. "It's okay. I get it."

Again Reagan stayed silent.

"He said as soon as I get my degree, I've got a job. And I can do ride-alongs once a week between now and then. Whenever it works with my schedule."

The relief stopped short. Four more years. That was a good thing, but still . . . one day she would most likely have to live with the reality. Tommy in a uniform. Doing the right thing. Putting his life in danger for others. People like those who saved Luke and her the other night.

It was time to tell him about his grandfather. There could be no better chance than now. She slid her chair closer and put her hand on Tommy's knee. "Son, there's something I've been wanting to tell you."

"About what I just learned?"

"Sort of." She folded her hands, her eyes on her son's. "I found out something about your grandpa Tom . . . a few months ago. He was a hero, Tommy." She paused. "But I found out new information the morning of the 9/11 anniversary. When we were in New York."

A puzzled look came over Tommy's face. "Why didn't you tell me then?"

"I . . . had to process the news. I planned to tell you when we got back, but then . . ."

"Then I told you I wanted to be a cop." Tommy was

tracking with her. "And if I knew Grandpa was a hero, I might want to be one, too."

"Yes. Exactly." Reagan was still ashamed of how she'd handled the whole matter. But right now she could make things better.

Sympathy warmed Tommy's eyes. "It must be quite a story."

"It is." Reagan started at the beginning. "Apparently Grandma got a call a few days before the 9/11 anniversary. From a woman who had been trying to track her down for nearly twenty years."

Tommy narrowed his eyes. "Okay."

"The reason she'd been looking for Grandma is because . . . her husband had worked in the same building as Grandpa Tom."

According to the woman, her husband, Bill, worked on the same floor as Reagan's father. When the plane hit their tower, Bill wasn't sure what to do, so he waited. After a while, though, it became clear that they needed to evacuate. So Bill tried to take the elevator down.

"But the elevators weren't working, so he rushed across the floor and found Grandpa Tom." Reagan felt her fingers begin to tremble. She'd told Luke the story, but it was difficult. Reliving her father's final moments.

As Bill stepped into her father's office, people were starting to panic. Smoke was streaming in at the edges of the walls, and the building was shaking. The weight of the jet, the burn of the fuel, all of it was melting toward them. So Bill did the only thing he could think to do.

He called his wife.

"From that moment until the tower collapsed, Bill was on the phone with her." Reagan couldn't imagine how horrifying, to be Bill's wife. Unable to do anything to help him. "So the story from that point is what Bill's wife heard while she was on the phone with him."

Apparently in the middle of the panic, with maybe thirty people frantic for a way out, a man jumped up onto his desk and began shouting for everyone to calm down.

"He told them his name was Tom Decker. He said, 'I'm going to heaven today, and I'd sure like to take the rest of you with me.'"

"Wow." Tommy leaned forward. "I can picture that."

"Bill hadn't been a man of faith." Reagan paused and chills ran down her arms. "But over the next fifteen minutes, your grandfather told the group about Jesus. How he had died on the cross for them, and how the gift of heaven was free to any who asked."

Bill's wife—still on the phone with her husband—could hear Reagan's father shouting this through the office space. *Whatever that man tells you*, she had said to Bill. *Do it. Please. Do it now.*

"And so all thirty of those people—including Bill—got on their knees and asked God to forgive them for whatever wrongs they'd done. Then they asked Jesus to be their Savior." Tears fell on Reagan's cheeks. "They were still praying together, when a terrible sound filled the phone line. And then the call went dead."

Tommy stared off for a moment. "He could've called Grandma with his final minutes."

"Right." That had been one of the hardest parts for Reagan. What her mom would've given for that final conversation. "The thing was, Grandpa's relationship with Grandma was so strong. So solid . . . they had shared those moments before he left."

Her mom had also told her that before her dad went to work that day—like every day—he had found her in their home office and hugged her. He told her he loved her and that he was easily the happiest man alive because of her. And that he couldn't wait to come home to her at the end of the day.

Only that never happened.

The story seemed to be landing on Tommy, making its way through his mind to his heart. The same way it had hit Reagan when she first heard it. "See, your grandfather had not chosen a dangerous job. He was a businessman, which should've kept him out of harm's way—at least at work."

"True." Tommy took Reagan's hand. "I can't wait to meet him one day."

Reagan smiled. "You've always had a little of him in you, Tommy." She brushed at her wet cheeks. "Especially lately."

"Thank you." Tommy's eyes glistened with unshed tears. "I bet Grandpa Tom would've loved me being a cop."

"Yes, Tommy. I think he would've." Reagan stood and

pulled Tommy to his feet. She hugged him and then stepped back. "And you know what? I think I like it, too."

Tommy looked at her for a long beat. "What are you saying?"

"I'm telling you I'm in favor." She lifted her face and smiled at him. "My son wants to be a police officer. What could make me more proud than that?"

"Mom?" Tommy shook his head. "Are you serious?"

"I am." She put her hand on his face for a moment. "I can't fathom losing you, Tommy. Four years from now when you put that badge on, I'll pray for your safety every day." She felt fresh tears. "But I won't stop you. Not when being a policeman makes you a hero . . . just like your grandpa Tom."

Tommy smiled, and they hugged again. Then for the next hour Tommy helped her hang ornaments on the tree. They sorted through the photo decorations and placed each one on just the right branch. The whole time, they talked about school and Annalee and Christmases past.

Reagan was sure she would remember this night forever.

And a thought occurred to her. Not only would her dad be proud of Tommy for wanting to be a police officer. He would be proud of her, too. For encouraging Tommy and affirming him. And for being brave enough to support him.

Brave . . . just like her daddy.

25

In the middle of the battle for her life, Annalee had looked forward to this day more than Christmas. It was the first Saturday in December and she and Tommy were going back to the zoo. Only they weren't on a double date this time.

Rather, the whole Baxter family and several others were coming together for a surprise they'd all been waiting for.

Dawson Gage was going to propose to Maddie!

Annalee wore leggings under her jeans, a turtleneck to go with her favorite winter coat, and her blond ponytail wig. Her mom stepped into her room just as Annalee finished getting ready. She stood there, studying Annalee. "You're so pretty, honey."

Annalee tilted her head. "Do you mean it?"

In the past, Annalee never would've asked that. She had been confident in her looks, not because she thought she was the most beautiful girl at church or school. But because she knew who she was on the inside. And that inner faith and peace and strength always shone through when she looked in the mirror.

But since her cancer diagnosis her eyes had looked sunken and dark. The kind of sick no makeup could hide.

Her mom came to her. "Yes, darling." She put her hand on Annalee's shoulder. "You're getting better. I can see it."

They wouldn't know until more than a month from now. After her final round of chemo and the scan that mattered most. For now, though, it was enough to know her mom thought she looked better.

They walked downstairs to the front room to wait for Tommy. Her mom sat across from her. "You're not too tired?"

"No." Annalee settled back into the sofa. She felt like she was floating. "I'm so happy for Maddie and Dawson. It's going to be the best day." She smiled. "Maddie has no idea."

"She knows you're all meeting up at the zoo, though, right?" Her mother raised her eyebrows.

"No." Annalee laughed. And for an instant she remembered how at her worst she couldn't even laugh without feeling tired. "Maddie thinks it's just her and Dawson. She has no idea."

The doorbell rang and Annalee looked over her shoulder. Tommy's black Jeep was out front. Right on time. The group was supposed to meet at the zoo entrance at noon and then walk together to the lion exhibit at 12:30. Annalee saw the handle of her wheelchair sticking out from his back window. He still had it from their time together yesterday.

Another sun break in this stormy season.

"Time to go." Annalee and her mother both stood.

Annalee kissed her mom's cheek and hugged her. It couldn't be easy for her mother to watch Annalee go to the zoo again. Not quite two weeks after she had come down with pneumonia her last time there. "Thanks." She smiled. "For always looking out for me."

Her mother nodded toward the door. "Tommy does a pretty good job, too."

"He does." Annalee's cheeks suddenly felt warmer than before. Because she adored Tommy. She couldn't wait to spend the day with him. She grabbed her gloves and scarf and a knit winter beanie from the end table.

"Annalee . . ." Her mom walked with her to the door. "You got so sick last time."

"You heard the doctor, Mom." She kept her tone kind, full of respect. "It would've happened if I'd been home. I had to have contracted the bacteria days earlier."

Her mother nodded. "True." She waited while her daughter opened the door for Tommy.

"Annalee." Tommy's eyes stayed on hers. "You look . . . breathtaking."

She hugged him. "Thank you." She turned and faced her mother. "Tell my mom you'll keep me warm."

Tommy laughed, but he looked nervous. Just like her mother. "I'll keep her warm. The whole time."

"There." She gave her mom one last hug. "See you in a few hours."

When they pulled away Annalee turned to him. "I can't imagine Maddie right now." She leaned her head back and stared at the sky. "She thinks it's a date at the zoo."

"Which"—Tommy chuckled—"shows you how much she loves the place. She works there, after all."

"I think it's beautiful." Annalee hadn't felt this carefree since September, before treatment began. "Maddie loves animals. I got that from our date last time. I really like her, Tommy. I mean . . . I've met her before, of course. But I know her so much better now. Her heart . . . her amazing story."

Tommy's eyes shone. "I mean . . . only God could've brought those two together."

Like other times since her cancer, they didn't spend the conversation talking about treatment and nausea and how many rounds remained. They both knew the answer. Just one. One more round of chemo and she'd be finished—for good, she believed. With every breath she trusted God for that.

Instead they talked about his classes and the finals he was studying for. Annalee had enough credits that the school had arranged for her to take the semester off. That way—if she was well enough—she could finish in the spring. Even if she had to take a few classes online over the summer, she would still graduate in May with Tommy and her class.

Typically the zoo was crowded on Saturday. Annalee and Tommy had been before. But today—with the clouds and the threat of snow, and with temperatures in the mid-thirties, the parking lot was practically empty. Tommy found a spot. "Looks like the perfect day for an engagement."

"They'll have the place to themselves. Amazing."
Annalee waited until he helped her from the passenger
side. She was still weak. Still unable to walk far without
the wheelchair. But she was getting stronger every day.
She could feel that, too.

Tommy had brought a thick blanket for the outing.
So in addition to Annalee's coat and gloves, scarf and hat,
once she was in the wheelchair Tommy tucked the
heaviest, softest blanket around her. She giggled. "We
could have a blizzard and I'd be warm."

"All right then." He sounded strong, confident. "Let's
get this show on the road."

They reached the front entrance and met up with
Tommy's uncle Dayne and aunt Katy and their kids.
Annalee hadn't met them yet, so Tommy made the introductions. Of course, she knew who Dayne Matthews
was, the famous actor who in the past ten years had been
making movies.

Tommy's aunt Katy put her hand on Annalee's
shoulder. "We've been praying for you." Her voice filled
with empathy. "You look wonderful, by the way."

"Thanks." Annalee stared up at Tommy and then
back to Katy. "I'm getting better. Definitely. And I have a
lot of love around me."

Tommy moved to her side and took her hand. "She's
easy to love."

Katy nodded. "I'm sure." She hugged Tommy. "The
two of you are the cutest."

More of the family arrived. Tommy's uncle Ryan and

aunt Kari and their kids. Also his uncle Landon and aunt Ashley and their kids—including Cole, who was home from Liberty University on Christmas break. Grandpa John and Grandma Elaine were here, too

Five minutes later Maddie's parents—Tommy's uncle Peter and aunt Brooke—hurried up. Maddie's mother carried a bouquet of white roses and hydrangeas, and her face was lit up with joy. Her daughter was getting engaged, after all.

For just a moment Annalee tried to imagine how her own mom might look at a time like this. Full of love and happiness, but also aware of the passing of time. The way Maddie's mother seemed to look right now.

Brooke was explaining why they were late and how the florist hadn't had the flowers ready like they were supposed to and how Peter had driven so fast that water sloshed out of the vase onto her pants. And everyone was laughing and talking and Annalee let the thrill of the moment wash over her.

She gazed at the sky. A hint of blue was breaking through the clouds. Exactly how she felt about her life.

Another few minutes passed and three people joined them. Tommy's grandpa John did the introductions. "Please say hello to Maddie's biological parents—Larry and Louise Quinn." Grandpa John's voice seemed choked by emotion. "And this"—he patted the other man's back—"is Dawson's father, David Gage." He grinned. "Today, we're all family."

At that, Maddie's parents, Peter and Brooke, and

their younger daughter, Hayley, approached the Quinns. According to Maddie, her real parents and her sister had never met her biological mom and dad. But she had expected they would one day.

This was that moment.

Annalee watched as the couples said a few words to each other and then Brooke and Louise Quinn embraced. For a long time. When they pulled away, both women were wiping tears.

Tommy leaned down and whispered near Annalee. "I can't imagine."

"Me, either." Annalee didn't look away from the two couples. To think the Quinns had given up a frozen embryo that had, years later, become the baby the Wests gave birth to. It was like something straight out of science fiction. Yet it wasn't. Because here—between the two sets of parents—was a love that could only be divine.

Finally Tommy's parents and his siblings rushed up the walkway out of breath. His mom tossed her hands and laughed. "Forgot my phone."

"We had to turn back." His dad gave a nervous laugh. "Lost ten minutes."

"But we're here now! And it's only twelve-twenty!" Tommy's mom waved at the group. "Hello, everyone! I see a few new faces."

More introductions and then Maddie's dad explained the situation. "Dawson asked us to wait till twelve-thirty." Peter looked at his watch. "Which is in one minute. Then we're supposed to stay together and head to the lion area." Peter went on to remind them that Maddie and Dawson had gotten here an hour earlier. "By now, they're probably watching the meerkats. Maddie loves those little guys."

"Here we go." Tommy bent down and kissed Annalee's cheek. "This will be one of the happiest moments in my cousin's life."

"I can't wait." Annalee felt a thrill as Tommy began to push her again. Slower this time, since they were in the middle of the group. Maddie had been engaged once before. To a longtime friend of hers. Connor something. A relationship that at first seemed like Annalee's and Tommy's.

But their dating days had always been a little off according to Maddie. Something she hadn't fully realized until she met Dawson. Apparently Connor was dating someone new now, too. Tommy said that Connor and Maddie had actually talked recently and they'd both agreed that their breakup was the best thing.

Hard as it had been.

The group reached the lions and Brooke's dad organized everyone to line up along the exhibit wall. As if they had never in all their lives been more intent on watching wild cats. Sitting in her chair lower than the rest of them, Annalee caught a glimpse of Dawson and Maddie walking their way.

Maddie didn't seem to notice the people crowded around the lion encounter. Dawson was grinning, talking to her about something Annalee couldn't hear. He walked Maddie to a spot just behind Peter. Then speaking in a louder voice he looked right in Maddie's eyes. "Maddie West . . . I have a surprise for you."

That was the cue they'd all been given. Those words.

And in a rush the group turned around and yelled, "Surprise."

Annalee had a front-row spot. Maddie put her gloved hands to her mouth and then looked up at Dawson. "What . . ." She turned to the group. "You're . . . you're all here!" Her eyes welled up.

Dawson couldn't stop smiling. He put his arm around her and drew her close. Then with gentle care he took off her gloves—one at a time—and slid them into her coat pocket.

Maddie made a sound that was more laugh than cry. "Dawson . . . what are you doing?"

Sunshine broke through the clouds and shone down on them as Dawson took Maddie's hands. "God alone could've dreamt this up, Maddie. This crazy, amazing story between us."

The crowd of family formed a half circle around them, so everyone could hear what Dawson was saying.

"You, Maddie." Dawson framed her face with his hands. Their chemistry made Annalee forget the winter cold. Dawson looked at Maddie for a long beat. "You are the one I've always prayed I'd find." He ran his hand over her hair. "And now you're here."

"Dawson . . ." Maddie put her hand on his. She seemed completely unaware of the rest of them. "What . . . what is this?"

"I found you and now . . ." He shook his head. "I don't want to spend a day of my life without you."

"Me, either." Her voice was softer than his. Like she was mesmerized by the magic of the moment.

Tommy took Annalee's hand and looked into her eyes. "One day," he whispered. "One day, Annalee."

Her heart felt light as air. *One day. Yes*, she wanted to tell him. This was all she wanted one day. When she was well and they were older and the time was right. But here all she did was nod and let her eyes do the talking. Then they both turned again to the beaming couple before them.

Dawson took a step back and dropped to one knee. From his peacoat, he pulled out a velvet box and opened it.

Again Maddie put her hands over her mouth as happy tears slid down her cheeks. "Dawson!" She danced in place a few seconds and squealed.

Suddenly one of the lions let out a ground-trembling roar. So loud Dawson couldn't have been heard if he shouted.

He laughed and lowered the box. For a second he looked down and shook his head and then, as the lion quieted, Dawson's eyes found Maddie's again. "Have I mentioned that I love how this is your favorite place? The zoo?"

Everyone laughed, and Maddie covered her face for a moment, her tears and laughter mingling in the most happy way.

In a heartbeat, the moment grew intimate again. Dawson took her hand once more and held up the ring. The diamond glistened in the sun. He smiled. "I've asked your parents and my dad . . . and I've asked our God above. Now . . . the only one left to ask is you." He hesitated. "Maddie West . . . will you marry me?"

"Yes!" Maddie danced in place again as Dawson rose to his feet. He took hold of her face and she settled down. Fresh tears spilled from her eyes. "Yes, Dawson Gage. A million times yes."

He kissed her. A kiss that made Annalee catch her breath.

The small crowd seemed lost in the moment as the couple kissed again. As if the sheer beauty of the passion and romance between Dawson and Maddie was something that made time stand still. And after a few seconds they all burst into applause.

"Way to go, Maddie," Tommy shouted.

And the rest of the family added their congratulations, too. The next half hour was full of hugs and pictures, and eventually all the parents took a photo together. When finally it was time for Tommy to take her home, Annalee could only hope that someday—if the Lord allowed—the moment that had just played out wouldn't belong to someone else.

It would belong to her and Tommy.

26

The five o'clock Christmas Eve candlelight service was exactly what Tommy needed. After their beautiful day at the zoo watching Dawson propose to Maddie, Annalee had gone in for another round of chemo. Now she was struggling with a low blood count, so she was back in the hospital tonight with her parents.

And Tommy was here at church with his family. Believing God. Trusting Him with every heartbeat.

This night was one of his favorite moments of the holidays. Sitting next to his parents and Malin and Johnny, soaking in the wonder of that first long-ago Christmas Eve.

Typically Pastor Dell Johnson would read from the Bible about Mary and Joseph and Bethlehem and they would sing "Hark the Herald" and "Angels We Have Heard on High," and Tommy's heart would fill with gratitude. That God had allowed him to be in this family, and that he had his health and his friends and his team. And Annalee. For the last three years she'd also been part of the reason he was thankful on this night.

But tonight after Pastor Dell read the Christmas

story, the man closed his Bible and looked long at the congregation. The place was packed—like usual on Christmas Eve and Easter Sunday. All generations gathered together, each person holding an unlit candle.

The pastor came a few steps closer to the edge of the stage. He was a fit man probably in his forties, born in Vietnam. He and his family had been at this church for twenty years. He took a deep breath. "Tonight . . . I want you to really think about Mary and Joseph. What it must've been like that Bethlehem night so long ago."

His voice grew soft and a hush fell over the room. "Just a couple kids following orders, showing up for a population count." He hesitated. "Mary's in labor. Joseph, scrambling for a place where the baby could be born."

Tommy noticed people sitting taller in their pews. Listening more intently. Even the children quieted down.

"You think they weren't scared to death?" He sauntered toward the far end of the stage. "Never mind that God had placed a baby in Mary . . . or the fact that they'd both been visited by angels. They were young and unmarried, about to have a child in a city with no room." He paused and looked the other direction. "They were scared to death."

Never had Tommy thought about the story like this. Mary and Joseph might've been the same age as Annalee and him. Just a couple of kids, young and in love and so afraid they could barely think straight.

Pastor Dell was walking closer again. "Here's what I want you to take away from this story tonight." He smiled. "Yes, Mary and Joseph were scared. They didn't know what was coming next. But . . ." He spread his arms out. "They trusted God. In their weakest moment, they trusted Him. And so they kept walking. Kept seeking God's plan. Kept believing. And by nightfall they weren't afraid any longer." He paused. "They were parents."

A chill ran down Tommy's arms. He looked at his mom and dad and saw their eyes glistening, their attention glued to the pastor.

Then the man went on to say something Tommy would remember forever.

"We're all afraid of something. We're human. But tonight God wants us to lay our fears at the foot of the manger. The way Mary and Joseph did. And do this . . ." He moved to the center of the stage and peered across the dark room. "Keep walking. Keep seeking His plan. And keep believing." He grinned. "The miracle you're waiting for might be closer than you think."

Tommy closed his eyes and let Pastor Dell's words fill him one more time. *The miracle you're waiting for might be closer than you think.* He could hardly wait to share that with Annalee later tonight.

Ushers came down the aisles then and lit the candle at the end of each row. Each small white candle had a plastic receptacle at the base so the melted wax wouldn't drip. Tommy watched his dad light his mother's candle. Then she lit Tommy's and he passed the flame on to Malin, who lit Johnny's.

In the time it took them to do that, a warm glow pierced the room and rose from the congregation. *The way we're supposed to shine in this world*, Tommy thought. Then—the way they did every year—Pastor Dell led them in an a cappella round of "Silent Night." This time, as they began to sing, the words hit Tommy differently.

"Silent night, holy night, all is calm . . . all is bright." Hope welled inside Tommy's soul. All was calm and bright because Mary and Joseph trusted God to get them through an impossible situation. That was the only reason.

"Shepherds quake . . . at the sight." The song grew and filled the church. "Glories stream from heaven afar . . . Christ, the Savior, is born . . . Christ, the Savior, is born."

His family's voices around him made Tommy smile as the song played out. "Jesus, Lord, at thy birth. Jesus, Lord, at thy birth."

The truth of the song had never meant so much. Tommy let the words breathe encouragement through his anxious heart. It was up to him this Christmas Eve to keep walking, keep seeking God . . . keep believing. And if he did . . . if he did then he wouldn't have to be afraid any longer.

Just like Mary and Joseph.

When the service was over, and they were on their way out to the parking lot, Tommy walked behind his parents. They held hands, smiling at each other. Laughing about something Tommy couldn't quite hear.

And a thought hit him. His parents had spent the last few months afraid, too. At least his mother. She hadn't wanted him to be a police officer, but not because she didn't honor and respect the badge and uniform.

Because she was scared to death.

And now . . . after taking one step after another in faith, his parents weren't just okay. They looked more in love than ever. Tommy put his arm around Malin on one side of him and Johnny on the other. Then he nodded to their parents. "It's going to be a beautiful Christmas."

Malin seemed to understand. "Ever since they went dancing, they haven't stopped smiling."

"Because . . ." Tommy smiled at her. "They never stopped believing."

TOMMY HAD DRIVEN separately to the Christmas Eve service. If the best part about Christmas was the giving, then tonight figured to be a blast. He had a number of deliveries to make before he would go home and wrap gifts for his family.

Tonight was the Christmas party for IMPD officers stuck working December 24. Tommy had heard about the event from Officer Raul. The man wasn't quite back to work yet, but he planned to be there tonight. "Wouldn't miss this," he had told Tommy.

"Tell you what." Tommy had thought of the idea mid-phone call. "I'll bring chicken sandwiches. The way your mom did when you were in the hospital."

The men and women on the Indianapolis force loved Chick-fil-A. So that was Tommy's first stop. He had ordered thirty sandwiches and a bucket of fries. Other people were bringing dessert and salad. But Tommy's part was a surprise.

His food was ready, lined up across the back counter when he walked in. Tommy paid for it and drove across town to the police station. The air outside was freezing, with snow expected tomorrow. He grabbed the bags and an oversized plastic container of his mom's Christmas snowball cookies, and jogged inside.

Raul was waiting for him. "Tommy, look at you. All dressed up!" He opened the door. "Suit pants and a tie!"

Tommy grinned. "Christmas Eve service! You'll have to come with me some week!"

"You know"—Raul took two bags from Tommy and led him into the building and through two security doors—"I think I'd like that."

Inside the break room a couple dozen police officers were milling about, laughing, celebrating. A few of them wore Santa hats and three had blinking Christmas light necklaces. "Tommy!" Officer Conway stepped out of the group and came to him. "Let me help you." He took the other bags and set them on the table.

Tommy opened the cookie container. "Had to share my mom's favorites!"

"These sandwiches, though!" Raul set the other bags down. "You must know someone at Chick-fil-A!"

A female officer clapped. "Christmas just came early."

"Tommy Baxter, everyone!" Raul pointed both hands at him. "Tell 'em what you told me."

When everyone had quieted down, Tommy looked around the room. These were the men and women keeping him and his family safe. He spotted Officer Green. Yes, these were the ones who had literally saved his parents' lives. "I brought dinner to thank you. All of you."

"No one does that, Baxter." Officer Conway gave him a thumbs-up.

"Well." Tommy grinned at Raul. "You've let me ride along with you way longer than I should've." He shifted his attention to Officer Green. "And you make life safer. For my family. For everyone in Indianapolis." He put his hands in his pockets. "So this is me saying thanks . . . and merry Christmas!"

Tommy stayed long enough to eat a chicken sandwich and chat with Raul. Then he was on his way again. More stops. More people to see. In the backseat he had a wrapped gift for Annalee. But his plan for tonight included more than a Christmas present.

He drove to the nearest Walmart and practically ran inside. Annalee had been on his heart all day and he couldn't wait to see her. But he didn't want to show up without this one special item. The perfect one was at the back of the store. Tommy bought it, and headed for the hospital.

Arms full, Tommy entered her room. Annalee was lying flat in bed, and her parents were in chairs beside her. "What's this?" She lifted her head and a slight smile brightened her face. "A Christmas tree? For me?"

"Yes." Tommy set the tree on the table next to her bed. "I can't let my best girl spend Christmas Eve at the hospital without a tree." He leaned over the bed and kissed her forehead. "How are you, love?"

She smiled with her eyes. "Tired."

"A tree?" Annalee's mom was on her feet, her arm around Tommy. "That's so thoughtful."

Her dad joined them on Tommy's other side. "This hospital room needed a little Christmas green."

Tommy looked back at Annalee. "She deserves it."

Annalee's dad nudged his wife. "Let's get coffee." It was nearly eight o'clock. He looked at Tommy. "Austin joined us earlier. He brought us all salmon and rice. Now he's at a friend's house."

"Glad you had time together." Annalee had wanted this evening with her family. Now Tommy waved to her parents as they left the room.

"They're so sweet." Annalee's voice was weaker than it had been since the beginning. "They always let us have our time."

"I know." He was still standing at her bed. "Otherwise I'd have to wheel your bed down the hall so we could talk."

"Tommy." She laughed and made a face. "You don't mean that."

"No." He took her hand and slid his fingers between hers. "I love your parents. But I don't think I'd have this conversation in front of them."

"True." She turned her head on the pillow. "I wish I felt better."

"What is it . . . nausea?" He pulled the chair as close to the bed as he could and sat down. Then he lowered the bed rail. Nothing was going to stand between them tonight.

"No, not like before." She shrugged one slim shoulder. "I just feel weak. My platelets are off." Her smile faded. "I'm glad it's the last round."

"And in a month you'll know the good news. No Evidence of Disease." This cancer thing had challenged Tommy's faith like nothing in all his life. But God was here. He was with them, even now.

Tonight all he could do was try to make her laugh. Hold her cold hands and tell her it was all going to be okay. Even when the fear breathing down on him tonight was just like Pastor Dell had talked about. Enough to consume him.

He still didn't understand why God would let Annalee go through this. Or how come she wasn't feeling stronger today. Shouldn't the treatment keep her moving in that direction? Was this a setback? Tommy closed his eyes for a moment. *Please, God, don't let it be a setback.*

"I'm glad you're here." She was watching him. Almost like she wanted him to say something, do something that might help her feel better. Something to pep her up and breathe strength back into her.

But he had nothing. Nothing but his faith.

Not on Christmas Eve sitting next to a cheap three-foot evergreen tree with Annalee stuck in a hospital bed fighting cancer. Not when he felt like hanging his head and crying for days over the situation. *How can I help her, God? Tell me, please?*

Then Tommy remembered the other gift. The one he was more excited about. He had bought it two weeks ago and put it together after Dawson and Maddie's proposal. The bag was beside him, so he reached inside and eased out the gift. So he wouldn't mess up the bow.

Tommy didn't know much about wrapping, so his mom had helped him. "Always use a bow," she had told him.

His gift wrapping wouldn't win any prizes. But as he handed the small package to Annalee, her whole face lit up. "More?"

"The tree was just . . . like Christmas flowers. That wasn't your gift, silly."

She took hold of her bed remote and raised the back up till she was in a sitting position. "Can you . . . adjust my pillow, please? It keeps sliding down."

Tommy had been here other days when Annalee could raise her own pillow. More proof of how weak she was. He did as she asked and then he remained standing near her bed. "Want me to help open it?"

"I think I can get it." She slid her finger under one end of the red and gold paper. Then her hand fell to the bed. A few seconds and she lifted one more flap. "What is wrong with me?" Annalee rarely sounded frustrated, but here . . . neither of them could understand this.

Panic seized him and he struggled to draw a full breath. *Please, God, don't let it be a setback.* He cleared his throat. "Here." He took it from her. "It's probably my wrapping. I made it ironclad." He shrugged. "I'm a guy. What can I say?"

She laughed. "There *was* a lot of tape."

"Exactly." Of course he had no trouble opening it. Inside the wrapping was a small box. But not a velvet one. He wasn't sure if she'd be strong enough to open it, but he wasn't taking any chances. No need to frustrate her. He popped the lid and handed the box to her. "Here, love."

The moment she saw what was inside she gasped. "Tommy! I love it!" She eased the necklace from the box and it dangled in front of her. It was a simple vintage gold chain with a small heart locket. He had bought it at an antiques store. She looked at him. "It's beautiful."

"Open it." As soon as he said the words, he changed his mind. Better for her to save her energy. He gently took it from her fingers and opened the tiny heart. Inside was a photo of him and Annalee on Karon Beach. His favorite from the trip. And next to it, on the other side, was a tiny Scripture reference.

JEREMIAH
29:11

This was the part of the gift he was most excited about. He handed it back to her and this time she smiled bigger than at any time tonight. "I can't believe this." She studied the locket. "I love that pic."

"It's us." He put his hand on her shoulder and tried not to notice how bony it felt. "Remember that day? We were both laughing at something your brother said, and your dad took the picture. Beach in the background, sun on our faces. Laughing like there was nothing tomorrow could do to take our joy."

"Mmm. You're the poet, Tommy Baxter. You should be a writer." She turned her eyes to him again. "There still isn't anything. That could steal our joy."

"Which is why I chose that picture. To help you remember . . ." He gritted his teeth. "When . . . when it's tough." *On nights like this,* he wanted to say. But he couldn't get the words out. He couldn't break down. Not here. Not tonight. *Help me stay strong for her, God. Please, help me.*

"And the Bible verse." Her smile looked almost angelic. Annalee's beautiful smile. "My favorite."

"Yes." He leaned closer, brushing his fingers across her forehead. "'For I know the plans I have for you,' declares the Lord. 'Plans to give you hope and a future.'" He took hold of her hand again. "'And not to harm you.'"

"Tommy." She held the locket to her heart. "I love it. I'll wear it always."

He thought for a minute. "Except probably not when you play tennis." With his free hand he made an exaggerated motion of an imaginary locket swinging from side to side.

She laughed out loud. "Oh . . . so not when I play tennis, then?"

"No." He tapped his temple. Like he was racking his

brain. "And maybe not when you're swimming." He nodded at the locket. "Because the picture and . . . well,
water. You know."

Again she laughed, and the sound was richer than
any Christmas carol that night. "You're so funny." She
made a mock serious face. "Okay. Not when I play tennis
and not when I swim."

"Because you love those things." He raised his brow
at her.

"I do, Tommy." Her laughter dropped off and the air
between them changed. "I do."

And suddenly there was no way he could stop the
tears that filled his eyes. Not just because she couldn't
do those things now. But because of her words. Soft
words spoken with the voice he loved more than any in
the world.

I do.

"One day . . ." He took the locket from her and set it
on the table near the little tree. Then he sat on the edge
of her bed and drew her close. So she was in his arms the
way he'd been wanting her to be since he got here. He
took her face in his hands and let himself get lost in her
eyes. "One day those are the only words I want to hear
you say, Annalee. I do."

He kissed her cheek. "And I'll say them, too. And we
won't be in this cold, gray . . . hospital room. We'll be in
front of our family and friends and you'll be the most
beautiful bride ever." He wiped a tear from her cheek.
"And I'll be yours and you'll be mine."

"That was my dream." She searched his eyes. "That day in the scan."

"About our wedding?" Hope warmed his heart. "Really?"

"Yes." She put her hand on his face. They stayed that way for half a minute. "I wish . . . you could kiss me."

A quick breath stopped him from acting on the sudden impulse. He couldn't kiss her. No matter how much he wanted to, he wouldn't. She was too weak, too susceptible to germs.

Instead his smile came easily. "Well . . ." He traced her cheekbone with his thumb. "Now you know. It's my dream, too."

He held her then, until they heard her parents returning. Once more he kissed her cheek, and then he whispered near her lips. The lips he wanted so badly to kiss. "Get better, Annalee. Get stronger."

As her parents entered the room he stayed there. Then he motioned them close and he prayed for her. That God would make clear the good plans He had for her, and that she would get stronger. By morning.

She couldn't wear the locket yet because of the port in her chest. But one day . . . one day soon. *Please, God, one day.* He leaned near her face one last time. "Merry Christmas, love."

"Merry Christmas."

And with that Tommy thanked her parents for the time, bid them goodbye and left her hospital room. On the way to the elevator he could barely see through his tears. What if the cancer was getting worse? Why would she be so weak?

Then as he made his way out of the hospital he realized something. He blinked so he could see better. This was exactly what Pastor Dell had been talking about. Okay, so he was afraid. The odds were against them and he couldn't do anything about it.

But he could do this. He could keep walking to his car, keep seeking God from now until Christmas dawned and every day after. And, like Mary and Joseph, he could keep believing.

That most of all.

27

Annalee had her answer.

A month had passed since Christmas and now she and her parents had just gotten back from the doctor. He had gone over her results and explained everything. And then he left them alone. Annalee and her parents had clung to each other, talking about what the news meant and what they would do next.

They had prayed together and then they had come home.

Now she had to tell Tommy.

Her text was short and to the point. *I know, Tommy. Can you pick me up? Please?*

His response was immediate. *I'm on my way.*

Her parents were in the kitchen, still talking about the results, no doubt. They knew Annalee needed time to process, time to get her mind around everything that came with this news. They always knew just how to handle things. This whole time since she first got sick, any doubts or frustrations toward God, they'd kept between themselves.

Annalee stared out the window at the barren trees.

January had never been her favorite month. Christmas was over and summer was a million days away. At least it seemed that way. But here, Annalee was struck by the trees. Every tree out front was bare, stripped of its leaves. Snow covered the ground from last week's storm, and bits of it still clung to the trees.

Look at them, God. She narrowed her eyes. As far as a tree knew, its branches would never bear leaves again. Yet outside her front window, every one of those branches was raised straight to heaven.

Then she remembered a Bible verse she'd read this morning. Before her one-month doctor appointment. It was from Isaiah 55. *The mountains and hills will burst into song before you, and all the trees of the field will clap their hands.*

And wasn't that what the trees were doing right now? The branches moving against each other in the winter breeze? *There's a lesson here,* Annalee thought. If the trees could praise God in the middle of winter, so could she. For so many things and for her energy. A month away from chemo and she definitely felt stronger. She didn't need a wheelchair.

Tommy's Jeep pulled up. Annalee wrapped her scarf around her neck and slipped on her gloves. She already wore her warmest coat and hat. "Bye," she yelled to her parents.

They both joined her in the living room. Their eyes were still swollen with tears. "Stay warm."

"I will." She nodded. "Thanks for letting me go."

"Don't be long." Her dad's tone was serious. "Just half an hour."

"Okay." A quick wave and she stepped out to meet him. The boy she loved with all her heart. The one who had been by her side through every day of this journey. And the one who deserved to hear her test results before any more time went by.

Despite the snow it wasn't cold today. Not really.

Tommy helped her into the car and the minute he was behind the wheel he looked at her. "Can you tell me?"

"Take me to our spot." Her tone was kind. But she couldn't tell him here. In his car. "Please, Tommy."

He didn't ask again, and she didn't have to tell him which spot. He began driving to White River Park as if he could read her mind and heart all at the same time.

Annalee leaned back into her seat and closed her eyes. The news swirled in her mind. This would change everything. She turned the radio to K-Love and let the song wash over her. It was one that had played when everyone gathered to cut her hair. A song about the titles God wore: *Way maker. Miracle worker. Promise keeper. Light in the darkness* . . . Annalee felt His peace come over her. *Yes, Lord, You are all of that.* Annalee hugged herself. God was with her. He was with them both.

Now more than ever before.

She could feel His holy presence here in Tommy's car and in her heart and soul.

Tommy parked at the lot near the swings. The basketball court here had been shoveled so it didn't require any extra walking. It gave them somewhere to stand. So she could look him in the face and tell him what she knew.

What they'd waited all these months to find out.

Once they were out of the Jeep, he took her to a spot on the asphalt. Near a trio of small evergreen trees. More privacy, which was a good thing today. Tommy's coach had allowed him to take off practice today. He'd been waiting at home with his phone since 2:30. An hour had passed since then.

Finally Tommy faced her. He took both her gloved hands in his. "No." She shook her head. "I want to feel your fingers against mine. Would that be okay?"

"Of course." They took off their gloves and Tommy gently worked his fingers between hers. "Tell me, Annalee. I need to know."

She wouldn't make him wait any longer. "Tommy . . . we prayed so much. But . . . I didn't expect *this*." No winter cold could dim the love she felt for him. The way she never wanted to leave him. Her eyes got lost in his for a few seconds. And then she did something that tipped him off to the results.

Annalee smiled.

"Wait . . . Love, tell me." He started to shake. Even his fingers trembled. "What did the doctor say?"

"The cancer is gone, Tommy." A quiet laugh took her by surprise. As if the joy inside her had a life of its own. "No Evidence of Disease. NED."

"What?" He leaned his head back and shouted. "Annalee are you serious?" Tommy searched her eyes. Desperate to know for sure. "Tell me it's true!"

"It's true." She laughed louder this time. Yes, she would have follow-up appointments—probably for the rest of her life. And she still had to take it easy until her strength fully returned. But she was healed. That's all that mattered. She put her hands on his shoulders. "Can you believe it, Tommy? God did it. He healed me." She raised both hands. "I beat cancer!"

Tommy stepped back and dropped to his knees. Right there on the frozen ground. "God, thank You. I'll never have enough words. Thank You for this." He scrambled back to his feet, then he pulled her close and picked her up. "Annalee Miller!" He shouted her name across the empty park. "You're cancer-free!"

As he set her down something happened that took Annalee's breath.

It began to snow.

Big chunky white snowflakes drifted down around them, landing in their hair and on their eyelashes. Annalee had worn her wig with the blond hair down today. It kept her neck warmer. Already a bit of fuzz had grown back on her head. But it would be a while before she had actual hair.

The snow was sticking to Tommy's cheeks and eyebrows. He had never looked more handsome. She framed his face with her hands. "I missed the winter dance." She was so close she could feel his breath against her skin. "You know that, right?"

He pressed the side of his face against hers. "Yes . . ." His voice was soft and marked by the miracle of the moment. "I seem to remember missing that."

She looked at him. "Would you dance with me now, Tommy? Could you?"

The smile on his face had never wavered, not since she told him the news. "Why yes, my princess." He stepped back and twirled her, just once slow and steady. As if he knew not to push the limits. Then he linked his hands at the back of her waist and swayed with her. "Do you hear the music?"

Her senses filled with the presence of him. "Yes." She blinked the snowflakes from her eyelashes. Mixed in the melody of the slight wind in the evergreen branches was a song of hope and praise and love . . . because they were here and she was whole and it was snowing. And Tommy Baxter was dancing with her. She looped her arms around his neck and moved just a little closer.

Tommy's eyes locked on hers and the world fell away. "Is it okay"—his voice was a whisper—"if I kiss you?"

Another quiet laugh came from deep in her heart. "That's all I want. In all the world."

And as the snow fell harder, as they danced on the basketball court at White River Park, Tommy kissed her. "Mmm, love. You're healed."

"And I'm going to make that app, Tommy." She looked deep at him. "I'm going to help those kids."

"I know. You will."

His body was warm against hers and Annalee savored the feeling. Everything about him, his kiss and his presence, his kindness . . . all of it was intoxicating. Tommy was whole and strong and he was hers. That alone gave her hope. "I've dreamed of this day." She drew her head back and smiled at him. "I can't believe it."

"Not me." He chuckled, and his eyes saw straight through her. "I believed the whole time." They both knew that wasn't true. But she appreciated his positivity. Always showing her his bravest face throughout her fight.

"I love you, Annie." With a feather-soft touch, he worked his fingers along the sides of her neck to the back of her head and he kissed her again. A kiss that told Annalee the depth of his feelings.

And how important this hour was in the story of their lives.

Annalee closed her eyes as they kissed once more. "I love you, Frank." Neither of them knew what tomorrow held. Not for Tommy after he got his badge or for her at those future scans. But they had this beautiful day, shining like a diamond. So she would thank God for every minute. For the answers this morning and the hope the news would breathe into her every tomorrow.

And she would ask God that one day in the not too

distant future, the dance might be indoors in front of everyone they loved. And she wouldn't be wearing a winter coat.

But a wedding dress.

IF SOMEONE WOULD'VE woken him up, Tommy wouldn't have been surprised. Everything about this moment felt like a dream. He pulled her close and swayed with her, his cheek against hers.

He had dreamed of this day, but he had been terrified of it, also. Putting one foot in front of the other. Always seeking God. Always believing. Like Mary and Joseph. He ran his hand over her hair. And yes . . . Annalee had told him to think of the wig as her hair. "It's mine," she had told him. And so it was.

Soon he had to get her home. She was cancer-free, but she needed to be careful. Take her time regaining her strength. He faced her. "This is real . . . right?"

"Yes." Her eyes sparkled brighter than the snow. "As real as us."

Again he held her close and this time he closed his eyes. How differently this day could've gone? He hadn't wanted to think about it, but sometimes—in the dark of night—his fears would wake him. Leave him gasping for air, his heart racing.

Like the night when the ice broke and Annalee disappeared in the freezing water.

He shuddered and let the image go. That wasn't happening. The ground beneath their feet was solid and she was dancing in his arms. She had no evidence of disease! And to celebrate the fact, God had given them this gentle snow. Falling all around them, landing on their faces and reminding them of His power.

His beauty.

His morning.

No matter how dark the night had been.

Tommy breathed in the sweet smell of her. He never wanted to let go, but in these last minutes before he took her back to her house, he etched the memory of this time forever in his heart. So he could remember it some far-off day when he was wearing a badge and the worst call came in and he was running toward the bad guys.

And when he would take her to the hospital for yet another scan and he would sit in the waiting room, praying and pacing and wishing with all his heart she'd finish, already. So they could get another clean report and go on with their lives.

So that when the hard times came—whatever they were—he could remember to keep walking . . . keep seeking . . . keep believing. So that this moment with Annalee would get him through whatever was ahead . . . every time.

He smiled and kissed her once more. Then he led her to his Jeep again.

Somewhere in time not yet lived, he would remember today. On a very special tomorrow that he believed would come in the next few years. A moment he knew would happen because he would pray it would happen. And whenever he was afraid of the future, he would just keep walking. God was in the lead, after all. They were just following Him.

And in that beautiful once upon a time still to come, before their first dance, he would remember this one. Here at White River Park at the end of January.

The day God gave him Annalee Miller back.

It would be the best day of his life. Their wedding day. And they would live and love and laugh till the end of time. Because their life together would never be ordinary. Rather the years would be unforgettable. The way the two of them already were.

Tommy and Annalee.

A love story for the ages.

Forever and ever, amen.

ACKNOWLEDGMENTS

A book doesn't appear in your hands without an entire team taking part in the process. A team of passionate, determined people working behind the scenes on a dozen levels. On that note, I can't leave this novel and the deeply emotional journey it's been without thanking the people who made it possible.

First, a special thanks to my amazing Simon & Schuster publishing team, including the keenly talented Libby McGuire, Trish Todd, Suzanne Donahue, , Lisa Sciambra, Paula Amendolara, and Dana Trocker, along with the rest of my gifted S&S team! I think often of our times together in New York and the way your collective creative brilliance always becomes a game changer. And to Carolyn Reidy, I miss you dearly. Your passing came far too soon, but I will do as you asked. I will keep writing the best possible book God places on my heart. To everyone at Simon & Schuster, you clearly desire to raise the bar at every turn. Thank you for that. It's an honor to work with you!

Also thanks to Rose Garden Creative, my design team—Kyle and Kelsey Kupecky—whose unmatched talent in the industry is recognized from Los Angeles to New York. Very simply you are the best in the business! My website, social media, video trailers and newsletter—along with so many other aspects of my touring and writing—are top of the book business because of you two. Thank you for working your own dreams around mine. I love you and I thank God for you every single day.

A huge thanks to my sisters, Tricia and Susan, along with my mom, Anne. You give your whole hearts to helping me love my readers. Tricia, as my executive assistant for twelve years; and Susan, as the president of my Facebook Online Book Club and Team KK. And, Mom, thank you for being Queen of the Readers. Anyone who has ever sent me an email and received a response from "Karen's mom" is blessed indeed. The three of you are making a tremendous impact in changing this world for the better. Love you and I thank God for you always!

Thanks also to Tyler for joining with me to write screenplays and books like *Best Family Ever* and *Finding Home*—the Baxter Family Children books. You are a gifted writer, Ty. I can't wait to see more of your work on the shelves and on the screen. Maybe one day soon! Love you so much!

Also, thank you to my office assistant, Aurora Galvin. You create space for me to write! My storytelling wouldn't be possible without you.

I'm also grateful to my Team KK members, who step in at the final stage in writing a book. The galley pages come to me, and I send them to several of my most dedicated reader friends. My nieces Shannon Fairley, Melissa Viernes and Kristen Kane. Also Hope Burke, Donna Keene, Renette Steele, Zac Weikal and Sheila Holman. You are my volunteer test team! It always amazes me, the typos you catch at the final hour. Thank you for loving my work, and thanks for your availability to read my novels first and fast.

Also, my books only happen with the help of my family, especially my amazing husband, Donald. Honey, thank you for your spiritual wisdom and leadership in our home, and thanks for talking through books like this one from outline to the editing. The countless ways you help me when I'm on deadline make all the difference. I love you!

And over all this, thanks to a man who has believed in my career for two decades, my amazing agent, Rick Christian of Alive Literary Agency. From the beginning, Rick, you've told me to dream big, set my sights high. Movies, TV series, worldwide reach. All for God and through Him. You imagined it, believed it and prayed for it alongside me and my family. You saw it. You still do! While I write, you work behind the scenes on film projects and my future books, the Baxter family TV series, and details regarding every word I've ever written. You are brilliant and driven, compassionate and dedicated. I used to dream of having you as my agent. Now Tyler and I are the only authors who do. God is amazing. Thank you, Rick, and thank you for praying for me and my family. That most of all.

ACKNOWLEDGMENTS

Finally, my greatest thanks to God Almighty, who is First and Last and all things in between. I write for You, through You and because of You. Thank you with my whole being.

Dear Reader Friend,

It seems so often when I write a book, real life is turning similar pages in the story of my life. That was the case with *Truly, Madly, Deeply*. As I was breathing the story of Tommy onto the pages, my youngest son, Austin, was talking more seriously about being a police officer.

Yes, I watched a thousand episodes of *Cops* with that boy and yes, I do think high school kids should have to watch a full season before they graduate. If for nothing more than to help them make good choices and appreciate the role of law enforcement in our cities and towns. So they can see that police officers have one of the toughest jobs around.

Also as in the book you just read, Austin was told by our local department that he should finish college before applying. If he applies.

People often ask me how I get my ideas. Well, there you have it! Life has a way of making some novels a little easier to write. Which is why *Truly, Madly, Deeply* is as much about love as it is about something we all battle.

Fear.

Each of us knows all too well the late nights worrying about a loved one, or the fallout after that fateful phone call. Anxiety creeps in and we sometimes become paralyzed. Yes, I loved the story of Tommy and Annalee. I laughed with them and cried with them.

But given my situation in life with Austin, my favorite part was this: It let me work through my fears and let them go. Jesus told us to think about today. That's all we're promised, and of course we all know that. But it's so easy to borrow trouble from tomorrow. Most often that trouble never materializes, and we have wasted a perfectly good today being afraid for nothing.

I feel more at peace for the journey of *Truly, Madly, Deeply*, and I hope you do, too.

As you close the cover on this book, do me a favor. Think about who you can share it with. A friend or a sister. Your mother or a coworker. The librarian at your child's school. Someone struggling to make sense of a loss or someone who needs encouragement, hope or simply a good love story. Maybe just a person who loves to read.

Remember, a story dies if it is left on the shelf. So please pass this one on.

By now you may have heard about the TV series— *The Baxters*. This was something I only dreamed about back when God gave me those very special characters. The series has the material to go on for a very long time, so look for it soon. I know you'll love it like the rest of us do.

To find out more about *The Baxters* on TV or any of my other books, television series, or movies, visit my website, www.KarenKingsbury.com. There you can enter your email address to sign up for my free weekly newsletter. I make my big announcements on my newsletter first! These emails come straight to you and with my blogs and devotions, event updates and a little something to encourage you.

Like I said, the biggest news will always be on my newsletter first, so sign up today!

At my website, you can also find out how to stay encouraged with me on social media or at one of my events.

Finally, if you are seeking a faith like that of the Baxter family, find a Bible-believing church and get connected. There is a reason you came across this book. Remember, the Baxters are not just my family. They are yours. And because of that, we are all connected. Until next time . . . I'm praying for you.

Thanks for being part of the family.

Love you all!

THE BAXTER FAMILY: YESTERDAY AND TODAY

For some of you, this is your first time with the Baxter family. Please know you don't have to read any other Baxter books to read this one. Like my other recent titles, *Truly, Madly, Deeply* stands alone! But if you read this and want to start at the beginning, the starting place is my book *Redemption*.

That's where the adventure of the Baxters begins.

Whether you've known the Baxters for years or are just meeting them now, here's a quick summary of the family, their kids and their ages. Also, because these characters are fictional, I've taken some liberty with their ages. Let's just assume these are their current ages.

Now, let me introduce you to—or remind you of—the Baxter family:

. . .

THE BAXTERS BEGAN in Bloomington, Indiana, and most of the family still lives there today.

The Baxter house is on ten acres outside of town, with a winding creek that runs through the backyard. It has a wraparound porch, a pretty view and memories of a lifetime of love and laughter. John and Elizabeth Baxter moved into when their children were young. They raised their family here. Today it is owned by one of their daughters—Ashley—and her husband, Landon Blake. It is still the place where the extended Baxter family gathers for special celebrations.

. . .

DR. JOHN BAXTER: John is the patriarch of the Baxter family. Formerly an emergency room doctor and professor of medicine at Indiana University, he's now retired. John's first wife, Elizabeth, died long ago from a recurrence of cancer. Years later, John married Elaine, and the two live in Bloomington.

. . .

DAYNE MATTHEWS: Dayne is the oldest son of John and Elizabeth. Dayne was born out of wedlock and given up for adoption at birth. His adoptive parents died in a small plane crash when he was 18. Years later, Dayne became a very visible and popular movie star. At age 30, he hired an attorney to find his birth parents—John and Elizabeth Baxter. He had a moment with Elizabeth in the hospital before she died, and years later he connected with the rest of his biological family. Dayne is married to Katy. The couple has three children: Sophie, 10; Egan, 8; and Blaise, 6. They are very much part of the Baxter family, and they split time between Los Angeles and Bloomington.

• • •

DR. BROOKE BAXTER WEST: Brooke is a pediatrician in Bloomington, married to Peter West, also a doctor. The couple has two daughters: Maddie, 22, and Hayley, 19. The family experienced a tragedy when Hayley suffered a near-drowning at age 3. She recovered miraculously, but still has disabilities caused by the incident.

• • •

KARI BAXTER TAYLOR: Kari is a designer, married to Ryan Taylor, football coach at Clear Creek High School. The couple has three children: Jessie, 19; RJ, 13; and Annie, 10. Kari had a crush on Ryan when the two were in middle school. They dated through college, and then broke up over a misunderstanding. Kari married a man she met in college, Tim Jacobs, but some years into their marriage he had an affair. The infidelity resulted in his murder at the hands of a stalker. The tragedy devastated Kari, who was pregnant at the time with their first child, Jessie. Ryan came back into her life around the same time, and years later he and Kari married. They live in Bloomington.

• • •

ASHLEY BAXTER BLAKE: Ashley is the former black sheep of the Baxter family, married to Landon Blake, who works for the Bloomington Fire Department. The couple has four children: Cole, 19; Amy, 14; Devin, 12;

and Janessa, 8. As a young single mom, Ashley was jaded against God and her family until she reconnected with her firefighter friend Landon, who had secretly always loved her. Eventually Ashley and Landon married and Landon adopted Cole. Together, the couple had two children—Devin and Janessa. Between those children, they lost a baby girl, Sarah Marie, at birth to anencephaly. Amy, Ashley's niece, came to live with them a few years ago after Amy's parents, Erin Baxter Hogan and Sam Hogan, and Amy's three sisters, were killed in a horrific car accident. Amy was the only survivor. Ashley and Landon and their family live in Bloomington, in the old Baxter house, where Ashley and her siblings were raised. Ashley still paints and is successful in selling her work in local boutiques.

• • •

LUKE BAXTER: Luke is a lawyer, married to Reagan Baxter, a blogger. The couple has three children: Tommy, 18; Malin, 12; and Johnny, 8. Luke met Reagan in college. They experienced a major separation early on, after getting pregnant with Tommy while they were dating. Eventually Luke and Reagan married, though they could not have more children. Malin and Johnny are both adopted. They live in Indianapolis, about forty minutes from Bloomington.

TRULY, MADLY, DEEPLY

KAREN KINGSBURY

1. Were you surprised to learn about sex trafficking being just as bad in the United States as overseas? How have you helped your family, friends and loved ones avoid this situation? What are some things you would tell young people?

2. There is a "no kissing in public" rule in Thailand and other countries. Do you think a rule like that is helpful? Why or why not?

3. Tell about someone you know who has battled cancer. How did they get through the treatment process? Share ways you know to help someone going through a health battle.

4. Have you ever visited the 9/11 Memorial in New York City? Would you want to visit? Why or why not? If you have visited the site, what was most memorable?

5. Were you alive when 9/11 happened? If so, share your experience of that day. What struck you the most about the attacks?

6. Tommy told his parents he wanted to be a police officer. Do you have any law enforcement members in your life? If so, share about their lives, their jobs and their struggles.

7. Reagan was deeply afraid when Tommy made his announcement about wanting to be a cop. Would you be afraid if someone you loved joined law enforcement? How would you handle that?

8. Did you agree with Reagan or Luke, when it came to their reaction to Tommy's announcement about wanting to be a police officer? Explain your answer.

9. Annalee and Tommy had agreed not to have sex until marriage. Some couples even agree to not kiss before being engaged or married. What are your thoughts about this? Explain.

10. When Tommy and Annalee witnessed the car accident while out getting coffee, Tommy ran toward the fiery wreck. Do you run toward danger or away from it? Give an example.

11. Annalee didn't for a minute think she would have cancer. Do you know someone young who has suffered a cancer or health crisis? Did people rally around them? How did the situation affect you?

12. The faith of Annalee and her family helped her handle treatment for her non-Hodgkin's lymphoma. How has faith helped you through a tough time?

13. Tommy and his mom often watched the show *Cops* together. Have you seen *Cops* or a show like it? Has that affected how you see the role of police officers?

14. At the dance studio, Luke and Reagan were held up at gunpoint by two masked robbers. Has something like this happened to you or someone you love? Tell about that time.

15. Has a police officer ever helped you or someone you love? Share that experience.

16. Luke took Reagan dancing because they'd had tension in their relationship. If you are married, how do you work through disagreements? Give an example.

17. As Annalee's treatment began, her hair started falling out. She held a ceremony of sorts at her home to be active, rather than passive, in that process. What did you think about that time for Annalee? What part was most memorable?

18. Officer Raul hoped that the teen he arrested for drug possession would turn his life around. Maybe even be a police officer. What can you do to help troubled teens in your area? If you're already doing something—or if you know of something that is working—share about that.

19. What did you think about Reagan's father's final minutes during the terrorist attacks of 9/11? Imagine you are in his place. How would you have handled a situation like that? Share about a time when you experienced a tragedy or terrible event. What helped you get through that?

20. Tommy brings sandwiches to the police officers on Christmas Eve. Do you and your family do something for police officers and firefighters at Christmastime or any time? Talk about how you show your appreciation to first responders.

21. What did you learn about fear while reading *Truly, Madly, Deeply*? Share about your greatest fears. How do you manage those fears?

YOU WERE SEEN
MOVEMENT

I'm thrilled to report that the You Were Seen movement is sweeping the nation and even the world, especially in light of the recent Coronavirus pandemic.

I started the You Seen Movement as a way of truly seeing people. "This is a movement of gratitude and generosity," I tell people when they ask about You Were Seen. "We have a chance to acknowledge someone every time we leave the house."

The movement centers around the "You Were Seen" cards. A card (a little bigger than a business card) can be given to food servers, baristas, medical personnel, delivery drivers, cashiers, and anyone in the service sector. Anyone you choose to thank. You simply take a moment to look into the eyes of a stranger, thank them, and hand them a You Were Seen Card.

Jesus says they will know we are Christians by our love, by the way we treat people. You Were Seen is a non-denominational way to truly love the people you interact with every day.

The movement also encourages generosity. Where

appropriate, people in this movement leave generous tips. One man wrote to me and said, "I gave the woman behind the counter a You Were Seen card and a fifty percent tip as I grabbed takeout the other day. I looked her in the eyes and said, 'Thank you for what you do. You matter. And today you were seen!' The woman had tears in her eyes as she took the card and the tip. It was the highlight of my week."

People say the "You Were Seen" cards give them purpose. Every encounter with a stranger is a chance to show the love of God to a hurting world. It's also a chance to fulfil our God-given calling—to share the love of Jesus to all the world.

Often we save money for an oversees mission trip. Then we spend the other fifty-one weeks of the year walking past people without really seeing them. But there are people in our own cities who desperately need hope and encouragement, faith and recognition. They need to be seen. By leaving a "You Were Seen" card and a better-than-average tip, you might change someone's life.

Always when you leave a Seen card, you will let a stranger know that their hard work was seen in that moment. They were noticed! What better way to spread love? The "You Were Seen" card will then direct people to the website—www.YouWereSeen.com. At the website, people will be encouraged and reminded that God sees them every day. Always. He knows what they are going through.

Get involved in the You Were Seen Movement today. Visit the website to get a pack of ten "You Were Seen" cards and read about this effort that is sweeping the nation.

Every day should be marked by a miraculous encounter.

www.YouWereSeen.com

ONE CHANCE FOUNDATION

The Kingsbury family is also passionate about seeing orphans all over the world brought home to their forever families. As a result, they created a charity called the One Chance Foundation.

This foundation was inspired by the memory of Karen's father, Ted C. Kingsbury. Ted always said, "Life is not a dress rehearsal. We have one chance to love, one chance to truly live!"

Karen often tells her reader friends, "You have one chance to write the story of your life!"™ Now, with Karen's One Chance Foundation, readers can join her in the belief that all of us have one chance to make a difference in the lives of orphans.

In the Bible, James 1:27 says people with pure and faultless religion are those who look after orphans. If you are interested in giving to Karen's One Chance Foundation and having your dedication printed in one of Karen's upcoming novels, visit www.KarenKingsbury.com. Below are dedications from Karen's readers who have contributed to the One Chance Foundation:

- To EK, my cousin, and to all the great police officers serving this country. Thank you. May God bless you and protect you always. – Love KK

- Brenda, Happy Birthday to my best friend! I love you! Amanda

- Happy Birthday, Rebecca Tope Olotu! Your smile makes my day & your passion for mentoring youths with AspireHub is an inspiration. Much love, Bayo

- In honor of Mom and Dad's faith legacy. BeckiJo

- Love You and Miss You Mom! Judy J. Knudsen 6/13/38 - 2/21/20 Love, Beverly

- To Scooter - Thank you! – Carol

- Margaret Miller, Enjoy this book! Love, Cherie

- Read & Bikes Caroline ♥ Chris

- Jen van der Vliet Amazing Mama, sister, friend -CB

- In thanksgiving for God's blessings. Diane Ferreter Weimer

- In honor of my husband, Brian, 30-year law officer! Love, Heidi

- To my loving wife, Donna Waters, my guide, my love, my everything! I'm not me without you. Love, Skip

- Gigi, may your books always be counted amongst your friends and may your best friend always be Jesus!

- To my mom Sandy Jackson. I love you! Joeii

- Evelyn Cripps - Thank you for your support, love in the Lord, and precious friendship! Karen Carlisle

- To the One Chance Foundation - Love, Carol Quick

- Scott - Celebrating 30 amazing years as Mr. & Mrs. Song of Solomon 3:4NIV. ILUSAGB-B4E&A+AWLM - Karen

- In honor of my forever sunshine, my Memaw-Lori Loo

- Laurie Jane Wiley is 16! Always Grandma's girl!

- Darlene Kriwiel - Dear sister & aunt, we miss you!

- My Adoptive blessings, Devin, Jason, Jaime & Jessica

- To my children Laura, Jody, and Joel and their families: I Truly, Madly, Deeply love each of you!

- My Beloved Dan, Our Love Never Had Enough Time. Soon, We'll Have Forever and A Day LOVE, Marilyn J.

- Mama, love U always! Marsha

- We miss you dad (Red Brummel)! Love, Dave and Marva

- Sophie, Noah, & Sarah-You are my world! Love, Mom

- IHO Bette MacWilliams, My Mother & Best Friend - MBR

- Evan & Caden, you are the most sweet, kind, and loving boys we know. Love you so so much! ~Dad & Mom

- Dedicated to Joy Dugan for loving unconditionally and making sure the sun rises every morning.

- Rick, My Love; Happy 10th Anniversary! Our song's a book by my favorite author! I love you! Patrica

- In memory of Shirley Spencer

- To my Grandmother, Doris, who taught us about Jesus and KK Books and is now in Heaven with her Lord!

- We love U Carol Ann Moore

- TO MY HERO ROCKY T! Love SALLY W

- Lovely Chris: You are and will always be LOVED and Cherished! Love from, Mom and Dad

- We love you, Lexi Wolfe. Love, Mom, Dad, and Easton

- To Gary, Robin, Eric, Gary II, Tiana, Jaeden & Jordon Bryant, Thank you for being the best family a person could ever ask for. Love Shaudonna

- Happy anniversary to the man I've loved truly, madly, deeply for 38 yrs. . . my beloved, Kurt! Forever yours, Sheila

- Daniel, You're Truly Loved! - Stephanie

- To LaDonna, who is truly special to me. Love, Tami

- To the One Chance Foundation - Love, Terilynn Knezek

- I love you to God and Back Ashley! May you always have the passion to read! Love, Thomas

- To my AMAZING Mom (Lori)! Love your 1st Born, Tianna

- Dedicated in memory of Frederick H. Corirossi

- To my Hubby, Dave, who cares daily through my health issues and truly lives his vows of "for better or worse!" Love, Jan

- Rebecca & Maria - God blessed Us with beautiful loving daughters! We love you Forever! Mom & Dad (Terilynn and Bob)

KAREN'S TOP FANS

To my top fans and most loyal readers listed below, this book is dedicated to you! I asked you to tell me why you were a top fan, and your letters filled my heart. What you wrote to me, I will treasure always. And so you were chosen out of countless thousands of my favorite readers. With each title, you tell other people about my books. And for that reason, each of you are a gift to me from God. May He bless you and yours, and may you—my top fans—continue to share these books with the people you love. Jesus is still healing hearts with the power of story. You are proof!

Abby Burns
Abby Douglas
Addie Pittman
Adebisi Amori
Adele Chang
Adele Musgrave
Adele Taylor
Adesayo Priscilla Ajiibade
Adikuor Essegbey
Adrianne Kincade
Adrienne Miller

Akogun Zainab
Alayna Givler
Alexxis Rudich
Ali Cobrin
Alice Biondi-Savino
Alice Moore
Alicia Groenendyk
Alicia Harvard Dunn
Alicia Mitchell
Alicia Prioste
Alicia Smith

Alicia Sorrow

Alicia Weber

Aliseea Hooker

Allie Emfinger

Allison Weinstein

Alma Nichols

Alma Snowa

Altheia Mason

Amanda Beukes

Amanda Claassens

Amanda Hackett

Amanda Harris

Amanda Kroening

Amanda McDowell

Amanda Neale

Amanda Schimmoeller

Amanda Secor

Amber Blake

Amber Harris

Amber Hawkins

Amber Holland

Amber Stuckey

Amy Anhaiser

Amy Blough

Amy Burt

Amy Carroll

Amy Conner

Amy Daugherty

Amy Franks

Amy Haralson

Amy Pleisch

Amy Poisal

Amy Priest

Amy-Leigh Smith

Andrea Brooks

Andrea Chaney

Andrea Grace Hnatiuk

Andrea Hayes

Andrea Hines

Angel Cooper

Angel Keyes

Angel Sturgeon

Angela Bosserman

Angela Gibbons

Angela Grissom

Angela O'Mara

Angela P Pope

Angela Phillips

Angela Williams

Angelina Quilimaco

Angelita Ali-Gonzalez

Angie Ehlen

Angie Lucas

Angie Purgason

Angie Rarey

Anice Marie Bradley

Anita Sikes

Anita Wright

Anjee Dencklau

Ann Berg

Ann Black

Ann Blair

Ann E. Johnson

Ann Petrich

Anna Noll

Anna Oliva

Anne Eichelberger

Anne Kingsbury

Anne Sperling
Annie Fleck
April Losekamp
Aramide Oluwa
Ariana Cruz
Ashleigh Kuchel
Ashley Bernard
Ashley Mallett
Ashley Patterson
Audrey Sharp
Ava Ramsey
Avayd Ann Lacy
Avery Ramage
Ayandele Ayomide
Bailey Lorraine
Barb Cummings
Barbara A. Krause
Barbara Fink
Barbara Garland
Barbara Hussong
Barbara Schad
Barbara Spillman
Barbara Wilcox
Barbie Monroe
Becki Basham
BeckiJo Disney
Becky Cabrera
Becky Carroll
Becky Joslin
Becky Lentz
Becky Simpson
Becky Thompson
Becky Vermeulen
Belinda Fortunato

Belinda Hallman
Belinda Rinehart
Bernice Ruff
Bess Brown
Beth Barina
Beth Farmer
Beth Johnston
Beth Magill
Beth Marshall
Beth McCarthy
Beth Price
Beth Smith
Bethany Chancey
Bethany Lyn Wolfe
Betty Caruthers
Betty Hellwege
Betty Medernach
Betty Monda
Betty Parrott
Betty Sandlin
Beverly Beck
Beverly Bowers
Beverly de Kruyf
Beverly Gray
Beverly Knotts Brown
Beverly Knudsen
Beverly Lilley
Beverly Potter
Bianca Herman
Bobbie A Wyzard
Bonnie Brooks
Bonnie Chaltry
Bonnie Johansen
Bonnie McGowan

Bonnie St Jean
Brandi Edwards
Brandi Menzie
Brandi Staudt
Brandi Stevens
Brandy Dixon
Brenda Brandt
Brenda Brown
Brenda Engle
Brenda Farris
Brenda Kay Chema
Brenda Lariviere
Brenda Line
Brenda Murphree
Brenda Pell
Brenda Provonsil
Brenda Veinotte
Brenda Wilkinson
Bri Leamon
Bridgette Williams
Briley Eliff
Britney Sininger
Brittany Phillips
Brittany Riley
Bronwen Powell
Brooke David
Brooke Helsel
Brooke Hoefnagels
Brooke Ratliff
Bruce Swart
Buddie Rose Rowell
Caitlyn Council
Camella Breaston
Candi Miller

Candi Wooden
Candice Story
Candy Dalton
Cari Sue Ewing-Durkee
Carl Hines
Carla Dawejko
Carla Lowery
Carleen Davenport
Carly McGee
Carol Baroch
Carol Fritz
Carol Haley
Carol Hyzer
Carol Meinnert
Carol Nappo
Carol Reynolds
Carol Rinko
Carol Rushing
Carol Thompson
Caroline Dethmers
Caroline Holladay
Caroline Kyle
Carolyn Akins
Carolyn Antley
Carolyn Brush
Carolyn Dillard
Carolyn Elaine Balch
Carolyn Keidge
Carolyn McCurry
Carolyn Munro
Carolyn Salley
Carrie Rushing
Carrie Smart
Carrie Woodruff

Carrington Kingsley

Casey Darnold

Casey Robison

Catherine Andrus

Catherine Stika

Cathy Bowyer

Cathy Cawood

Cathy DiBella

Cathy Dunlap

Cathy Hunt

Cathy Johnson

Cathy Schmidt Sims

Cathy White

Cathy Whittington

Catie Dullaghan

Celeste Anderson

Celeste Lacey

Chanelle Fairlene Pillay

Chantle Uthe

Charity Rodrequez

Charlene Jackson

Charlene Keller

Charlene Smith

Charlese A. McCloskey

Charlotte Boudreaux

Charlotte Fisher

Charlotte Heck

Charlotte Hess

Charlotte Morrison

Charlotte Smith

Charmaine Tan

Chelsey Novak

Cheri Bonkowski

Cheri Bovee

Cheryl Ardus

Cheryl Baker

Cheryl Henry

Cheryl Johnson

Cheryl L. Fields

Cheryl Perry

Cheryl Rawlings

Cheryl Rose

Cheryl Van Berkel

Cheryl Van Norman

Chibuzor Nwanguma

Chioma Chukwunyelum

Chris McCoy

Chris Vroman

Christa Richmond Gruener

Christabelle Pillay

Christi Mendoza

Christie Dannenmiller

Christie McFarland

Christin Bumgardner

Christina Evans

Christina Troyer

Christina Wilson

Christine Evans

Christine Hall

Christine Johnson

Christine Magnusson

Christine Shaw

Christy Blanchard

Cindy Broker

Cindy Burns

Cindy Carlson

Cindy Carver Bond

Cindy Gabbard

Cindy Hamilton
Cindy Harkcom
Cindy Lippincott
Cindy Lovins
Cindy Myers
Cindy Newman
Cindy Power
Cindy Pritchard
Cindy Reeder
Cindy Shively
Cindy Tudor
Cindy Washburn
Claire Pascavis
Clara Olson
Claudia Globerger
Claudia Muniz
Claudia N. Turkson-Ocran
Claudia Samford
Claudine Pruitt
Colleen Jansen
Colleen Moses
Connie Graber
Connie R. Kruse
Connie Salcido
Coralie Walton
Courtney Bales
Courtney Matis
Courtney Young
Craig & Jill Morrow
Cris-Annette Nicholas
Crissy LeAnn Robbins
Crissy Nichols
Crystal Doll
Crystal Freda

Crystal Matelski
Crystal Wynn
Cyndi Armstrong
Cyndi Martinez
Cyndie Hunter
Cynthia Thompson
Dacia Pitzer
Daisha Cronier
Dana Bruce
Dana Garrett
Danielle Brezina
Danielle Knowles
Daphne Gazdagh
Dara Brewer
Darla Crowder
Darlene Jarrett
Darlene Mitchell
Darlene Morgan
Dave Lubben
David Clough
Dawn Groves
Dawn Jenkins Foust
Dawn Kesterson
Dawn M. Medley
Dawn Marshall
Dawn Smith
Dawn Thompson
Dawn Whittington
Deanna Whitehurst
Deanna Wickizer
Deanne Mills
Deb Kennedy
Deb McCoy
Deb Paschall

Deb Zurawski
Debbie Beeler
Debbie Black
Debbie Coffey
Debbie Derrenberger
Debbie Dewhirst
Debbie Fox
Debbie Haakenson
Debbie Harmon
Debbie King Taylor
Debbie Marro
Debbie Mitchell
Debbie Newman
Debbie Pollock
Debbie Schniederjan
Debbie Stewart
Debbie Troski
Debbie Wadsworth
Debbie Williams
Debbie Workman
Deborah Burgett
Deborah Fadare
Deborah Greene
Deborah Raley
Deborah Shawver
Deborah Thompson
Debra Hunter
Debra Johnson
Debra K. Illies
Debra Leigh Coe
Debra Thompson
Dee Thompson
Deidra Kronstedt
Denise Gilreath

Denise Levesque
Denise Westra
Denise Wiggins
Desiree Swenson
Diana Mancinelli
Diana Nelson
Diana Wilson
Diane Barnard
Diane Bassett
Diane Bickel
Diane Cary
Diane Crile
Diane Hammond
Diane Hicks
Diane K. Weimer
Diane Peacock
Diane Ryscamp
Diane Walsh
Diane Waters
Dianne Estabrooks
Dianne Werner
Dolly Bauer
Dolly Lowe
Dolores Bailey
Donna Becker
Donna Bullock
Donna Clare
Donna Clouse
Donna Cochrane
Donna Hadley
Donna Keene
Donna Nunn
Donna Perry
Donna Powers

Donna Preston
Donna Smith
Donna Sue Jolliffe
Donna Toxey
Donna Tuttle
Donna Walker
Dori Mitchell
Doris Beckman
Doris Ciarlo
Doris Havard
Doris Meinecke
Doris Webber
Dorothy Powell
Dorothy Thevenet
Dot Baker
Dottie Jones
Dr. Danon Carter
Earlene Edwards
Egwuatu Chiamaka Glory
Eileen Deelstra
Elaine Hoffman
Elaine Hons
Elaine Minnett
Elida Liederbach
Elise Cotuna
Elise Kirschenmann
Elizabeth Brooke Westerfield
Elizabeth Duff
Elizabeth Julius
Elizabeth Mote
Elizabeth Schuldt
Ellen Beck
Ellen Bilotta
Ellen Janney

Elna Buys
Elretha de la Rey
Elya Brubaker
Emi Lyons
Emily Dotegowski
Emily Gail Webster
Emily Jennings
Emily Kelley
Emily McAbee
Emily Potter
Emily Thompson
Emma Lottes
Emmalee Parnell
Emogene Oliver
Equilla "Scoop" Bruce
Erica Barwick
Erica Glass
Erica Hodges
Erica Magilke
Erma Lee McMinn
Esther Marmelo
Evelyn Seaton
Evelyn Tomlinson
Evonne Shepherd
Faith Hargett
Faith Novak
Faye Bertelmann
Faye Stubblefield
Felicia Ann Holmes
Felicia Courtney
Felicia Heuett
Felicia Holmes
Feyisayo Oke
Flame Burns

Florence Evans Hewett
Florence Ramer
Fontella Jamison
Fran Stanek
Francine Maffit
Frenette van den Berg
Gabrielle Hatley
Gail Brandt
Gail England
Gail Erwin Hale
Gail Graham
Gail Hollingsworth
Gail Jenkins
Gail Seibert
Galina Mahn
Gary Snyder
Gay Case
Geneva McClanahan
Genevieve K. Lynch
Gennifer Winger
Georgiann Wilson
Geraldine Ferguson
Geri Button
Gerry Ann Sweeney
Gillian Moulton
Gina Stephenson
Ginger Graber
Ginger King
Ginger Shriver
Ginger Summerlin
Ginnie Montoya
Ginnie Varnam
Ginny Metts
Ginny Paradis

Glenda Jones
Glenda Mason
Glenda Spurlin
Glenn Winningham
Gloria G. Blakeney
Gloria Seipel
Gloria Stahl
Grace Cirillo-Fiore
Grace Normand
Gracie Conner
Gracie Jones
Grayce Kidwell
Greta Charles
Gwen Nelson
Hadassa van Vilet
Hallie Johnson
Hannah Keasling
Hannah Layman
Hannah Miller
Hannelie Scheepers
Harriette Brinkley
Heather Beard
Heather Davis
Heather Fahlfeder
Heather Harris
Heather Hawkins
Heather Hoffmeyer
Heather Howell Harris
Heather Mansfield
Heather Nicholson
Heather Stevens
Heidi van Doorn
Helen Hayes
Helen Welch

Holly McKnight
Holly Milam
Hope Burke
Hope Grimball
Hunter Martin
Imogene Baldwin
Irene Ammacher
Isabel Hanes
Izumi Kawakami
Izunna Amakwe
Jacki Holleman
Jackie Eades
Jackie Jacezko
Jackie Lawrence
Jackie Robedeau
Jacqueline Drumwright
Jacqueline Shannon
Jacquelyn Brown
Jacquelyn Smith
Jamalyn Norman
James and Donna Woods
Jamie Barnard
Jamie Norman
Jamie Smith
Jamie Toler
Jan Brands
Jan Knecht
Jan Kukkola-Miller
Jan Moore
Jan Morse
Jan SaintAmour
Jane Beswick
Jane Daughdrill
Jane Houde

Jane McDaniel
Jane Poplin
Jane Tjarks
Janel Lewis
Janene Van Gorp
Janessa McNutt
Janet Decker
Janet L. Putney
Janet McCarter
Janet Smith
Janet Stenger
Janet Tomes
Janet Wiggins
Janice Birge-Wagner
Janice Crow
Janice Grizzel
Janice M. Daley
Janice Roye
Janice Troglia
Janie Lynch
Janine Bryant
Janis Boossarangsi
Janna Rutkowski
Janyse Heidy
Jayden Anderson
Jayme Porter
Jayne Wiltshire
Jean Gloudemans
Jean Morgan
Jean Walton
Jean Westergaard
Jeanette Bigham
Jeanette Cronan
Jeanine Hodges

Jeanne Jacobs
Jeanne McAuliffe
Jeannie Pratt
Jeff Owens
Jen Barren
Jen Pascoe
Jene Abrams
Jenna Evans
Jenna Pearl
Jennifer Ann Miller
Jennifer Baezner
Jennifer Brake
Jennifer Chalmers
Jennifer Chapman
Jennifer Cigainero
Jennifer Cunningham
Jennifer Diedrich
Jennifer Finch
Jennifer Goodwin
Jennifer Gray
Jennifer Lasseigne
Jennifer Moore
Jennifer Munn
Jennifer Okano
Jennifer Payne
Jennifer Pitman
Jennifer Rice
Jennifer Smith
Jennifer Stephenson
Jennifer Zwickl
Jenny Davis
Jenny Foreman
Jenny Propst
Jeri Gossett

Jeri R. Dolvin
Jeri Soll
Jerica McCracken
Jerri Dunn
Jess Leed
Jess Morgan
Jess Wayner
Jessica Caroe
Jessica Davison
Jessica Forbes
Jessica Morgan
Jessica Sizemore
Jill Dilyard
Jill M. Orosky
Jill Von Boeckman
Jim Krueger
Jo Ann Clark
Jo-Ann Mhishi
Joan Balthazor
Joan Fessler
Joan Hawkins
Joan Marsh
Joan Paris
Joan Patton
Joan Rickett
Joan Walker Hahn
JoAnn Wellman
Joanne Burruss
JoAnne Haynes
Joanne May
Joanne Molstad
Joanne Orris
Joanne Sumption
Jodi Edwards

Jodi Jordan
Jody Brinks
Jody Meier
Jody Nieto
Joelle Mann
Johannah Maxwell
John Letourneau
Joline Murphy
Josie Bourgeois
Joy Armstrong
Joy Jewel Yeshua
Joy Lee
Joy Sewell
Joyce Holdren
Joyce Jackson
Joyce Joblonski
Joyce Mcculley
Joyce Mullen
Joyce S. Ramsey
Joyce Spamer
Joyce Welsh
Joyce Yoder
Judi Hunt
Judith Hiler
Judith McCormack
Judith Strausser
Judy Boshart
Judy Buiter
Judy Church
Judy Connor
Judy Davison
Judy Eaton
Judy Elswick
Judy Eudy

Judy Garrett
Judy Goudreau
Judy Jeffreys
Judy Meador
Judy Mowry
Judy Resley
Judy Roberts
Judy Snyder
Judy Swible
Judy Williams
Judy Wilson
Julie Clark
Julie Conard
Julie Dykxhoorn
Julie Lutz
Julie Mills
Julie Petersen
Julie Swigert
Julie Wood
Kaeti Roberts
Kaitlyn Calicott
Kaleena Foster
Kara Zufall
Karen Ann Steich
Karen Blubaugh
Karen Carrington
Karen Cossett Evans
Karen Davison
Karen Dingler
Karen Fitchett
Karen Green
Karen Hollenbeck
Karen Jones
Karen Kempf

Karen Kruse
Karen Mathena
Karen Mercadante
Karen Merklin
Karen Quesnelle
Karen Raudenbush
Karen Simpson
Karen Williams
Kari Hyden
Kari Lostocco
Karma Bradley
Karma Smoke
Karyn Stoneberg
Kasy Long
Kate Kauffman
Kathleen Grieser
Kathleen Pietron
Kathleen Waffle
Kathy Bement
Kathy Crowling
Kathy Fletcher
Kathy Giannone
Kathy L. Booker
Kathy McCulloch
Kathy Price
Kathy Smith Johnson
Kathy Szatkowski
Kathy Tatsu
Kathy Tingle
Kathy Walters
Kathy Waters
Kathy Whitman
Katie Beavers
Katie Cleary

Katie Combs
Katie Haas
Katie Hickly
Katie Neblett
Katie Richtsmeier
Kay E. Freeman
Kay Jennings
Kay Munson
Kay Murry
Kay Price
Kay Rhinebeck
Kay S. Rose
Kay Tarrant
Kay Wilson
Kaye Turner
Kayla Mize
Kayla Salazar
Kaylee Rodriguez
Kayleigh O'Neal
Kaylie Olson
Kellee Bosket
Kelli Dart
Kelli Dingus
Kellie Miller
Kelly Brassington
Kelly Isenberg
Kelly Kendall
Kelly Lusk
Kelly Osborne
Kelly Price
Kelly Tanger
Kelly Williams
Kendra Spees
Kennedi Williams

Kerri Naylor
Kerri Schnulle
Kerry Michael
Keshia Wood
Kiersten Oxenreider
Kim Brown
Kim Callihan
Kim Forman
Kim Green
Kim Groves
Kim Herring
Kim Hunter
Kim Payne
Kim Reynolds
Kim Wecht
Kimberly Frazier
Kimberly Gwaltney
Kimberly Rogers
Kimberly Staton
Kimmi Goldman
Kingston Painter
Kirsten Jonora Renfroe
Kris Bradley
Kris Maurelli
Kristen Harrison
Kristi Crook
Kristi Lambert
Kristi Sill
Kristie Jarmusz
Kristin Lee
Kristin Rollins
Kristy Backus
Kristy Crow
Kristy Hatch

LaDona Peavler King
LaDonna Fager
Laura Eddy
Laura Herron
Laura M. Jones
Laura Newell
Laura Parsons
Laura Pepper
Laura Sunday
Laura Wagenaar
Laurel Milam
Lauren Basham
Lauren Kay
Lauren Pajunen
Laurie Barrett
Laurie Elizabeth Mercier
Laurie LeBlanc
Laurie McGowan
Laurie Mercier
Lavinna Ashwell
Leah Bickler
Leah Duke
Leandra Smith
LeAnn R. Noak
Leanna Colonna
Lee Ann Wright
Lee Mishler
Leeta Stevens
Leia Ancheta
Leigh Ann Allen
Leigh Stone
Leigh Wallace
Leigh-Ann Bogle
Lena Johansson

Lena Reimer
Lesa Mote
Leslie Arnold
Leslie Bentley
Leslie Blair
Leslie Hartzog
Leslie Rhyne
Leslie Ward
Lettie Hoots
Leyitnen Vivian Lenka
Lianna Burkovskaya
Libby Ballew
Lily Del Boccio
Linda Allen
Linda Alvord
Linda Critcher
Linda Ford
Linda Hendrix
Linda Huddleston
Linda K Fenster
Linda Litton
Linda Orr
Linda Rafferty
Linda Stauffer
Linda Tom
Linda Vandivort
Linda Wagner Brown
Linda Welch
Linda Woodury
Lindsay Bryant
Lindsay Clifton
Lindsay DeVries Herndon
Lindsay Shigemoto
Lindsey Sentef

Lindsey Weihmeir
Lindy Anastis
Lindy Peterson
Linnea Kinney
Lisa Bean
Lisa Dahl
Lisa Davis
Lisa Elliott
Lisa Falkenberg
Lisa Fundingsland
Lisa Gallup
Lisa Gentry
Lisa Green
Lisa Gretch
Lisa Halvorson
Lisa Hammond
Lisa Harris
Lisa Healy
Lisa Hobbs
Lisa Hogue
Lisa Keeley
Lisa Lovell Cromwell
Lisa Ross
Lisa Thompson
Lisa Thompson Grant
Lisa Townsend
Lisa Webster
Lisa Wright
Liz Naylor
Liz Winship
Lois Shaw
Lora Chastain
Lora Wright
Lori Camp

Lori Diehr
Lori Heimbach
Lori Huelskamp
Lorna Palevich
Lorna Priddy
Louise Hershey
Louise Hicks
LuAnn Hayden
Luann Sippy Way
Luanne George
Lucille Griffin Watkins
Lucille Watkins
Lucinda Spires
Lydia Young
Lynda Fields
Lyndsey Young
Lynn Hunt
Lynn Robbins
Lynne Fowlkes
Lynne Kelley
Lynne Kratzer
Madelein Steynvaart
Madelyn Mathias
Madison Carroll
Madison Chrestman
Madison Gannon
Mae Joudry
Maelyn Riley
Maggie Foster Wemmer
Makayla Lee
Malinda Wolfe
Maliska Bothma
Mallory Ellis
Mallory Smolen

Marci Varney
Marcia Casteel
Marcia Clark
Margaret Blankenbeckley
Margaret Burnam
Margaret Fraleigh
Margaret Harding
Margaret Henley
Margaret Mihm
Margaret Rooney
Margaret Stallings
Maria Davenport
Maria deSa
Maria Gundorin
Maria Heehn
Maria Smith
Maria Wickham
Maria Zembrowski
Mariah Havens
Marian Houston
Marian S Ainsworth
Marianne Terpstra
Maribeth Griessel
Marie Bahr
Marie Cannon
Marie Crider
Marie Seals
Marie Waters
Marieke van Keulen
Marilyn Coleman
Marilyn Garrelts
Marilyn Johnson
Marilyn Konkoly
Marit Joys Wigart

Marjie Bonner
Marley Mansfield
Marlo Jaques
Marlon Pritchett
Marsha Stephens
Martha DeLong
Martha Farace
Marty Inman
Marva Lubben
Mary Ann Anderson
Mary Ann Brann
Mary Ann Stauffer
Mary Anne Joyce
Mary Beavers
Mary Ellen Yeager
Mary Ellerman
Mary Evelyn Terry
Mary Gildemeister
Mary Harris
Mary Hysell
Mary J. Marchand
Mary Jane Estabrooks
Mary Jett
Mary Kay Delavan
Mary Kensinger
Mary Kilora
Mary Lou Barlieb
Mary Lou Keener
Mary Marchand
Mary Milner
Mary Mosbey
Mary Novinger
Mary Redford
Mary Riggins

Mary Terry
Maryann Quinn
MaryBeth Carr
Marylou Anderson
Maxine Garon
Maxine Penney
Megan Brown
Megan Cottle
Megan Hoyng
Megan Landman
Melanie Cummings
Melanie Mills
Melessa Segal
Melinda Olsberg
Melissa Beasley
Melissa Craigen
Melissa Dodgen
Melissa Dykeman
Melissa French
Melissa Fryer
Melissa Lambrechts
Melissa Maples
Melissa Mayoral
Melissa Pierson
Melissa Reeves
Melissa Rice
Melissa Sauter
Melissa Tuthill
Melissa Young
Melody Forbes
Melody Okke
Melody Weston
Melonie Brown
Mercy Atuhaire

Meredith Clifford
Merete Aasemoen Aardal
Meri Long
Mette Mydland
Meza Lee
Michael Ray Judd
Michaela Grinder
Michele Hadder
Michele Kallberg
Michele Moore
Michelle Cook
Michelle Dickey
Michelle Fettig
Michelle Flores
Michelle Hume
Michelle Leone
Michelle Newton
Michelle Pals
Michelle Watkins
Milisa Gardner
Mindy Colton
Mindy Snider
Miranda Chewning
Miranda Overholt
Miranda Quinn-Tolle
Miranda-Afa Uyeh
Missi Porter
Missy Barth
Missy Dietz
Missy Savage
Misty Lou
Misty Westbrook
Molinah Matodzi
Mollie Halpin

Molly Hail
Molly Jaber
Morgan Teague
Mrs. A. M. Alexander
Myndi Downs
Myra Cordova
Mysti Totten
Nadia Tymciw
Nadine Colwell
Nadine Glass
Nadine Mauldin
Nancy Craft
Nancy Gibson
Nancy Green
Nancy Hoskinson
Nancy Lentz
Nancy Lewis
Nancy McDonald
Nancy Miller
Nancy Minor
Nancy Overcash
Nancy Palmer
Nancy Peterson
Nancy Quiggle
Nancy Rader
Nancy Stein
Nancy Ware
Nancy Wayman
Natalie Lewis
Natalie Manning
Natalie R. Hudgens
Natasha De Almeida
Natasha Schmidt
Nelda Bishop

Neshma Riggs

Ness McNutt

Nicholas Sullivan

Nicola Reid

Nicole Anderson

Nicole Blanchard

Nicole Engel

Nicole Skinner

Nikita Wells

Nita Armstrong

Norma Neill

Norma Pratt

Nyle Potthast

Oakli Van Meter

Olamide Makinde

Olive Smyth

Oluwadamilola Mobolanle-
  Babatunde

Pam Aylesworth-Streekstra

Pam Clark

Pam Edmiston

Pam Holycross

Pam Mitchell

Pam Russell

Pam Salmoni

Pam Schipper

Pam Smith

Pamela Edmiston

Pamela Sheldon

Pat Elsberry

Pat Inman

Pat Wise

Patience Neal

Patrica Davis

Patricia Belanger

Patricia Wagner

Patricia Whitlock

Patricia Yarbrough

Patsy Burnsed

Patti Heacock

Patti Skipton

Pattie Barton

Patty Clouse

Patty Kleck

Patty Miller

Patty Painter

Patty Pettingell

Patty Wingler

Paula Meinhardt

Paula Miksa

Paula Myers

Paula Oakley

Paula Sulzle

Paula Walker

Paula Watkins

Paulette Wiens

Pauline Dewey

Pauline Lottering

Peggie Hoffman

Peggy Bullock

Peggy Burroughs

Peggy Kasaba

Peggy King

Peggy Singleton

Penney Albright

Penny Battershell

Penny Mossbrucker

Penny Reinhard

Penny Sullins
Penny Taapken
Perlina Nelson
Peyton Mottern
Phyllis Burckhard
Phyllis Fish
Phyllis Guajardo
Phyllis Hines
Phyllis Osbourne
Phyllis Perry
Rachel Baker
Rachel Chapman
Rachel Curtis
Rachel Cyphers
Rachel Deely
Rachel Dorman
Rachel Engbers
Rachel Midyette
Rachel Mims
Rachel Richardson
Rachel Sacco
Rae Johnson
Rafaela Cavazos
Rainbow Zoyiopoulos
Ramelle Collins
Ramona Chappell
Randy and Lisa Cox
Reagan Lynn
Rebecca Burkhart
Rebecca Parker
Rebekah G. Shipley
Rebekah Gough
Rebekah Johansen
Reeva Gordash

Rene Allen
Rene Lubbe-Hendricks
Renee Decker
Renee Stalker
Renette Steele
Renita Kelly
Rhoda Mason
Rhonda Barnhouse
Rhonda Cole
Rhonda Cordova
Rhonda Defoor
Rhonda Harrell
Rhonda McDaniel
Rhonda Robertson
Richele Herigan
Rita McClure
Rita Reitman
Robbie Temple
Robert Storrs
Roberta Gigis
Roberta Hubbard
Robin Crenshaw
Robin Dix
Robin Lewis
Robin Lindsey
Robyn Wynn
Rochelle Ann Ness
Roma Downey
Ron Hadley
Rosa Gross
Rose Pierce
Rosella Elifrits
Rosemary Liebmann
Roshe Olaonipekun

Rosie L Perkins
Roxanne Rossano
Roxanne Ruble
Ruby Metcalf
Ruth Bowerman
Ruth Sharp
Ryan Senior
Sabrina Grobleben
Sabrina Hodges
Samantha Bailey
Samantha DeBerry
Samantha Lutz
Samantha Novak
Samantha Simon
Samaria Driscoll
Samuel Marsala
Sandi Nagel
Sandra Adams
Sandra Brown
Sandra Crone
Sandra Livingstone
Sandra Needham
Sandra Varner
Sandy Bloesch
Sandy Bowman
Sandy Glomski
Sandy Heller
Sandy Lee
Sandy Moore
Sandy Morgan
Sandy Schlosser
Sandy Wood
Sanette Taljaard
Sara Beth

Sara Kiplinger
Sara Moore
Sara Rollins
Sara Taylor
Sara Vassallo
Sarah Arnold
Sarah Beth Lichtefeld
Sarah Bolduc
Sarah Carnes
Sarah Hanna
Sarah Helber
Sarah Jane Fields
Sarah Nelson
Sarah Palmer
Sarah R. Kilbreth
Sarah Salazar
Sarah Taylor
Sarah Williams
Sasha Zackrisson
Sedi Graham
Shaelyne Leamon
Shaina Brown
Shannon Anderson
Shannon Castonguay
Shannon LaNasa Henry
Shannon Welsby
Shari Fox
Shari Jones
Sharon Bridges
Sharon Dean
Sharon Howerton
Sharon Kimberlin
Sharon Koss
Sharon Ramsey

Sharon Sherron
Sharon Sloan
Sharon Sommerkamp
Sharon Turner
Sheeba Liz Ninan
Sheila Ann Turner
Sheila Boonie
Sheila Brady
Sheila Coleman
Sheila Gilliam
Sheila Glisson
Sheila Holman
Sheila Hughes
Sheila Keeler
Shelia Gillman
Shelley Childress
Shellie Oftedahl
Shelly Satterfield
Shelly Townsend
Sherri Brock
Sherri Hayes
Sherri Hayes
Sherri Wheeler
Sherry Clapp
Sherry Dennis
Sherry Dorsey
Sherry Jesick
Sherry Jones
Sherry Miles
Sherry Sayers
Sherry Sayers
Sherry Sutton
Sheryl DeJonge
Sheryl Ewing

Sheryl Trumpet
Shirley Delp
Shirley Dollar
Shirley Hickman
Shirley Jones
Shirley Koestler
Shirley Lantrip
Shirley Mabry Thomas
Shirley Olson
Shirley Traynor
ShirleyAnn Loomis
Sonia Burden
Sonia Matthews
Sonja Fisher
Sonya Westbrooks
Stacey Morrison
Stacey Swift
Stacie Campbell
Stacy Mason
Stacy Sobieck
Stephanie Bare
Stephanie Conlee
Stephanie Dulac
Stephanie Fidelak
Stephanie Kobelinski
Stephanie Lamb
Stephanie McCaslin
Stephanie Wood
Stephenia Payne
Sue Baird
Sue Barnes
Sue Collins
Sue Ellen Tucker
Sue Falkner

Sue Flowers
Sue Furlan
Sue Herflicker
Sue Kennedy
Sue O'Sullivan
Sue Parrish
Sue Taylor
Sue Thrappas
Susan Birkins
Susan Bisbing
Susan Bohannon
Susan Edwards
Susan Glasgow
Susan Hewett Rutter
Susan Kane
Susan Lederer
Susan Marcuccio
Susan Newman
Susan Rackley
Susan Reagan
Susan Schroyer
Susan Shoemaker
Susan Thevenard
Suzanne King
Suzanne Parrigan
Suzanne Stack
Suzette Bailey
Suzette Kluttz
Sylvia Kiers
Sylvia Miller
Taiwo Akindele
Tamela Cohen
Tami Davis
Tami Wedll

Tammie Hicks
Tammy Chidester
Tammy Hillmick
Tammy James
Tammy Layton
Tammy Lowder
Tammy Rogers
Tammy Stahl
Tammy Stewart
Tammy Victor
Tammy Williams
Tanya Koski
Tara B Calliham
Tasha Hamil
Taunya Pittman
Tega Bazunu
Teresa Bowden
Teresa Diener
Teresa Fuqua
Teresa Kenyon
Teresa McKinney
Teresa Mims
Teresa O'Dell
Teresa Sonnier
Teresa Yocham
Teri Aldridge
Teri Scanlon
Terri Combs
Terry Grimshaw Micks
Thalia Kirindongo
Thelma L. Quest
Theresa Korneisel
Theresa Roderick
Thomas & Amy Hudak

Thuso Masikhwa
Tiffany Baccus
Tiffany Day
Tiffany Hulsey
Tiffany Stephens
Tina Campbell
Tina Loewen
Tina Sohl
Toni Lucky
Tonya Helveston
Tonya Sims
Tonya Szepanski
Tracey Hagerman
Tracie Powell Duncan
Tracie Smith
Tracy Baker
Tracy Craven
Tracy Curse
Tracy McDaniel
Tracy Peoples
Tricia Brann
Tricia Kingsbury
Trina Mills
Trinity Kupe
Trish Shinn
Trisha Parra-Gonzalez
Trisha Tonne Ontiveros
Trista Burkett
Trista Kittle
Tyler Brady
Uzumma Ozeh
Valarie Fischer
Valerie Adcock
Valerie Ganter

Valerie Kyte
Valerie Lacroix
Vanda Human
Vanessa Guidry
Vanessa Wheeler
Vangela Roeder
Vasiliki K. Koleas Whitten
Velna Schilling
Venessa Crawford
Vicki Maynard
Vicki McKim
Vicki Scott
Vicki Temple
Vicki Thomas
Vicki Widger
Vickie Deal
Vickie Watts
Vicky Glover
Victoria Mason
Victory Friday
Viola Dondo
Virginia Greene
Vivian Molisee
Wanda Buckley
Wanda Mattox
Wendy Biach
Wendy Jacobson
Wendy Morris
Wendy Myers
Wilhemina Boyd
Yamilia Quinones
Yolande Kuystermans
Yvonne Gill
Yvonne Hargreaves-Beatty